CRIME CLASSICS

# Close Up On Death

Also in the Crime Classics series:

CRIME CLASSICS

# Close Up On Death

## AN INSPECTOR BRIGHT MYSTERY

## MAUREEN O'BRIEN

## ABOUT THE AUTHOR

Maureen O'Brien (1943– ) is best known for her role as Vicki in the iconic BBC series *Doctor Who*, starring alongside the first Dr, William Hartnell. She went on to have a distinguished career in theatre as well as television. She has twice won the Sony Best Actress award for her work on radio, and has written plays, directed, and taught acting workshops. She has written seven crime novels, all of which feature DI John Bright. *Close Up on Death* is the first in the series.

This edition published in the UK by Arcturus Publishing Limited
26/27 Bickels Yard, 151–153 Bermondsey Street, London SE1 3HA

Design and layout copyright © 2012 Arcturus Publishing Limited
Text copyright © Maureen O'Brien, 1989

Cover artwork by Steve Beaumont, coloured by Adam Beaumont
Typesetting by Couper Street Type Co.

AD002460EN

Printed in the UK

For Michael

# CHAPTER ONE

I had trouble with the keys.

The outside door, on the street, was a solid wooden affair, high, and wide enough to take a car. There were enough keys to unlock every cell in Wormwood Scrubs. I tried each of them in turn. To no avail. A man was parking his car. A woman negotiated a push-chair over the snow. I started to feel a fool. Cursing the estate agent under my breath I began again. It was impossible to keep track of which key was which. At the third try I got one to work, a bent Yale that someone had had trouble with before.

I found myself in a small courtyard: high walls, cobbles and weeds. The house, on my left, was Georgian with mock-Georgian additions, a dinky little canopy over the door, bottleglass bow windows. The front door was blue; it had two locks. I'd tackle this one in private; I shut the courtyard gate.

It took five minutes to achieve the combination, then two keys turned like knives in butter. I pushed the door. It opened less than a foot, hit something and swung back. I pushed again, exerting pressure. Whatever was behind it was hard to shift. I squeezed inside.

The body was lying with its back to me behind the door. The clothes were exquisite: perfect new shoes – I could see the soles – Italian, expensive, hardly worn; the beautiful legs were drawn up to the stomach. It was strange that in death the hair should spring and shine more vividly than it had in life.

I leaned against the wall. Everything had stopped: my heart, my pulse, my pumping blood. I was one vacant eye, being filled.

There was no question this was Liza, just as there was no question this was death. I saw my hand take her wrist: no pulse; no warmth; dead flesh. There was a phone in the corner of the dusty hall, on the floor. I lifted it. That too was dead. I sat beside it staring at the blossomy hair which had absorbed and was radiating all the spilt life. I felt neither need nor desire to see the face. I had no ability to move. I sat for some time. I don't know how long. It may have been hours.

The estate agent, however, said. 'You're back fast.' So time had altered for me.

'Did you like it?' he said.

'Can I use your phone?'

'It's a nice little place, isn't it? Lots of possibilities.'

Perhaps he hadn't heard. Perhaps I hadn't spoken.

'I must use your phone.'

'Oh! Oh yes, all right.' He looked puzzled. 'It's a very good price for where it is. And they might accept an offer.' There was a wink in his voice. 'You never know.'

I dialled Paul. There was no thought before this. I had not deliberated. I needed to tell him first.

'Paul?'

'Yeah?' He sounded sleepy: just woken up, a reminder it was early in the morning still.

'It's Millie.'

'Oh. Hi, Millie.'

'Hi.'

'Liza's away, I'm afraid. If you—'

'No. I . . . I must see you.'

'Oh?'

'Now.'

'I'm still asleep, Millie.'

'I'll be there in five minutes.'

'Oh?'

I put the phone down and left. The estate agent was calling after me, something about the keys, but I was in the car and away. Paul was near.

He opened the door, tousled in clothes hastily dragged on.

'My God, Millie, what's the matter? You look terrible.'

'You have to come.'

'Where?'

'Come.'

'Okay, I'll just—'

I sat on the step. My legs shook too much to hold my weight. He came back.

'Will you drive?' I held out the car keys. He took them.

'Where are we going?'

'Belsize Lane.'

'Come on then.' He tried to lift me. 'Millie, what is this? What's upset you so much?' I couldn't say it.

'Are you ill?' My head shook.

'Oh no,' he said. 'It's Liza, isn't it?'

I didn't even nod. It was in my eyes.

'What? What?' He started to shake me. I heard myself wailing. I sank back onto the step. He hit my face, once this side, once that. The third slap made the wailing stop. He sat on his haunches in front of me and held my head.

'Tell me, Millie. Tell me.'

'I can't, Paul.'

'You can.'

'It's beyond telling.'

'Nothing is.'

'Except this.'

'Whatever it is that's happened to Liza, I've got to know.'

'Just come. Please come.'

'You have to tell me first. If Liza's ill, if she's been in an accident, even if she's only left me for another man.' He laughed, sort of. 'Just tell me now. Come on; I've said all the worst things it can be.'

He looked into my face. 'Haven't I?' I looked back at him. He saw that he had not.

He pulled me up and almost carried me to the car. We drove in silence till I told him to stop. There was no trouble with the keys this time. Nothing was locked.

His face when he saw her was stone. He was prepared. He stood and looked, like a man confirming something, grim. Then he ran.

I heard him start the car. The door let in the snowy air and too much light. I pushed it to. This was the last time I should be alone with Liza.

I sat on the stairs and watched with her. My vigil. The last silence. The two of us waiting in the wings for the action to begin. It didn't seem a long time.

A silver-haired man in uniform pushed the door open. Liza's hair moved in the draught. There was a boy, all navy serge and silver, at his heels. Paul was with them. They looked but didn't touch. The young one stayed with us. Silver-hair walked round the ground floor. He came back.

'Take a look upstairs.'

The young one's feet nudged me as he passed. Silver-hair walked round to Liza's head. He bent to see her face. Young-one came down the stairs. Silver-hair said, 'This is one for the CID. Better get on the talking brooch.' I thought I had misheard. He spoke to his lapel, which crackled and hissed. It went on for some time. He seemed to be calling the world. We waited. Silver-hair looked up. He seemed to remember where he was.

'Anything upstairs?'

Young-one shook his head. No one spoke. Footsteps crunched outside. Had they got here fast? I don't know. My sense of time *had* gone.

It's odd how you can always recognise policemen even without the hats and silver bits. It may be the haircuts, it may be the casual clothes which aren't quite casual enough; perhaps it's the way they stand and walk. One of these was a big, solid man in his forties, the other smaller and younger in a brown leather jacket that stopped at his waist. They had eyes like mouths, gobble, gobble, everywhere they looked. The four of them moved into a huddle round Liza, murmuring, a ritual of standing and kneeling.

'You found her?' The big one turned to me. I nodded. He nodded.

'Touched anything?' I gazed around, trying to remember.

'Phone?' he said. I nodded again.

'Touch the – er?'

'Wrist,' I said. My voice was like dry leaves, 'To see if . . .'

'Yeah. That all?'

'I think so. Yes.' Rustling in a cold corner.

'Okay.'

'You, sir?' said the small one. Paul shook his head. He looked like a man on a mountain watching the earth burn below. Medusa had touched him. Big-one, Silver-hair and Young-one stayed with us. The small one moved over the house. He was light on his feet.

Silver-hair said, 'Sent for everyone. The works.' Big-one nodded, looked at Paul.

'Just waiting for the doctor,' he said. Paul gave a short noise, not quite a laugh.

'Got to find out what happened, sir.'

There were footsteps in the courtyard. A slight man with a bag came in. A man with a camera bounced in after him. Suddenly the tiny hallway was full of people, men in grey suits. A woman, also in a grey suit, pulled on a pair of surgical gloves. Using tweezers she picked bits of – dust? – off the body and the floor and popped them into little plastic bags. A young male assistant took them from her and labelled them. She stood and peeled off the gloves. It was the camera's turn with Liza. It flashed and clicked at her from high and low. She was used to that: 'She doesn't have a single bad angle,' an awed make-up girl had told me once. The doctor stood by, holding his bag in front of him with two straight arms, like the priest waiting to follow the acolytes. A thin man stood next to Silver-hair, taking notes. They were like the chorus of an opera with the sound turned off. My mind had got out. It was watching everything from somewhere else.

Camera stopped and stood about. Lady in grey departed with assistant and polythene bags. Doctor moved in – for the final flick with powder and lip gloss before the next take? He knelt. His back was to us, hiding his hands, and her. We waited. Camera and Big-one discussed an accident that had occurred in the Finchley Road, not here.

'Bit of a mess,' said Camera.

'Mmm,' said Big-one.

The doctor had cleared to upstage of Liza. We saw that he had turned her face.

There was a white hole where her mouth should have been.

I heard the sound of screaming. The sound was coming from me. Water seemed to be running from every orifice in my face. My body, crouched on the stairs, was thrown back and forth out of control.

When I came to, the little one in the brown leather jacket was behind me holding my neck, the doctor was by my side with cloudy liquid in a small paper cup. I drank it. Paul was standing by the door, his face pressed against the wall.

The big one helped me to the door. He tried to shift Paul. Paul looked as though he might break if moved, arms splintering, fingers dropping to the floor. He came out backwards and walked like that all the way to the car.

'This yours?' Big-one asked Paul. Paul didn't hear, staring at the house.

'Mine,' I said without voice. 'My lips felt thick and numb; my throat was dry. I touched Paul's hand. It was hot. It didn't feel like stone. I had to prise the car keys out of it. Big-one was gentle with him. 'Get in please, sir.'

A police station is like a hospital in that you pass it a hundred times without any wish to see inside. We followed Big-one up the steps, into a tiny lobby fenced with a counter. There was hardly room to move. Ahead of us in a far room policemen strode to and fro with sheaves of paper. There was a low hum of voices, coldly comforting. A man in uniform shirtsleeves greeted Big-one from behind the counter. They mumbled together briefly. Big-one opened a door on our left.

'This way, sir. And you, love.'

So this was the backstage area: bleaker, as in the theatre, than the front-of-house; an unspeakable little room, six foot by six, two doors, a deal table, four metal chairs with their seat stuffing hanging out. It smelt of wet dog. Uniform Shirtsleeves came through the second door.

'Found you an empty office,' he said. Big-one left. We and Shirtsleeves waited, staring at the walls, silent. Big-one came back, opened the door and beckoned Paul.

'Come along if you don't mind please, sir.'

Paul stood, blind and obedient. And went. I sat. And waited. Shirtsleeves stood, arms folded, back to the door. Big-one opened it. They held a whispered discussion. Someone said, 'Nothing else for it, then.' Big-one's face appeared round the door.

'Come on, love. Sorry to keep you waiting.' I followed him.

A stone corridor lined with doors. He opened the third on the left. Like the dog room, it was windowless. The walls were cleaner and the chairs unchewed. The desk was metal, painted grey. Paul sat rigid on one of the chairs. We stood and looked at him. Big-one said, 'Look, love, the chap's in a bad way. I can't get anything out of him. It's highly irregular but I'm going to have to question you together. Okay?' I nodded, dumb. He sat me in the chair next to Paul. Paul was unaware of our presence in the room. He was unaware of the room.

Big-one settled himself behind the desk, reached a pen out of his breast pocket and shuffled his papers about. He wrote on a form my name, address, date of birth, marital status, profession. On a separate form he wrote my answers to the same set of questions about Paul.

'Now.' He leaned forward and clasped his big hands. Just a few simple queries,' he said. 'You're both in a state of shock so we won't take long.'

There was a knock. A rosy young policewoman came in with three mugs of tea on a tin tray.

'Thanks, Irene.' She placed the tray on the desk and sat behind us against the wall. I put Paul's cup into his hands and closed his fingers round it. He looked at it. He wondered how it got there, what it was. I gently lifted it towards his mouth. He drank, but didn't swallow.

'Now,' said Big-one again, 'are you aware of the identity of the deceased?'

I nodded, for us both.

'Who was she?'

'Liza Drew,' I said.

'What, Liza Drew the actress?'

'Yes.'

He wrote on his form, lifting his eyebrows. They were two furry caterpillars with an independent life. 'How well did you know her, sir?'

Paul moved his lips. No sound came out. I said, 'They lived together.'

'I see. How long?'

I looked at Paul. He was gazing at the surface of his tea.

'About eight years,' I said. 'I think.' He wrote.

'And you?' he said to me. 'How long have you known her?'

'Longer. We were at drama school together. Fifteen years,' I said. 'I suppose.'

'Close friends?'

'Yes,' I said, and tears started to run down my face. Big-one looked at the policewoman. She got up and handed me a box of tissues. I nearly said Thanks Irene. I said, 'Thanks.'

'So you're an actress as well?'

I nodded.

'And you, sir?' Paul was bewildered. 'Are you an actor, sir?'

He formed the shape of Yes with his mouth, then said, 'Yes.'

Big-one wrote. His eyebrows moved at me.

'Now take your time and just tell me in your own words what happened this morning.'

'I went to look at the house,' I said. 'It's for sale. She was lying there when I went in.'

'Could you see her face?'

'No, she was lying with her back to me.'

'How did you know it was her?'

'I don't know. Her clothes. Her hair.' The tears were running down again. I wiped them up.

'I see. You were together? When you found her.' He looked from me to Paul. Paul whispered something we couldn't hear.

'No,' I said. 'I went to get him. The phone was dead.'

'So you both went back there. Anything different when you got back?'

'No, I don't think so.'

'Then what?'

'Paul came and got you.'

'And you?'

'What?'

'What did you do?'

'I waited. I sat on the stairs.'

'Touch anything? Touch the er – touch her at all?' They had asked me that in the house.

'Not then, no. Before I went to get Paul, I told you, I touched her wrist. And the phone.' I wiped my face again. Not many tissues left in the box.

'Okay,' said Big-one. 'Any idea how she got there? What might have happened? What she was doing in the house?'

Paul made a sort of quiet moan. He had started to shake. He managed to say something that sounded like 'No'. I said, 'She rang me on Wednesday to ask me to go and see the house with her. I said yes but then my agent phoned to say I had an interview that afternoon—'

'An interview?'

'Yes. For a job. So I called Liza back to say I couldn't go. She must have gone on her own.'

'Or with you, sir?'

Paul again moaned. 'No.'

'Paul wasn't here,' I said. 'In London I mean.'

'Oh? Where were you, sir?'

'Sh—Sh—'

'Sheffield,' I said.

'And what were you doing in Sheffield, sir?'

'Sheffield,' Paul said.

I said, 'He's working there.'

'So when did you get back from Sheffield, sir?' I wished he'd stop saying sir.

'Last night.' His voice was like paper. 'Last night.'

The eyebrows rose and fell. 'Thursday night,' he said. And wrote. 'And was your – was Miss Drew at home?'

'No.' The fluttering paper voice.

'Not at home.' The pen and eyebrows moved together. 'Did you expect her to be at home?'

'No. No.'

'Why was that, sir?'

'She was at her . . . She was . . . She said she was going to her mother's.'

'When, sir?'

'On Wednesday.'

'She said this on Wednesday?'

'No – No. She – said it the . . . night before. She was going on –

Wednesday.' There were long breaks between the words while he pulled himself back from a distant place.

'And she said this, how, sir?'

'How?' I watched Paul searching – an actor's search: cheerfully? resignedly? tiredly? crossly? How had she spoken to him?

'Were you *with* her on Tuesday night?' Big-one spelled it out.

'Oh.' Paul got it. 'No. On the phone. She told me on the phone. She phoned me. In Sheffield.'

'I see.' Big-one wrote. 'Was that usual?'

'Going to her mother's in the middle of the week? No. Her mother was sick. Is sick.'

'Phoning, sir.'

'Oh, phoning. Yes. Every evening.'

'She phoned you every evening?'

'Or I her.'

'I see. She phoned on Wednesday evening?'

'No.'

'Did that surprise you?'

'A bit. I rang but assumed she was on her way to her mother's.'

'You didn't ring her mother?'

'No.' Paul, for the first time, looked ordinarily puzzled. Taken aback.

'Why not?' said Big-one.

'I don't know.' Paul saw something he didn't like the look of. Shook his head to get rid of it. Big-one was writing. He made a determined full stop and sighed. He retracted the point of his pen with a loud click, returned it to the warmth of his breast, patted it with a beefy hand.

'Right,' he said. 'Well. That'll be all for now.'

We stared at him, blank.

'We'll be in touch,' he said. 'Bound to be some ends to tie up.' He chose his words with unerring finesse. The stuff the doctor had given me was sending my mind in an upward spiral. Words spun in it, out on their own. I had to get out of there. Big-one stood up. We stood up.

'What happens now?' I said. Big-one looked perplexed.

'Happens?' He looked blank.

'Yes. I mean—' I didn't know how to go on.

'Ah yes. We do an autopsy, you see. We'll get the autopsy report. That will establish time of death, cause of death hopefully etcetera, etcetera. And then we'll get back to you. Might take a couple of days. Depends how much they've got on. At the er – laboratories, see.'

Paul and I did not reply. Big-one went to the door. We filed out of the windowless room. I handed the few remaining tissues to Irene. She received them with an expression of mute concern.

Like a good host after a party, Big-one saw us right to the door. On the step Paul stopped. He turned quickly to Big-one. It was a shock. He'd been in slow motion up to now.

'When do I—?' He was having trouble with the words. 'When will she—? How—?'

'Ah yes, sir. Well now. We have to complete our investigations before the er . . . before we can release the—. And I'm afraid at this present moment in time it is too soon for me to say when that will be.'

I felt Paul shudder but his face was still.

'Yes,' he said. 'I see. Thank you.'

Big-one nodded, in a final manner, and turned on his heel. He disappeared into the dimness of the police station doorway, leaving us standing on the steps.

# CHAPTER TWO

Paul and I stood blinking in the light, not even feeling the abnormal cold. There were islands of black snow in the busy traffic on the hill. Paul looked as if he might walk under a car. I touched his arm. He gazed at my hand, mystified, slowly connected it with a person and looked at my face. 'Paul,' I said.

What were we to do now, where were we to go? I couldn't leave him alone, I couldn't be left alone. We were adrift.

'My place,' I said. I was too shaky still to drive. It was a longish walk to Fortune Green, but downhill. He walked blindly into people, lamp-posts, bollards, holes. I held on to him, steering him.

My flat isn't much. One flight up, a huge room. Cooking arrange-ments in a cupboard, share bath. He sat on the divan-by-day bed-by-night. He looked at his hands clasped between his knees. I put a match to the gas fire, filled the kettle. The chill remained in the room. I crushed a Valium into his coffee, not knowing if it was the right thing to do, having to do something. I was suddenly aware that my bladder was about to burst and went off to the shared bath. When I came back he was asleep, flat on his back, face to the wall, arms by his sides, coffee untouched. I covered him with my coat and sat in the armchair. Silence and white light. Only his breathing and the gas fire, continuo and counterpoint, the same sound. I kept watch over him.

I was in love with Paul once. And he with me. Years ago, before he met Liza, I'd sat in another bedsit watching him sleep. The back of his neck was as vulnerable now as it had been then. For a moment, so distant was I from reality, I was back there waiting for him to wake, turn his head and hold out his arms. I got up, looked out of the window at the lumpy snow, the black trees. A cat sat on the wall, hunched, keeping itself warm. The doctor's sedative was wearing off; desolation started to echo round me, a cave, a maze. I swallowed Paul's cold coffee in one draught. I wanted to beat the cushions, shake the sheets, climb the walls. I sat still so as not to wake Paul.

He woke me, after dark, coming back from the bathroom. His face and hair were wet. We looked at each other. He sat down. I felt afraid. He said at last, 'I can't believe this. But it's happened. I have to believe it.'

'Yes.'

'But I don't understand – understand it.'

'No.' There was another long silence.

'Will you help me?'

'How?'

'Tell me the truth.'

I looked lost. 'What do you mean, Paul?'

'I mean don't fear hurting me.' I didn't know what he meant. I said so.

'If there was – anyone; anyone she knew; anything – going on, anything she feared or was suffering. Anything. She would have told you, in confidence perhaps. I'm asking you to tell me. Everything you can. I've got to know what was going on in her mind. In her life. I've got to know.'

'You think—' My astonishment was genuine. '—You think that there was someone else?'

'It's all I can think of.'

'Another man?' He didn't speak. 'The idea is ludicrous. There has been no one in Liza's life but you. Right from the start. You must know that.'

'I know nothing. In one day I don't know anything. Tell me what was going on.' He was shaking me. It was horrible.

'Paul!' He stopped.

'I'm sorry.' He sat down. 'To do that. To go off to an empty house and do that. To herself. What was going on inside her head?' He was rocking now, his face in his hands.

'To herself?' It had not occurred to me, either that she had done that, or that anyone could think she had.

'What else?' he said. What indeed? 'She had no enemies,' he said. 'No woman was ever more loved.' It was the truth.

He was forcing me to think. I didn't want to think. We all know the easy ways of doing it: the pills, the polythene bag, even the slashed wrists. I started to see the hole in her face. It was inconceivable.

'No,' I said. 'No. Not that way, Paul.'

He saw what I saw. He spoke quietly: 'What are you saying then?' My mind jumped but wouldn't land.

'An accident?' he said. I didn't speak. 'What possible kind of accident would—' We stared. 'Oh God,' he said.

'Paul.'

'Oh God.'

'No, don't.'

'If I find out,' he said, 'that someone did that to Liza, I will kill them slowly with my bare hands.' I shivered. 'She was pregnant,' he said. I ran away from him, across the room. I was bouncing off the walls. He had to gag me with his hand. When he had calmed me down he started to put his jacket on.

'I'm going to see her mother.'

'You can't drive in this state.'

'I have to tell her before she finds out some other way.'

'Don't leave me alone.'

'Come on, then.' He threw my coat at me. 'Come with me.'

As we got to the door the phone rang. For a wild moment I thought someone was calling to tell me that there had been a mistake, that Liza was alive. The man said he was Inspector Bright. 'We met this morning,' he said. The small one in the leather jacket, I guessed, nasal south London voice. 'We can't locate Mr Paul Mannon. Any idea where he might be?'

'He's here,' I said.

'A-ha.' He did not sound surprised. 'What was Miss Drew's car, do you know?'

'An Alfa Romeo,' I said. 'Silver.'

'A-ha. Number?' I asked Paul: 'What is the number of your car?' He rapped it out automatically; I repeated it into the phone.

'A-ha,' he said again. 'We've found it.'

'Where?'

'In Belsize Lane. Did you see it there this morning?'

'No,' I said. 'But I didn't look. I mean I wouldn't have noticed. I didn't – expect.'

'A-ha,' he said. 'No, of course not. Erm . . . Neither of you is thinking of going anywhere, are you?' Was this man psychic?

'Well,' I said. 'Just a moment, please.' I covered the mouthpiece. 'He wants to know if we're going anywhere.' Paul hesitated, a bull checking the red rag.

'Tell him yes.'

'Yes,' I said. 'We're going to Suffolk to tell Liza's mother.'

I waited for him to say 'A-ha'. He did. I said, 'We don't want her to find out some other way.'

A horror struck me. 'You haven't told her yet, have you?'

'No,' he said. 'Not yet.'

'Let us tell her first,' I begged him. His pause seemed a minute long, then:

'All right,' he said. 'Can't do any harm I suppose. Do we have her address?'

'Yes,' I said. 'I gave it to the Big – the other policeman this morning. It's near Saxmundham.'

'Right then,' he said. 'We'll be able to reach you there.'

'Yes,' I said, and he hung up.

# CHAPTER THREE

We used my car. Felt as though we were stealing it, outside the police station in the dark, out of breath from climbing up the hill.

Driving through the dark disembodies you: the motion, the speed, the lights flashing out of black and into it again; the mind floats. You're nowhere, between lives, like a convalescent, a baby. Carried, lulled. How else could we have got through the night? Paul drove. I didn't look at him. We both stared at the rushing black. We were as separate, and as together, as two people can be.

I don't know what time we got there; my little 2CV doesn't go fast. It was not yet dawn. The house was in darkness so we stayed in the car. The country is a noisy place; the rustling, the owls, the attenuated cock-crow and even the cold were a welcome diversion from the hole in her face and 'She was pregnant'. We – I – may have slept for a short time, frozen, though when I opened my eyes Paul was sitting upright, eyes straight ahead, arms folded, shoulders set, shivering.

A casement closed upstairs. Of course Mrs Drew would sleep with her window open even in this hard winter. The cottage is nearly four hundred years old, most of it, thatch and lattice, small panes to keep the dark Suffolk magic out. Pretty, if you like that sort of thing. I don't much.

Paul turned his head, then got out of the car. I followed. The door knocker was a graceful brass hand. As he touched it, I touched that cold wrist in Belsize Lane. I shut my eyes. When I opened them she was standing there in a dressing gown, Liza thirty years hence. Her face lit up when she saw Paul, became puzzled when she saw me, then an awful fear started in her eyes as she looked back at him. Her face was as expressive as Liza's and her eyes the same blue-green. Paul took her by the shoulders and turned her into the hall. I closed the door. He led her into the living room. I went with them. But as he sat her down I left.

I could hear their voices from the kitchen, his soft and hesitant. I heard her say, 'No' and later call out, 'No! No!' When I took in the coffee they were sitting hand in hand on the sofa, yesterday's fire dead in the grate. She looked at me. I was unnerved by the hatred in her eyes. It blazed. I gasped as though she had struck my face. 'I've made coffee,' I said. She sat upright, hands clasped on her knees.

'Thank you, Millie. How kind.' She lowered her eyes. The loathing in them must have shocked her almost as much as it had me.

'Paul tells me you found her,' she said in that beautifully modulated voice.

'Yes,' I said. We could have been discussing the stock market – 'Paul tells me that the price of steel has dropped' – except that her cup rattled as it met the saucer.

'Did she tell you she was pregnant, Millie?'

'No,' I said. She put her hand to her throat and seemed to relax a little. I saw she couldn't have borne it if Liza had confided in me before her. I could understand that.

'She said she would have some wonderful news to tell me when she arrived,' she said. 'She refused to tell me on the phone.'

'She said the same thing to me,' I said, 'when she asked me to look at the house with her. Only—' I stopped for a second. '—Only I never got there. I wish . . .' I stopped again. The burning hatred was directed at me once more and I realised what I had said. She had been going to tell me before she told her charming, elegant mother. 'Or perhaps,' I said, 'it was something else she was going to tell me – a job perhaps. That's what I thought at the time.'

'I think not,' she said.

We sat in silence. The cold was dreadful. Couldn't I have kept my mouth shut? 'I could light the fire,' I suggested. No one replied. I dared not move. There was an atmosphere of violence in the room. I felt it to be directed against me. I wished I hadn't come.

Paul said to her, 'You were ill.'

'It's over now. Just a flu.' She spoke to me again. 'Paul believes she killed herself. Do you?'

'No,' I said. 'I don't.' She turned her head to me on its upright stalk, her face full of surprise.

'Why not?'

'It's just not possible. The – means, and in the—'

'Particular circumstances. Quite.'

Paul said, 'I think I am going to go mad.' She touched his hand, lightly.

'It is cold in here. Will you light the fire, Paul? Thank you. I shall go and dress. You will perhaps prepare us some breakfast, Millie. You know where things are.' She left the room. We obeyed her. While I made toast and boiled eggs, the smells sickening me, I could hear Paul scraping out the grate, crumpling paper, positioning logs.

We ate in silence, she with an apparently normal appetite, Paul and I barely able to swallow. Halfway through his egg, Paul abruptly got up. We heard him retching in the scullery. She patted her mouth with her napkin, and rose. I listened to her say, 'You need a hot bath. There are warm towels in the airing cupboard. And you will take one of these.' I found myself all at once ragingly hungry. My last meal, also breakfast, had been twenty-four hours ago, before driving to the estate agent to pick up those terrible keys.

'What did you give him?' I asked when she came back. 'Valium,' she said. 'I was prescribed them recently during a period of – finding it difficult to sleep.'

'You?' It escaped me.

'Yes, Millie, even I. A short-lived problem, however, quickly cured.' She turned her head to the window and said casually, 'Was the child Paul's?'

'Mrs Drew!' She made my blood run slow, like treacle.

'Such things have been known, Millie. And in your world—'

'Not Liza,' I whispered. 'You must know that.'

'Then why would Paul think suicide?'

'Because he knows no one hated her enough to – how much Liza was loved. By everyone.'

'Ah yes,' she said. 'Her friends. So many. Friends. And you, Millie. Would you say you were her closest friend?'

'And oldest,' I said.

'And would you say you – loved her, Millie?'

'What do you think, Mrs Drew?'

'Friendship is a complicated matter, Millie. Love is not always uppermost. There is often as much anger and hate.' She paused, idly watching the sparrows in the snow. 'And envy of course.' She looked at me. Unlike her earlier look, this one was cool but there was no mistaking now what that piercing blaze had meant. So pointed was her accusation that for a moment I was drowning; I had to get to the surface, fast.

'Did you not envy her, Millie?'

'Envy her what, Mrs Drew?'

'Her career. Naturally.'

'Mrs Drew, there are many actresses whose careers are more successful than mine. Do you think I am starting a campaign of mass murder, eliminating every actress in England so that when a decent part comes up one day, I shall be the only one left? Sounds like a good idea. I must give it some thought.'

'Oh,' she said. 'I did not mean to suggest . . .'

'Yes,' I said, 'I think you did.' She raised her brows; she wasn't used to the direct approach. 'Mrs Drew, of course I envied Liza from time to time; there's probably not an actress in the country who didn't. But I loved and admired her as well.' The tears were rolling down again. There was no Irene hovering with the tissue box; I used the napkin, pale pink linen. 'And I gloried in her success.'

'I wonder,' she said. I was shaking with – anger?

'You wonder what?'

'Oh . . . Envy is a powerful emotion. I wonder, that's all.'

'And what about you, Mrs Drew?' It was anger now.

'I?' Imperious.

'Yes, you. Envy *is* a powerful emotion. You seem to know a lot about it; certainly more than I do. What about you, Mrs Drew?'

'You appear to be suggesting that I felt envy for my own daughter.' The coolly raised brow.

'Motherhood is as complicated a relationship as friendship is. Why not?'

'Preposterous.' A dismissive sound. She folded a towel. 'You have suffered a great shock and read more into my words than I meant to suggest. I was merely conjecturing that those who seemed to love Liza so dearly might have been harbouring other feelings in their hearts. Please do not think, Millie, that I doubted your loyalty for a moment.' She paused. 'You are distraught.' She was right there. 'I am trying,' she said, 'to examine all the possibilities. It is the only way to occupy my mind.'

Paul said, 'I killed her.'

He was standing in the doorway shaved and clean, his black hair spiky with damp. There was a silence in the room. 'Don't start accusing each other,' he said, 'for what is my fault only. Don't spread the ugliness further than it has to go.' He sat down. 'I was – having an affair is how they put it. It was nothing: a bit of fun and friendship; nothing serious on either side. As far as I'm aware, Liza didn't know. But things get round; any kindly interfering busybody could have enlightened her. When she told me she was pregnant last weekend—' He stopped talking for a second. The gentleness of his mouth was hard to watch. 'She was happier than I have ever seen her. I knew it had to stop, my – playing around, I mean. But of course there had to be a final – a fond farewell. That took place on Wednesday night. I phoned Liza from her place, the girl's. Liza wasn't in. I meant to call here later. I – forgot – to phone again.'

Out of the silence, I said, 'Paul. If Liza didn't know . . .'

'You don't understand what I'm saying,' he said. 'Between last weekend and – whenever she did that – someone must have spilt the happy news. Liza was trusting. You know how trusting she was. That's partly why she was so successful; no one could ever bear to disappoint that trust. She wasn't used to her trust being abused. And for me to abuse it . . . Why she did it there I don't know. Or why she used – whatever hideous thing it was. I can only think she wanted the most violent – I can only think—'

'You have done more than enough thinking,' said Mrs Drew.

She gently touched the back of his neck, and swiftly withdrew her hand. She always snatched back her intimate gestures; they escaped from some secret weakness in the fortress of her self-control. I was surprised that she, searching around for solutions in the wilderness of conjecture, should not be convinced by this one. She evinced neither shock nor blame at Paul's self-confessed betrayal of her daughter's faith. I saw that she loved him, that for her he could do no wrong. I heard Liza say gaily, 'Oh, Mummy adores Paul; she always has. I sometimes think she loves him more than she loves me; it's wonderful.'

Mrs Drew went on, 'Liza did not kill herself. You must get that idea out of your head. Or if she did, it was by accident, not intent. She most certainly did not know about your – silly behaviour in the North.' She made Sheffield sound like Alaska. 'When she rang me on Tuesday night she was as happy as a bird. She had no need to pretend with me.'

'That was Tuesday night,' Paul said.

'But, Paul,' I was insistent. 'She phoned me on Wednesday morning. I spoke to her twice. She was on top of the world.'

'Then she found out after that,' he said. As I turned away in helpless exasperation to wash the plates I heard her say softly, 'Oh my dear boy.' I suddenly felt sick, and as tired as I had ever been.

'Can I have a bath?' I asked. 'Is there enough hot water left?'

'It is constant in this house,' she announced.

# CHAPTER FOUR

I felt stoned. There was too much steam to see myself in the mirror. It confirmed the sensation I had that I simply wasn't there. Steam and a pinkish glow. My mind floated on the surface of the water, miles away. It was a kind of sleep. I was quite surprisingly angry when Paul's voice jolted me back. 'Millie. Are you all right in there?' I couldn't reply. His face, when it appeared round the door, showed that he had wept. So she had done that for him.

'Yes, Paul, I'm fine. I'll get out now.'

As I was going downstairs the knocker rapped on oak. Mrs Drew answered it. The little one stood there in the snow. Brown leather jacket and sleek hair. He introduced himself. He hadn't wasted any time. A teddy bear in uniform chaperoned him in. They seemed to do everything in twos. The broker's men.

'Come in, Inspector Bright. Yes, I know Sergeant Simmons. Do come in. Could I ask you to make us some coffee, Millie? Thank you. There's a fire in the drawing room; this way.'

'Hello,' I said.

'Good morning, Miss Hale.' His little brown eyes were sharp. Like blades.

'Coffee is served, ma'am.' I didn't say it. But the scene was set for the entrance of the maid, aggravated Cockney, apron and cap. The set was good: gleaming diamond window panes, snowy light on the oriental carpets and comfortable chintz, even a log fire blazing in the oak-beamed hearth. As I entered, Little-one was actually saying, 'I hope you won't mind if the sergeant jots down a few notes?' in that nasal voice like a thumbscrew. The sergeant was on the window seat staring at his boots.

'Is that necessary?' said Mrs Drew.

'We might all be glad of a record for future reference.' Smooth.

'Very well.' She sighed. 'Ah, Millie, thank you so much.'

Her hands were not shaking now as she poured and stirred and lifted and handed round. Such comfortable sounds – crackling fire, clink of silver spoon on fine china, 'No sugar thanks', 'A little milk' – about as comfortable as a nightmare from which you can't wake.

'Now,' said Little-one, 'I'd like to tell you what we've been finding out. Not a lot, I'm afraid, till all the reports come in, but for what it's worth – time of death, sometime on Wednesday. Probably. Very late Tuesday night. Possibly. Till we get the full autopsy report we can't fix it more firmly than that. It looks as though it happened in that house, where she was found. Though we're not certain of that either. Yet. Cause of death we don't yet know.'

'You don't know?' Paul came to life.

'Not yet.'

'But the—'

'The appearance . . . yes. But that *may* turn out to have nothing to do with the actual cause.'

'I don't understand.'

'Well, it was a corrosive substance of some kind. Could have been administered afterwards.'

'Corrosive.' Paul flinched.

'A-ha. Any number of things it could have been. Still being analysed. Some ordinary household cleaning agent possibly – bleach, ammonia, spirits of salts.'

'What?' Paul said.

'Sorry, sir?'

'What is that?'

'Spirits of salts? Used for cleaning bricks, getting scale off baths, that kind of job. Powerful stuff. Never heard of it?' Paul shook his head slowly. His eyes were black.

'It is a curious – way – for anyone to have chosen,' Mrs Drew said.

'It is, yes.'

'So – violent.'

'Yes, it looked violent. There were no other marks on the body. The way it looks so far, she was a perfectly healthy young woman. No inherent weakness, heart condition, anything like that. Would you agree?' Paul hid his eyes. Mrs Drew said, 'She has had no illness since she was a child. Just the ordinary childhood maladies.'

'A-ha. What I need to know from you is this: was there any reason you know of why she might – if anything had happened recently to cause her to—'

'To take her own life?' Mrs Drew was unperturbed. 'No, Inspector. It is out of the question. She was expecting a child.' The knife-blade eyes flashed towards each of us in turn. Village-bobby looked up from his notebook, shaken.

'A-ha. And you all knew that?' We conveyed silently that we did. 'Was it generally known?'

'I don't think anyone knew. Apart from us.'

'How long have you known, Mr Mannon?'

Paul was grey.

'She told me last weekend.'

'You, Mrs Drew?'

Her head was high. Her hands tight on the arms of the chair.

'My daughter intended to tell me when she got here, I believe.' There was a movement in her throat. She controlled it. 'She did not arrive, of course. Paul told me this morning.'

'A-ha. And you – Miss Hale?' He put my name in quotation marks.

'Paul told me this morn – yesterday morning.'

'Was it a surprise to you?'

'Yes. She'd been trying for a long time. She'd almost given up hope.'

'You were close friends, I hear. Odd that she didn't tell you. Big news. She'd known since last weekend.'

'She said on the phone she had something to tell me when I met her at the house. I didn't go to the house. Till yesterday. A little late,' I said, 'to hear the news.'

I was shocked. I don't talk like that, not to policemen. He had rattled me; his look stripped me; his manner invited me to collusion.

'A-ha,' he said.

The corner of the thin mouth twitched. Mrs Drew slightly turned her head. He said, 'So she was pleased about this pregnancy, you would say?'

Mrs Drew said, 'There is no doubt about it.' Paul started to cry. It was terrible.

Knife-blade ignored it.

He was not to be put off. 'Wouldn't it have had a bad effect on her career, a child?'

Mrs Drew said, 'Liza would have managed that.'

Paul said, 'She didn't give a – damn about her career.'

I said, 'Women don't have to drop everything these days just because they have a child.'

'A-ha.' The Village-bobby coughed behind a fat fist. He didn't like Knife-blade either. I realised I had stopped calling him Little-one. No name could have suited him less, wiry though he was. He said, 'I'm sorry to have to ask these things. It's painful I know. But we have to get to the bottom of this. It's a question of eliminating possibilities. So. You'd all say you knew of no reason why she should – take her own life? And that of her child?'

Mrs Drew said, 'Inspector, as I have said before, it is out of the question.'

Paul had his head down, still crying. He made no reply. The eyes glinted round to me. I noticed now that there was the slightest of casts in one of them. It perfectly expressed his untrustworthy character. 'She never mentioned the idea to you, Miss Hale?' I shook my head.

Village-bobby jotted: 'Interviewees replied in negative'?

Knife-blade looked at me a moment longer.

'A-ha. Now. Also you understand, just for the purpose of eliminating possibilities, I would like an account of where you all were from, let's say, Tuesday – shall we? – until, well, now.'

# CHAPTER FIVE

There was a sense of shifting in the room, though no one moved, except Village-bobby who crossed one big leg over the other. Knife-blade removed his amused squint from me and turned it on Mrs Drew.

'I understand you were ill,' he said.

'Yes. It was a flu of some sort. It started with a headache and sore throat, slight temperature, nausea, that sort of thing.'

'When did it start?'

'Last weekend.'

'Did you see a doctor?'

'Certainly not. The only way to treat a flu is go to bed with a hot-water bottle and drink plenty of honey and lemon. I should not dream of wasting a doctor's time on such a trivial matter.'

'A-ha. Carry on.'

'When Liza rang on Tuesday to say she would come here on Wednesday, I was not at all well.'

'What time was this?'

'Her phone call? I'm afraid I cannot give you a precise time. The phone woke me, you see. It was dark.'

'It gets dark soon after four these days.'

'Yes. After the call I went back to sleep. I'm sorry.' He nodded resignedly. 'As I said, I was not at all well. I told her there was no need to come. I don't like being fussed when I am ill, but she was determined to tell me her exciting news in person. And, of course, I am always – I was always pleased to see her here. When she had not arrived by Wednesday night I was a little worried.'

'A little?'

'Yes. Liza is not naturally punctual and anyway in her business – things are always cropping up. I did call her. On Wednesday evening. About nine o'clock.. There was no reply. I assumed either that she was on her way or that something had occurred to prevent her and she would let me know in her own good time. When I didn't hear anything on Thursday, I was a little puzzled. I was feeling, if anything, somewhat worse. I am not accustomed to being ill; it is something that happens to me rarely. I have to admit that I was – aggrieved. It was simply pride that prevented me from ringing her again. Also my throat was painful; it caused me a certain difficulty even to speak. And anyway such things have happened before. Once, she was supposed to come here; she did not arrive at the specified time, and she rang me two days later from Cornwall where she had been called at short notice to film some scenes for a series in which she was involved. So this time I simply felt a little cross and hurt that she had not had the courtesy to let me know. When Paul arrived this morning – with Millie – I expected it to be Liza.'

'So you haven't left this house since last weekend?'

'I did not leave my bed till yesterday morning. Except for the usual reasons. It would have been foolish to go outside.'

'Anyone called here?'

'No. Oh yes. My cleaning woman, Mrs Banks, from the town. Mrs Banks comes to me on Tuesdays. She was here last Tuesday all day till about four. Since then I have seen no one. You have only my word.'

'Spoken to anyone on the phone?'

'Apart from Liza, I am afraid not.'

'Thank you. Now, Mr Mannon.' Paul rubbed his eyes. He had himself under control now.

'Yes.'

'You have been working in Sheffield, I believe.'

'Yes.'

'For how long?'

'I've been up there since – it must be now – nine weeks. I started rehearsing this play two weeks ago, after the first one I was in closed.'

'You get back to London much?'

'Every weekend. I come home every weekend.'

'I thought actors performed on Saturdays.'

'I come after the show on Saturday night if I'm performing. Saturday afternoon if not. I'm not performing now, just rehearsing.'

'This weekend you came back on Thursday evening.'

'I wasn't needed on Friday. Or Saturday morning either. They were doing – rehearsing – bits I wasn't involved in.'

'You believed, then, that Miss Drew was here with her mother?'

'Yes.'

'But you didn't come straight here?'

'It's easier to go via London. And I needed to pick up some clean things.'

'You didn't phone here either.'

'It was late. I didn't want to disturb – anyone.'

'A-ha.'

On it went. When had he last spoken to Liza? When had she told him about the pregnancy? How had she seemed? Paul's so resonant voice was hardly audible. Mrs Drew stared out of the window at the white Suffolk sky. The bobby strained to hear and jotted. I winced each time Knife-blade uttered his punctuating nasal 'A-ha'.

'Now, Mr Mannon, where were you exactly on Tuesday?'

'I was at the theatre, rehearsing.'

'All day?'

'Yes. All day.'

'With other people, I presume?'

'Yes, the whole company. We had two runs.' Knife-blade raised an enquiring eyebrow. 'We ran through the play twice.'

'A-ha. Till what time?'

'Six. Or a little after.'

'I see. And then what?'

'We went to the pub. Then I went to eat.'

'Alone?'

'No.' Paul went quiet. He clasped his hands tight. Knife-blade simply waited. 'A friend from the company.' Knife-blade waited again. 'Jane Barnes.' Village-bobby looked hot, but wrote. Knife-blade nodded.

'A-ha. Till what time?'

'I don't know. Quite late. They were closing. It was an Indian restaurant. I suppose about midnight.'

'Then what?'

'I walked Jane back to where she lives. And then went back to my digs.'

Village-bobby coughed. No one else moved. Knife-blade had not lost his amused look.

'A-ha. See anyone there?'

'Where?'

'At your digs.'

'No.'

'Wednesday morning?'

'The theatre.'

'Yes. Before that.'

'Before?'

'Yes. From when you got up.'

'I woke about six and worked.'

'Worked?'

'Yes.'

'Alone?'

'Yes. On the script.'

'I see.'

He didn't.

'Had breakfast.'

'Where?'

'In the flat. It has a kitchen.'

'So, alone again?'

'Yes.'

'Look, Mr Mannon,' he said patiently, 'what I want to know is if anyone saw you Wednesday morning before you left for the theatre.'

'Oh.' Paul tried to concentrate. 'Oh yes. I share a bathroom there. I must have gone along about half past six. Jack Hill was in there. He didn't see me exactly; we talked through the door.'

'What about?' Paul showed a flicker of life.

'I gathered he'd had a heavy night the night before. He told me to piss off. It seemed he was going to be in there for some time. I went back to my room and peed in the sink.'

Village-bobby laughed, then looked sheepishly at Mrs Drew. The knife-blade eyes did not move. 'I went to Jack's room with some coffee about half past nine to get him up for work. We walked to the theatre together.'

'And you were at the theatre all day again?'

'Yes. And Wednesday night I spent in the flat of my "friend" ' (the quotation marks were his), 'Jane Barnes, from finishing at the theatre till going to work again on Thursday morning, and I hope you appreciate just how much satisfaction it gives me to be able to tell you that.' Paul got up and walked the length of the room. He'd have walked up the wall if he could. He stopped with his forehead pressed against a window. Knife-blade said: 'I wasn't going to ask you about Wednesday night; she was already dead by then.'

Paul shrugged. 'What does it matter?' he said.

Knife-blade glanced at the bobby. 'Strike out anything Mr Mannon said after yes he was at the theatre all day Wednesday. Irrelevant.'

'Yes, sir,' said Plod clearing his throat. Knife-blade turned to me. The look of concealed amusement intensified though his face didn't move. It was one of the stillest faces I have ever seen.

'And now, Miss Hale. How was your Tuesday night?'

'Event-less. I was reading at home. Alone.'

'A-ha. And your Wednesday morning. How was that?'

I stared at his squint, defying his mockery. I told again how Liza had phoned me on Wednesday morning.

'What time?'

'About ten.'

'A-ha.'

I told how she had asked me to meet her at the house and I had agreed, how excited she had been about the news she had to tell me, how I'd asked her to tell me now, how she'd said it was too wonderful to say on the phone; how then my agent had called about the interview at Television Centre at three, how I had rung Liza back to say I had to wash my hair and make myself presentable so couldn't go to the house, how disappointed Liza had been.

'Couldn't you have met her there after your interview?'

'I suggested that. She said it would be dark by then. She wanted to see it in the daylight.'

'A-ha.'

That noise was getting on my nerves.

'What time did she want you to meet her?'

'Twelve noon.'

'And you couldn't have managed it?'

'In simple terms of time I could, but I get keyed up before interviews, I need plenty of time to prepare.'

'What does the preparation entail?'

I sighed. Paul looked at me from the window, even gave a sort of smile. Sort of.

'Hair,' I said. 'Make-up, nails, long soak in the bath imagining how I'm going to play it.'

'The part?'

'The interview. Choosing the clothes, light lunch, plenty of time to get there so's not to be late.'

'Pretty elaborate.'

'Hard for you to imagine.'

'I'm learning. See anyone Wednesday morning?'

'No. Yes. I did. A bathroom encounter; not quite like Paul's. There's a couple on my floor—'

'Bathrooms?' He was winding me up.

'People.'

'A-ha.'

'The woman was coming out as I was going in.'

'Name?'

'What?'

'The woman's name?'

'I don't know. I don't know my neighbours by name.'

'How long have you lived there?'

'About six years.'

'How long have they lived there?'

'About a year.'

'I see. Time?'

'Time? Oh. I should think about, I don't know, eleven-thirty or just before. After the phone calls anyway.'

'See anybody else after that?'

'Afraid not. Not till I got to the car park at Television Centre.'

'What time was that?'

'About a quarter to three.'

'How did the interview go?' Bastard.

'Very well, thank you.'

'When did it finish?'

'Half past three.'

'Go straight home?'

'No, I went for a cup of tea. In the canteen.'

'Alone?'

'No, with a friend I'd met in the foyer. An actor. James Clegg. You wouldn't know him.'

'I can look him up.'

'He's not in *Who's Who in the Theatre*.'

'Are you?'

'Yes, as it happens.'

'I'm impressed.' I looked patient. 'When did you leave?'

'About half past four, I should think. I gave him a lift to Baker Street.'

'And after you dropped him?'

'I went straight home. Well, I stopped in West End Lane to do some shopping: bread, milk, something for supper; went home, cooked, ate, washed up, read a book, went to sleep.'

'Anyone phone?'

'No one phoned.'

'You phone anyone?'

'Yes, my agent to tell her how the interview went.'

'What time?'

'Oh, I suppose about five-thirty.'

'Back to Tuesday night – Did you see anyone? Coming out of the bathroom perhaps?' How amusing he was.

'No.'

'Mmm,' he said. It was a change from A-ha. 'Tough.'

Was he joking, or threatening me? I couldn't tell.

'Well,' he said, 'we'll have to see if anyone saw *you*. Never know, we might be lucky.' I still couldn't tell.

Paul said, 'Millie is Liza's best friend. They go back years. Before me, even.'

'Yes,' he said, looking away from me for the first time since he started his questions. 'I know that, Mr Mannon.'

Mrs Drew made a slight movement. I glanced at her. Knife-blade didn't miss much: 'You agree with that, Mrs Drew?' She let a little pause stretch a little.

'They were friends, yes,' she said slowly; implying I could say more but I won't. She and Knife-blade were stitching me up. I was helpless.

Paul said, 'Millie has stuck by Liza through thick and thin; I don't think her loyalty can be questioned. Or her friendship. There was nobody closer to Liza or more supportive of her. Apart from me.' He saw a black vision and stopped.

'Got all that, Simmons?' Knife-blade said.

'Yes, sir.'

'Good. Well. That's about all. Thanks for being so helpful. Will you mind, Mrs Drew, if we just look round the house and garden a bit while we're here?' She gave him a long hard look. He smiled like a cat smiles, without moving his face, and waited.

'For what, Inspector Bright?' He didn't quite shrug.

'We could go through official channels but that takes time.'

He waited again. She sighed and stood up.

'I will accompany you, if you don't mind,' meaning whether you mind or not.

'Certainly.'

The look of reproach she shot at Village-bobby was rewarded: embarrassment oozed from every inch of blue serge.

'Paul,' she said, 'put another log on the fire, would you? Thank you so much.'

The very room seemed to let out its breath when they left. Paul came over and dealt with the fire. He turned to look at me. We suddenly clutched each other and held on tight. The rough warmth of his sweater against my face and his arms protecting my back, it felt like the first human comfort for years. I don't know how long we stood like that. We could hear their footsteps overhead, marching about. We sat on the sofa side by side. I poured some cold coffee. Paul said, 'I don't know what to do, Millie.' Whether he was referring to the immediate future or the rest of his life, I didn't ask.

'Nor I,' I said. 'If only I had gone to meet her at the house.'

'Don't talk about the If Onlies. Mine are worse than—' He walked the length of the room again and came back; said, 'I don't think I can live with this.'

'We have to get through it bit by bit, one moment at a time.'

'Get through it to what?' he said. I had no answer to that.

I put my arms around him again. I was holding a husk; he had gone somewhere my arms couldn't reach. But Mrs Drew wasn't to know that when she came in. Over his shoulder she pierced me again with a look of consummate loathing, and began to collect the coffee cups.

'They are looking round the garden now. I decided they could do that by themselves; it is extremely cold. What are they looking for?' Ignoring me, she asked Paul.

'They are looking for the common household substance—'

'I see,' she said. 'Presumably I am thought to keep it in the kitchen to flavour the soup. Or in the garden to poison the plants.'

'No doubt they'll search our flat. And Millie's too.'

The thought appeared to console her; they were bound to find a sack of the stuff under my bed.

'It's their job,' said Paul.

We heard them beating their feet on the back doormat. When they appeared they were purple with cold.

'Did you find what you were looking for, Inspector Bright?' She was sarcastic. His eyes glinted.

'No, Mrs Drew, we didn't. Just got a little bit chilled.'

'I'm so sorry,' she said. It didn't sound like she meant it.

'Not your fault, Mrs Drew.'

'I did not suggest that it was.'

Sergeant Simmons turned a deeper shade of mauve.

'Now, Mr Mannon, Miss Hale,' Knife-blade's eyes slid over to me. 'I think you ought to be getting back to London quite soon.'

'What for?' Paul asked.

'Well. Let's say we'd like to have you on hand.'

'I see.'

Mrs Drew braced herself to say something difficult.

'Mr Bright. My daughter's – the arrangements will have to be made. With as much dignity as we can manage in the circumstances.'

'There'll have to be an inquest, of course. It will depend on the result of that.' Paul winced. Mrs Drew remained stony. 'I'm sorry,' Knife-blade said. It did sound like he meant it.

'It is so – *disgusting* – all this,' she flung out.

There was silence. She was suddenly fragile, vulnerable.

'And there will be the press,' she said on an inward breath.

Paul sat beside her and touched her hand. Knife-blade said, 'We'll keep them off it for as long as we can.'

'That won't be long,' said Paul.

'No.' Knife-blade agreed.

Paul said, 'We've probably got the rest of the weekend.'

'You'll be used to them, of course.'

'You never get used to them.' Mrs Drew stood up. 'I shall get my coat and pack a bag.'

'Where are you going?' Knife-blade asked for us all.

'I shall accompany Paul to London. If he doesn't mind.'

Paul was in no state to mind; you could have put him in a pram and wheeled him anywhere; but I minded.

'I shan't know what to do here and I may be able to be of some help. Only if Paul wishes, of course.' Paul wished.

'Thank you,' he said.

I felt a rush of rage and devastation so strong I had to turn away to hide it. I picked up the poker and prodded the spitting logs. Now it was I who didn't know what to do. She was locking me out of the only place I wanted to be. I controlled myself, concentrated on the fire-guard.

She walked past me without a glance. As she left the room, Paul said, 'She's a rock.' Knife-blade said, 'Quite a lady, yes.' Plod nodded his large head and cleared his throat:

'Oh yes, that's a fine woman, Mrs Drew.'

Knife-blade raised an eyebrow in my direction. 'Don't you think so, Miss Hale?' Amused behind the mask.

'Remarkable,' I said, and went to fetch my coat.

# CHAPTER SIX

We were all in the hall ready to leave when Knife-blade said to me, 'I'd like to offer you a lift, Miss Hale.'

'What?'

'Would you like to travel in my car?'

'No,' I said, 'I wouldn't, thanks. I'm going with Paul.'

'I'd be glad of the company.' He was inexorable.

'But—' I was incoherent with panic, and angry too. 'It's my car.'

'What about it?'

'Paul is driving my car. We came here in my car.'

'You live quite close to each other in London, don't you?'

'*Quite* close, yes.'

'Well, that shouldn't be a problem, then.'

Paul tried to help. 'If Millie would rather come with us—'

'There are a few more questions I'd like to ask Miss Hale. It seems as good an opportunity as any.'

'Paul,' I said.

But Mrs Drew was merciless: 'You might as well go with Inspector Bright, Millie, since he wishes it. You will certainly have a more comfortable ride than we shall. I almost envy you.'

'Perhaps you'd like to take my place,' I said.

'If you don't decide soon—' She pulled on one smooth suede glove. '—we could be standing here in the hall for the rest of the day.' She pulled on the other.

'Miss Hale?' Knife-blade waited. I was defeated.

'It seems I have no choice,' I said.

It was cold outside. I handed the car keys sadly to Paul. He held Mrs Drew's bag on one arm; he hugged me with the other and kissed me lightly on the cheek. 'I'll bring the car round tonight,' he said, and to Knife-blade, 'Look after her.' I didn't speak; someone had shoved a billiard ball down my throat. It hurt. I watched him tuck Mrs Drew solicitously into my car and drive away.

We dropped Village-bobby at his police station on the outskirts of the town, an incongruous seventies pile, grey brick and blue paint, with a wide concrete forecourt. 'We'll get the notes telexed through, sir.' He clambered out of the car and plodded away.

'Unexpected, isn't it?' Knife-blade said. 'I bet you imagined a little house with a blue lamp.' I didn't reply. 'County Constabulary Head-quarters,' he said. 'Computers and everything.' I stared ahead. Silence I had decided on and silence I maintained. 'I see,' he said. He turned the car in an easy arc, and from then on neither of us spoke. To me the silence felt like stone; he was unaffected by it. He sat back relaxed and content; I burned with misery and fear.

He drove well, I had to admit; by an instinct higher than thought, at one with the car and the road, through the flashing snowy landscape. It was a drive that felt more like flight. In different circumstances I'd have enjoyed it. But all I could see in the grimy snow was Mrs Drew, not even turning to say goodbye, hands folded in her elegant lap, setting off to London with Paul.

'What's with that Mrs Drew?' he said.

'What?'

The granite silence had lasted an hour or more. By his choice of subject, his way of putting it and, worst, by his slicing into my thoughts, he had startled me into speech.

'Well?'

'What do you mean?' I said stiffly.

'A bit weird, isn't she?'

I didn't reply. 'Don't you think so? Or don't you want to say?'

'She's very brave.'

'Oh yes, she's that all right.'

'And very strong.'

'I wouldn't argue with you there.' He laughed quietly. 'How did she get like that?'

'What do you mean?'

'Well, gradual, you know, over the years, or sudden, like this morning?'

I pulled myself together. 'I will answer no questions about my friends.'

'A-ha,' he said. Then, 'You should know who your friends are. She's no friend of yours.'

I stared bleakly ahead.

'Look,' he said, 'what we say in this car on this journey is strictly off the record. I'm not asking you to betray your friends.'

'Ha,' I said briefly.

'You don't believe me,' he said.

'In a job like yours,' I explained carefully, 'as in a job like mine, there is no such thing as off the record. The record is inside your head and it goes round whether you like it or not. Anything I say you will remember, and if you remember, it's cut in wax. There's no wiping it even if you try.'

'Different kind of record,' he said.

'The same thing applies.'

'So you'd like your lawyer to be present before you say another word?'

'On this subject, yes.'

'Quite tough, aren't you, in your way?'

'You have to be in my business.'

'Not as tough as you have to be in mine.'

'That is very clear.'

'What I mean is, if you fight me I'll win.'

'I know what you mean, thanks. But knowing you're going to lose is no reason for giving in.'

He laughed, a sort of nasal snicker of delight, his horrible little eyes screwed up. He had surprisingly nice teeth. All the better to eat you with.

'Look, Millie,' he said, 'you're a strong girl, but that woman is out to get you and you're not as strong as her.' Millie indeed! He ignored my outrage and went on, 'Also she makes a good impression.'

'And I don't?'

'And you don't. You're rude, belligerent and scornful. She's polite.'

'Oh yes.' Horrified, I heard myself say, 'She's polite all right.'

'She'll be polite to the end. She's not going to lose her cool.'

I pulled myself up short.

He would get no more collusion out of me.

'You're talking,' I said, 'about a woman who has lost her only daughter in the most—'

'Disgusting?' he said.

'Horrifying of circumstances. If she didn't keep up that iron control she'd break into little pieces which she might never be able to assemble again. She's got to be like that. It may not be sympathetic, but you have to respect it.'

'Oh, I respect it,' he said. 'I've a healthy respect for tempered steel.' His little eyes swivelled round to me, amused. I responded with a cold stare. Not many people frighten me; this rattish little man put me into an ecstasy of fear. Even anger can be a kind of fear. I felt exhausted suddenly. I seemed to have known nothing but violent emotions for so long. I felt my power to resist and fight him ebbing away. I had no strength any more. I closed my eyes.

'You're tired, Millie,' he said. 'Mind if I call you Millie?'

'Yes,' I said, 'I mind.'

'Sorry,' he said. 'Have a sleep.'

I heard myself say dreamily, 'Macbeth hath murdered sleep. Macbeth shall sleep no more.'

'Macbeth was the one who did it, wasn't he?'

'Yes. With a little help from his friends.' And then, to my great surprise, I slept. The welcome velvet black descended on me.

When I woke we were bowling along the bleak A12, lumps of dirty snow littering the drab verges. I felt marvellous as I woke; Paul was by my side and the sun was shining. The happiness lasted three seconds. The sallow capable hand expertly changing gear jolted me into gear too. I was immediately on my guard.

'Feeling any better, "Miss" Hale?'

'No . . . Thanks.'

I could see that sleep might be the only solace for some time to come. I wished I could go there again.

'Look,' he said, 'tell me something about Mrs Drew; she interests me. Work it out: what possible harm can it do her for you to tell me her personal history? I want to understand, and I'll never get anything out of her; I know when I'm beat.'

'Apparently you don't.'

'What harm can it do her?' he said again.

'That has ceased to be the point.'

'Ah. Not that it might do harm to her but that it might do good to me?'

'I didn't say that.'

'No.' He grinned. 'You didn't say it.'

There was a silence. Then:

'All right, then. If you won't tell me about her, tell me about you. Any objection to that?'

'Many objections to that.'

'But you will, won't you?'

He must have sensed my weariness.

'What do you want to know?'

'Everything. Where you were born, grew up, everything, the lot.'

I couldn't explain my capitulation. I was a safer subject than Mrs Drew? At least I could *bore* him to death? I sighed. 'I was born in Norwood,' I said. 'Thrilling, isn't it? My dad worked on the railways, my mother cleaned other people's houses. I cleaned ours. No brothers and sisters, she only had miscarriages after me. I was a disappointing child, I used to read. Books. Learning to read was the most exciting thing that ever happened to me. I recognised a means of escape when I saw it. And when I went to Stratford with the school to see *As You Like It* I recognised another.'

'How old were you then?'

'I don't know, fourteen, fifteen. I never told anyone what I'd decided to do; I arranged auditions for the drama schools and when they accepted me at RADA I arranged for my own grant; I just got the parents to sign the forms.'

'When they found out, didn't they object?'

'No point in objecting to a *fait accompli*. Anyway it would have created a precedent; they never in their lives had the energy to object to anything. They suffered from terminal apathy.'

'See much of them now?'

'Saw my mother at my father's funeral.'

'What did he die of?'

'I told you. Laziness. It became too much trouble to breathe . . . Oh, all right. He had a dicky heart.'

'Where's your mother now?'

'Still in Norwood. Still cleaning other people's houses.'

'She must be lonely.'

'Everyone's lonely.'

'Bitter.'

'Not really, just a fact. I see her now and then. Maybe twice a year. Enough for us both.'

'A-ha. Enjoy drama school?'

'Yes, after the first year.'

'What was wrong with the first year?'

'Not it. Me. I was scared shitless. Then I made friends with Liza and—' I stopped.

'A-ha.'

'It made a difference. I also started to realise I was the best. Liza was the prettiest; I was the best.'

'Is that when you met Mrs Drew?'

I gave him a look. He grinned.

'Yes,' I said. 'We used to go there at weekends. She was nice to me. Liza was so much prettier than I was, prettier than anyone was; she didn't see me as competition. When I won the medal her attitude changed.'

'Won a medal did you?'

'Yes. They give them every year. Seems a big deal at the time. Not much cop really.'

'Oh?'

'No. It gets you some good jobs for a year or two; then it wears off.'

'You got good jobs?'

'Yes. I was good at the ingenues. A bit out of the ordinary. You know.'

'A-ha. And Liza?'

'She played maids and pretty secretaries for about four years. No one thought she was much of an actress but everyone loved her so she got work.'

'Did you?'

'Did I what?' I knew what he meant.

'Love her?'

'I love Liza more than – anybody in the world.'

Silence.

'Then she got the first telly series and everyone discovered she could act. It was just on stage she wasn't very good. From then on she was a star.'

'Did she change?'

'Liza? No.'

'Success didn't spoil her, then?'

'It's not success that spoils people,' I said. 'It's failure. Haven't you noticed?'

'Has it spoiled you?'

'It hasn't happened to me.'

'You're not a star.'

'There are other things.'

'Like what?'

'Respect. Within your profession.'

'A-ha. What sort of parts do you play nowadays?'

'Difficult ones.' I snapped.

Silence.

'Where did Paul Mannon come in then?'

'I met him at Coventry about three years after drama school. We were playing the leads in three plays.'

'So he met Liza through you?'

'Yes. She came up to see the second show.'

'Love at first sight?'

'Not quite. While she was visiting she got asked to play a small part in the third show.'

'Love at second sight.'

'More or less.'

'How did you feel about it?'

'How do you mean?'

'Well. Feel left out?'

I said, 'Of course. A bit. Who wouldn't? But I was also really glad for them. And, as everybody said, they were such a perfect couple. And I wasn't left out. We all stayed friends.'

'And how long did that last?'

'What?'

'The perfect couple.'

'Always. It never stopped.'

'Oh?' He raised a sceptical eyebrow. 'He said he was playing around.'

'Oh that,' I said. A needle of fear slipped down my throat. His weasel mouth was set in the line of one who takes more than a pinch of salt with everything. How should I play it now?

'That happens,' I said.

'Oh, does it?'

'Yes, it does. It's not important.'

'Oh, isn't it?'

'No. You go away from home to work, you're with new people day and night, working very hard. You're lonely. It happens. It's normal.'

'Would Liza think it was normal?'

'Of course she would, she's – she was – not a fool.'

'A-ha.'

'If people in our business let those things upset them – she knew there was no one for Paul but her.'

'He was very keen to tell me all about it,' he said.

I turned blazing eyes on him. You bastard, I thought. You've walked me into the centre of a maze, and in the centre of the maze was a trap and I've walked Paul straight into its mouth. I had difficulty breathing.

'That's because he felt so terrible about it,' I said.

'It's also, possibly, his alibi,' he said, very quiet.

We turned into Fortune Green Road and stopped. 'Thanks for the lift,' I said with considerable sarcasm. I was struggling with the seat belt. Nowadays there's no making a clean exit from a car.

'What will you do now?' he said.

'I'll take a lot of Valium,' I said, 'and phone Paul.'

'A-ha.'

'If you have no objection, of course.'

'Sounds fun,' he said.

'Don't you want to search my flat?'

'Not just yet, thanks.'

'Giving me time to clear all my household cleaning substances from under the sink? How kind.'

'Not allowed to do it on my own.'

'I see.'

'Miss Hale—' He'd dropped the quotation marks. He leaned across the passenger seat and gazed at my face. What was coming now? 'Is there anything you know, or anything Liza told you that you didn't want to say in front of them, that might give me some headway on this?'

I didn't need time to think. I'd thought enough. Wearily I shook my head.

'There was nothing. There is nothing. There's nothing I can think of at all.'

'If you think of anything, will you be sure to let me know?'

'Oh yes, I'll be sure to let you know.'

'Okay. You take care of yourself.' His eyes didn't let me go. 'I'll be seeing you,' he said. It was a threat, not a promise.

'I'm sure you will.'

He smiled. His eyes undressed me down to the bones.

I hated him.

# CHAPTER SEVEN

My flat was awful: dusty, grey, damp, dead; cold air, emptiness congealed. I felt I'd been away for years, Rip Van Winkle rubbing the sleep out of his eyes on the side of a cold mountain. I'd felt alone before, it was a feeling I was used to; but not like this. I lay on the bed in my coat and stared at the ceiling. The diagonal crack that zigzagged across it was nothing to the fissure that had opened in my life. Life after Liza. I'd reached an abyss. There must be a way to reach the other side but at this moment I couldn't see it. It was lost in fog. I had spent my life looking forward, not back. When you're climbing a mountain you don't look down. But when you can't see the future and can't bear the present, where else is there to look but the past? That man in the car had tricked me into recalling the bitter images, and now they refused to go away. I was too weak to chase them back into the dark where they belonged. They were flashed onto the cracked ceiling one by one. I was powerless even to shut my eyes. The life of Amelia Hale and how she at last became me.

Amelia Hale at home. Home! I never knew the meaning of the word till Liza took me to hers. The 'living' room: mean, shabby. The parents: he crouched in the Parker Knoll with the *Evening Standard,* working away at the dandruff with a blackened little hand; she with the knitting; the telly mumbling in the corner. Amelia: at the table doing her homework, shutting them out, biding her time. It was only a matter of waiting. I never went out, never brought anyone 'home'. I was working for my future, tunnelling my escape.

Liza's home. Liza's beautiful mother opening the door with a dazzling smile: 'You're Millie, I've heard so much about you, do come in.' Books and paintings and the china like feathers on your lips. Such welcome. Every weekend. Wandering in the garden, swaying on the swing. The sun always shining as in other people's childhoods. That was my true childhood; the only time I was touched by innocence and hope.

The exit from the garden. I won the medal and watched the smile stiffen on her mother's face. *My* mother's face. I'd thought the adoption was mutual. I believed in it. But the smile grew stiffer in my first successful years. It softened a bit when Liza became a 'star' but it was too late. I was shut out of the garden by then.

Paul. Paul. The one good thing in my life, apart from my work, that I didn't get from Liza. She wasn't there; her mother was lost to me. Paul was my own. I watched him even when he slept, learning him by heart. I never touched down, that three months with him. I thought he felt the same. So did he.

Paul meets Liza. Enter the court with hautboys and trumpets. His bewilderment was comical. I couldn't fail to recognise in him the symptoms he had caused in me.

Exit Millie, leaving the stage to her two dearest friends. A touching scene. Oddly, Liza's mother and I drew close again. It seemed almost worth the loss. But it didn't last. Paul was lovable. She loved him. He responds to love like a flower to the sun. He loved her. Millie returns to being family friend.

Liza dies. Re-enter Millie, centre stage, Millie the comfort and support. Paul reaches out his empty arms; Millie enfolds him in hers. Mrs Drew stretches forth a hand; Millie grips it in hers and mops the tear-stained eyes. Ha!

You don't know what your fantasies are until you see them unfulfilled. The scene faded fast. There was nothing on that side of the crack but grubby ceiling, flaking paint. No one can accuse Millie Hale of not facing facts. I lay on my bed and laughed into Knife-blade's mocking face. 'But I haven't given up,' I said. 'Amelia Hale didn't and neither will Millie. I owe her that much. I will not be beat.' I was confused suddenly: his foxy little face had become my father's face; it was my father I was talking to. And then I knew why I loathed Knife-blade so. They were alike, he and my father. Same wiry little body, cunning intelligence, even the slight strabismus in the eye. One a railway man, the other a cop; either could have been a petty crook, slipping past dustbins in the dark.

That night and Sunday were a black hole. Sunday morning, Paul came round with my car.

'The police are keeping ours,' he said.

We smiled cold comfort on the step.

'How's Mrs Drew?' I said.

'Bearing up. Bearing me up too.'

'She has the strength for four.'

The number came out of the air, but hung there: she only needed strength for three now. Paul swallowed nails. There was truly nothing one could say. We held each other's cold hands and shivered with more than cold.

'Want a cup of tea or something before you go?'

'No, Millie, I'd better get back to her.'

What about me? I thought.

'All right,' I said.

We held each other briefly. Then I watched him loping down the street. Later, Knife-blade rang.

'John Bright here,' he said.

For a second I was at a loss. Who?

'Oh! Yes. Yes?'

'You all right, Miss Hale?'

'Never been better; what did you think?'

'Are you spending the day alone?'

'I don't know yet. I've made no plans.'

'I shouldn't. If I were you.'

'You're not me.'

He laughed. 'The press,' he said. 'I imagine they'll be on to it tomorrow. Try to say as little as you can.'

'I'm not a fool.'

He ignored that.

'If you can't manage no comment, make it the bare bones.'

'You're full of good advice.'

'And try not to be too much alone.'

The bastard. He had an unerring way with a raw nerve.

'Right,' I said. 'Thanks. I'll throw a party tonight. Like to come?'

'Funny you should say that.'

'Oh no!'

'A-ha. A colleague and I will be dropping round about three, if that's all right.'

'Oh that's great. Everybody welcome. Drinks on the house.'

'You'll be there?'

'Be here? I'll kill the fatted calf.'

The words dropped into a deep well, reverberating all the way. When they hit bottom and the echoes died, he said. 'That's the sort of thing I mean, Miss Hale. Watch yourself with the press.'

It was something to look forward to, having your place searched by the police on a wintry Sunday afternoon. I tidied up, tried to make it look like home. I hated the idea of Knife-blade seeing how I lived.

He came with a chap in an overcoat and jeans. He hardly looked at me. He hardly looked at the flat. They went through everything like two old women in an Oxfam shop, with fastidious attention to detail and delicacy of touch, but as though they were thinking about something else. I stood in the middle of the room, arms folded across my thumping heart, looking detached and keeping mum. I almost expected them to find a sack of – quicklime? – under the sink. Will you please accompany us . . . Anything you say . . . I'll have to leave this place, I thought. Everything in it is now contaminated by touch. It didn't take them long. There wasn't much of it. Knife-blade asked if he could wash his hands. I'd heard it used as a euphemism before but not for 'May I search your bathroom?'

'Be my guest,' I said. 'Round the corner on your left.'

I looked at Overcoat. He was just a boy, with flawless English boy's skin.

'Awful weather,' he said.

'Yes,' said I.

Knife-blade came back.

'That bath could do with a spot of spirits of salts,' he said. 'Takes the scale off like magic.'

Nobody smiled.

'The inquest opens Wednesday afternoon. You'll be required to attend, Miss Hale. Two o'clock at St Pancras Coroner's Court. See you there.'

Then I watched them roaming the scrubby garden, peering over the walls. Knife-blade turned over a dustbin lid distastefully with his foot.

He looked up at me as they left and gave a sort of salute. I nodded. At this distance he looked almost all right. I even felt a reluctant gratitude that he had treated myself and my belongings with respect, as much as was compatible with his job, that is.

Paul rang at nine. They'd done his flat over too.

'It wasn't as bad as it might have been,' he said.

'No. Not much worse than your average burglar,' said I.

'They took away Liza's address book. He's going to question every person in it, he says. I told him some of her fans are fairly loopy; he took some of their letters as well.' He sounded weary and much at sea. We talked about the press.

'They'll have a field day,' he said.

'Yes. Wonder who'll win the egg and spoon.'

'Good luck, Millie.'

'And you, Paul. Take care of yourself.'

'No need. Mrs Drew is taking care of me.'

I don't suppose he meant it to be cruel.

'See you at the inquest,' I said.

His goodbye was cut off by Mrs Drew. 'Are you all right, Millie?' she said to me.

'No.' I was surprised into response. 'I can't truly say I am.'

'I must apologise for my behaviour to you yesterday morning.'

I made an inarticulate noise. What was I supposed to say? Oh no, really, not at all, any time?

'Forgive me, Millie, I was in a state of some shock. It is no excuse, I know. I needed to hit out at something, somebody. It was simply that you were there.'

I heard myself saying: 'I understand.' And then: 'Don't worry about it, Mrs Drew.'

'Have you anything to help you sleep?'

'Oh yes, like you and everybody else, I've got the stash of Valium in the medicine chest. Thanks.'

'Be careful of the press, Millie.' It came out like an afterthought, almost teasing. 'Remember not to joke with them. They are not good at understanding irony, still less conveying it. Resist temptation. Some of your comments may appear less than amusing on the pages of a newspaper.'

I was stung. 'I learned that for myself some years ago. I am always very earnest with the press.'

So that was it. Warmth and penitence. Forgive and forget. Catch Millie off her guard. Then give her a warning to hold her tongue. I took three Valium that night. Thank you, Mrs Drew. And didn't catch so much as a glimpse of Liza in my sleep.

# CHAPTER EIGHT

You don't feel too witty on the doorstep at seven-thirty in the morning, freezing cold, your best friend violently dead, a pack of dogs pawing you all over with insinuation, excitement in their eyes. I refused to let them into the flat. That's what they wanted: photo of star's best friend getting out of tousled bed. So I shivered on the step. They were too excited to feel the cold.

'How did you feel?' Good question, isn't it? I didn't say fine, just great, never better. And how many answers can you give to the question, 'Was it a terrible shock?' 'Well, no, it's generally what I expect to find when I go to view a house for sale; especially with this estate agent as a matter of fact.' I didn't say that either. I started to take a certain pride in the variation of my conventionally sorrowing replies. Mrs Drew would be proud of me. 'Terrible,' I said. 'Awful,' I said. 'Indescribable,' I said.

'What do you think happened, Millie?'

'I just don't know,' I said. 'I can't bear to think,' I said.

One or two of them even seemed genuinely upset. They'd all known Liza. She'd been a good bone to gnaw at. She had always been nice to them. I tried to emulate her. I tried hard. I had to feel like Liza inside in order to do it well: open, eager, simple; no cynical reserve, no holding the dogs at bay, just straight and sweet. It worked; my diaphragm relaxed, my throat loosened, my facial muscles softened out. This softness spread to feelings. I had a hard job controlling the tears, in the eyes, in the voice. And having worked on me, it started to work on them. Their barking got gentler, their manner solicitous. They were licking my hands.

So that was how she did it. I'd always wondered. Well, now I knew. Funny way to find out.

'I'm sorry,' I said, on the edge of breaking down. 'I don't think I can – I have to—'

'Okay, Millie, we'll go now, you've been great.'

'Just look this way, love.' Click.

'A quick shot before you go in, love.' Click.

'Thanks a lot.'

The news cameras arrived later. Same questions, same answers, different style; the respectable end of the news business. I knew the lines by now. I was so soft and vulnerable I got scared I was going too far. I didn't have the appearance to go with it, the aureole of silk-spun hair, the eyes, the mouth. It was a momentary fear; I squashed it fast. The way I'd started was the way I had to go on: you can't change your performance halfway through the show. And anyway I'm not used to people being so nice to me. It made me feel good; too good to relinquish for an artistic scruple. I played it to the hilt. It was easy, it was luxurious. Liza was inside me now, working away like yeast.

We made the afternoon editions, Liza huge on the front page, 'Interview with Liza's best friend see page two.' And all the television news. I couldn't resist the temptation to watch. I came over straight and nice and honest and upset. And I looked good. Weeks ago I'd decided to lose some weight and the past few days were better than any diet; I was all cheekbones and eyes and trembling mouth. You can't help thinking these things: it's professional, not personal; you're an actress, a commodity: you've got to see if it works. It worked.

By Tuesday I'd made the front page. And they'd looked up my credits. I was no longer 'Liza's Best Friend.' I was 'Actress Millie Hale', 'Millie' in the tabloids. I'd achieved fame. Over Liza's dead body. What a way to do it. Makes you feel really good.

And I hadn't talked so much in years. In those two days I was phoned by everyone I'd ever met. And some I hadn't. They wanted the story from the horse's mouth and were prepared to buy it by paying their respects. They were shocked, sorrowing, sympathetic. And avid. People who could claim only casual acquaintance invited me to lunch. My social calendar could have been filled from morning till night for the next six weeks. I was pleasant and adamant. I refused them all, and told them no more than I had told the journalists. What more was there to tell?

They interviewed Knife-blade on the evening news. People look different on the box. The cast in his eye didn't show so much. He looked less like a petty crook. He was terse, unsentimental. Yes there were injuries to the face, but no sexual interference. No, there were no clues, nothing had come out of questioning acquaintances, relations, friends. I didn't believe a word of it. The case remained a mystery but 'There's an answer somewhere,' said Knife-blade, 'even to the apparently in-explicable. And we'll find it,' he said. He ended by asking anyone who had been in the vicinity of the house on the morning in question or who had information that might be relevant to come forward. And I ended by almost liking him. Only till I turned the telly off. Being Liza hadn't affected me that much.

But being Liza was affecting me. It was weird. Those two days, I was alone, except for the telephone and the journalists. But I didn't feel alone. Sure, I was busy answering questions from morning till night, with no time to brood, but that didn't account for the good feeling I had. Liza was like a soft light spreading inside me, de-fusing horror and fear. I was keeping her alive. In return she kept me sane. It was our reciprocal agreement, friendship's reward. Sounds ghoulish? The world was a ghoulish place at that time. Shadow puppets waving on the wall. Liza sustained me. Liza gave me peace enough to sleep. She stayed inside me day and night. And she was my secret. Nobody would ever know.

On Wednesday the letters started to arrive. I answered them. It kept me occupied; I didn't want to dwell on the inquest in the afternoon. There was even a note from Mrs Drew. She and Paul were answering no questions and had unhooked their phone, which was why I was taking the brunt. She thanked me for handling the journalists 'with dignity and charm'. In her scale of human attributes they were the tops. Higher praise you couldn't get.

I replied to the letters in Liza's style. It was an effort not to do it in her handwriting. Some of them were touching; I even found tears in my eyes. Maybe I was rehearsing for the inquest. I was nervous. It was on my mind. By the last reply my hands were sweating. It was lunchtime but I couldn't eat. Neither could I stay in the flat any longer. I was glad when it was time to go. At least I would see Paul. I was missing him like hell. And Mrs Drew? Her note had been kind.

The coroner's court was hard to find. I parked on the one free meter I could see and walked through the concrete desert that surrounded the railway terminal. In a dismal back street I found a notice next to a secret-looking flight of steep and narrow steps. I went up them to a pink brick building like a nineteen-fifties public lavatory, which was grafted onto a little Victorian Gothic edifice that might have been a chapel once. I went into its tiny entrance hall. A notice said, 'All enquiries to coroner's office' with an arrow pointing down the corridor; and another, 'Please do not enter the court until you have announced yourself at the office.' I could hear voices but there was nobody about. I was early. I went out. I stood in the cold, feeling frozen. There was a small gate next to the court. It was open. I walked through it. I was in a public garden, one of the secret gardens of London, half-buried under snow, ancient trees, gravestones, paths, winding one way to a church, another to a hospital; there were benches, patches of wintry grass. Opposite me a pair of huge iron gates were open to Pancras Road. I walked about a bit, alone. There was a moment when I almost ran to the main gates and out into the road. I decided to announce myself instead.

The coroner's office was like a counter at the labour exchange, but with a push-button bell to get attention. I pressed it and stood. On the other side of the glass was a room with a row of tall metal cupboards, their doors open showing piles of stationery; on top of the cupboards several dozen eggs and a small mound of empty egg boxes, three bulging plastic shopping bags and a bottle of orange liqueur. The coroner's men were planning an omelette party?

A big man with a big moustache appeared at the counter.

'Yes?'

'I am Millie Hale.'

'Yes?'

'I'm attending the inquest at two o'clock.'

He consulted a list.

'Oh yes. The waiting room is there if you'd like to sit down,' indicating a door behind me. 'We'll call you when it's time.'

'Thank you.'

The waiting room had a virulent turquoise carpet and a turquoise door that didn't match. There was a metal coatstand in a corner and a fire extinguisher with a plastic bucket underneath it. On the table a tin ashtray spilled cork stubs out of a cushion of ash. The room smelt of it. On the windowsill was a neat display of leaflets, blue and white: *Income Tax and Widows, Your Benefit as a Widow, How to Obtain Probate*. I wished Paul would turn up. I heard his voice.

But he didn't speak to me. Mrs Drew was in black, elegant. None of us spoke. We sat on the grey plastic chairs. The tall silver-haired policeman came in.

'Good afternoon,' he said.

We nodded. He sat next to Paul and folded his arms. The big man from behind the counter appeared.

'Would you like to go into the court now?'

Funny questions people ask.

'This way please.'

We trooped after him back down the corridor. He opened a heavy arched door on our left.

It was more like a chapel than a courtroom. Four vaulted windows faced the secret garden, too high in the wall to see anything but grey sky. One of them was mended with plywood. The bare bricks were painted a shiny pale green. At the far end was a dais. On one side of it three rows of pews; a sort of pulpit on the other. In the middle of the dais stood a throne with a coat of arms hanging over it on the shiny green wall behind. Rows of pews faced the dais.

The big man said, 'You go and sit in the front row, that's it. The coroner won't be long.'

We sat on the crimson plastic cushions. The pews were caked with syrupy brown varnish as was all the wood. An unhealthy-looking young man in a navy-blue raincoat that had seen better days came in and sat at the table in front of us below the throne. He took out a spiral note book and started to bite his nails. He went through them methodically, spitting out the bits. He was joined by five colleagues, no one I knew. They had sent second strings? A shirt-sleeved policeman with red hair came through the door and stood to one side with his back against a radiator; it wasn't warm in there. Silver-hair walked past him and sat at the end of our pew. We waited. The nail-biter started on his left hand. The Gothic door, stage left of the throne, opened. Red-head said in a monotone without punctuation, 'Will the court rise please be seated,' as a small grey man in a suit came in at the door and sat facing us on the throne. Red-head continued without a break, 'Sir will you open the inquest in the case of Liza Drew Inspector Grahame please.' Silver-hair got up and stood in the pulpit and Red-head followed him without pause or change of tone saying, 'I swear by Almighty God . . .'

'I do,' said Silver-hair.

'You are?' said the coroner.

Silver-hair gave his name, 'Inspector Alan Grahame', and his police district.

'Can you tell us what happened on the morning of Friday the tenth of January?'

'Yes. Would you mind, sir, if I refer to my contemporaneous notes?'

A long word for a policeman, I thought.

'Please do.'

He described that morning, surprisingly graphically.

'Thank you.'

He got down. Red-head piped up. 'Amelia Hale please, I swear by Almighty God . . .'

I found myself on stage facing the audience. Knife-blade was leaning against the back wall. My view was clouded by my own breath which hung on the cold air. The little coroner looked at me kindly.

'You are Amelia, known as Millie Hale, an actress,' he consulted his notes and told me my address. 'And you found and identified the body I believe.'

'Yes. It was Liza Drew.'

'You knew her well?'

'Yes, she was my closest friend.'

'Thank you.'

Bewildered, I found myself back in the pew as Paul was being informed of his name and address.

'Millie, Miss Hale, came to my flat and fetched me to the house.'

'And you confirmed the identity of the deceased?'

'Yes.'

'Thank you.'

Paul, also looking bewildered, stumbled back to his seat.

'I am adjourning this inquest in order that inquiries may proceed, thank you.'

'Court rise please thank you sir.'

The little grey man had already made his exit and shut his door. We sat baffled, looking at each other. The five reporters scuttled out. Nail-biter was studying the tube map in his diary with an aggrieved expression. Silver-hair stood up.

'Is that it?' I asked him.

'Yes. All over,' he said. 'For the time being.'

The big man from the office was in the corridor.

'Do we just leave now?' I asked.

'That's right, love. You're adjourned while the police investigate.'

There was another group of people straggling towards the court with the uneasy expression of hospital visitors on their way to the wards. We found ourselves out in the cold. Of Knife-blade there was no sign. Had I imagined him? The cameras clicked. Paul and I said 'No comment' three or four times. We were left alone. Mrs Drew shivered and took Paul's arm. Paul looked at me. A coffee somewhere might have been nice, his place perhaps? Before I could suggest it, 'Take me back, please, Paul dear,' Mrs Drew said.

I followed them down the icy steps.

'How are you getting back?' I asked.

'Taxi,' Paul said.

'I can take you,' I proffered. 'My car's quite near.'

He looked at Mrs Drew.

'Thank you, Millie, but a taxi, I think.' She sounded exhausted.

I wasn't going to beg. Paul pecked my cheek. I watched them go off down the street arm in arm. So much for seeing Paul. So much for the kindness of Mrs Drew.

# CHAPTER NINE

On Thursday it was obvious why there had been only second string reporters at the court. The wife of an RUC officer had been kidnapped in Derry. It was a bigger story. The dogs had leapt in full cry over there. On Radio Four at lunchtime they said, 'The inquest into the death of the TV Star Liza Drew was adjourned yesterday at St Pancras Coroner's Court. Police say they are still questioning those who knew the actress and people who live near the house in Belsize Village in north-west London where the body was found. So far nothing has emerged that might indicate how or why the tragedy may have occurred.' Knife-blade's voice was suddenly in the room, nasal and nasty; they should never have put him on the radio.

'Most police work is routine. We are sticking to our routine. My men are questioning meticulously and eventually they'll find what they are looking for.'

'Is this, as the newspapers have implied, a murder inquiry?'

'Not necessarily,' declared Knife-blade, blandly. 'No, we're just looking for some indication as to what might have happened.'

'Is suicide suspected?'

'It seems unlikely but we haven't entirely ruled it out. Anything anyone has to tell us will be treated in strictest confidence. I ask anyone who might have seen Miss Drew or spoken to her any time last week to please come forward and talk to us.'

Trust a man with a voice like that to split his infinitives.

And that was that. As far as the news business was concerned, the case was dropped. The caravan moved on. Everything seemed to have stopped. Except the phone calls: they went on. Nosiness is underestimated as a human motivating force; Knife-blade and his ilk have made a career out of it. Not that Knife-blade rang me up. But Robin Foxe Mills did.

It was Friday morning, grey and early. I was woken by the screaming instrument with the sensation that it hadn't stopped ringing all night. I answered it, furry of speech.

'Robin Foxe Mills here.'

'Yes? Who?'

'Foxe Mills, we met last Wednesday.'

'My God!' The BBC director I'd gone to see instead of Liza. Was it only last Wednesday?

'Millie, I'm sorry to ring you in the midst of all this, but I wonder if you could come in to see us again. The producer would like to meet you. Would you mind?'

No, I wouldn't mind.

'Could you possibly make it this afternoon?'

Yes, I thought I could.

They were all there: Robin, the producer, the writer, a secretary. The atmosphere was hushed.

'Terribly sorry. She was a wonderful girl. It must all have been a frightful ordeal for you. Sorry to bring you in to see us so soon but BBC schedules wait for no man.'

'Did you know,' said the producer, a small plump man tending to the bald, 'that Liza was our first choice for this part?'

I went pale. I stood up and turned towards the door. 'Oh no,' I said. 'Oh no.'

Gentle hands were laid upon me. I was drawn to a chair and lowered into it. The secretary proffered a paper cup of water. I tried to drink. It slopped on my skirt. She took it from my hand. I looked up. The room was in fragments. Robin was apologising for giving me a shock; the producer was looking at his feet. He was wearing scuffed suede shoes. I couldn't take my eyes off them.

'Would you like Sarah to take you to the canteen . . . a cup of coffee, perhaps?'

'No. It's all right, I'm all right, let's carry on. I'm sorry, I'm all right.'

'If you're sure.'

'Yes.'

'You are a very different type from Liza, of course.'

'Yes.'

'But we have seen something of the same quality in you, and we feel that it might work.'

'Oh God.'

'I know you are very shaken and upset but I wonder if you'd mind reading for us. Would that be too much of an ordeal?'

'No. I'll manage. But please don't expect too much.'

'We'll read the scene starting on page thirty-five where Jackie's talking to the inspector about the loss of her child.'

There was silence in the room while I looked over the script. It was a big emotional scene. I was in the right mood.

'Okay,' I said.

'I'll read in the inspector's lines, very badly, I expect. In your own time, Millie.'

No one spoke at the end of the scene. The producer stood and looked out of the window. Then he came over and shook my hand.

'Thank you, Millie,' he said, and shuffled out of the room.

Robin said, 'Look, Millie, I might as well tell you: we're down to a short list of three. Obviously since Liza was first choice—'

I winced.

'Sorry. But you can see from that that they were going for a star. They'll find it hard to give up that idea. But I think you're the best for the part. Better, though it's a terrible thing to say at this point, than Liza would have been.'

I dumbly shook my head.

'We've got to decide this weekend, so I won't keep you in suspense for long. I'll do my best but, of course, I can't promise to win.'

'Thank you, Robin. You've been incredibly kind.'

'Not kind,' he said. Promising to let me know by Monday, he gave me to the secretary who led me to the lift.

'You read marvellously,' she whispered shyly as the doors slid to.

In that lift I had the experience of pure fear. There were no grey walls, no floor; I was plummeting in a high wind down a black well that had no bottom. When it jolted to a halt on the ground floor I crossed the desert of the foyer to one of the padded seats, blindly picked up a newspaper from the table and sat with it shaking in my hands. A woman in reception came from behind her desk and touched me on the shoulder. I looked up. I saw mirrored in her glasses the terrified expression on my face.

'Are you all right?' she said.

My mouth made a movement but nothing came out.

'Put your head between your knees,' she said, and stood with her hand on the back of my neck. I started to breathe again. Objects came back into view. When her sturdy legs came fully into focus I looked up again.

'Thanks,' I said. 'I came over faint for a moment in the lift.'

'You've been going through quite an ordeal,' she said.

I looked at her wildly.

'We've all been seeing you on the box. It is you, isn't it?'

'Yes.' I smiled wanly. 'Yes, I suppose it is.'

'You sit there, dear, till you feel better. Can I call you a taxi to take you home?'

'No, I'm okay, honestly. I've got the car.'

'Are you sure you're fit to drive?'

'Yes.' I wasn't. 'It was just a bad moment. It's over, I'm fine.'

I drove on automatic pilot while I tried to work out what had been happening to me. I'd been playing Liza to the hilt. Not just in the reading but in the whole interview from beginning to end, her softness, eagerness and vulnerability, her niceness through and through. It was a darn sight easier than playing myself. Playing yourself you have to make up the lines as you go along and mine tend not to come out right. Playing Liza I knew the lines, I just had to say them as I got the cues. But when the doors shut me in the lift they left Liza floating outside with the secretary's face. She had taken me over so completely that when she was gone there was nothing left, I was the void I was dropping through. And if I got this part, Liza's part, which one of us would have got it – Liza or myself? And did it matter? And if I got it, what would people think? What would Paul think? What Mrs Drew? What, and this did matter, would Knife-blade think?

I must have looked odd when I parked the car. Paul was standing outside my flat.

'Millie! Are you okay?'

He didn't look so grand himself, hyacinth shadows under his eyes. 'Let's get inside,' I said.

'They returned the car to me today,' he said. 'I forced myself to drive it. It felt pretty bad. I decided to come here. I don't think I can drive it back.'

'Oh Paul, I've missed you so.'

We went into the flat. I lay face down on the bed.

'I need someone to talk to about this,' I said, 'but I'm not sure you're the one.'

I told him, however. Not about my 'playing' Liza; that was between me and her; nor about the experience in the lift: impossible to explain, and my secret too. Just about the interview.

'Paul,' I said, 'I'm horrified. This was Liza's part. She never mentioned it to me.'

'Yes, they offered it to her but she told them she would probably turn it down. Then the—' He swallowed. '—the pregnancy was confirmed. She couldn't have done it. It's eight episodes, she'd have been showing by the fifth. So it's not as though you're robbing her of anything.'

'That's how it feels; it feels like stealing,' I said.

'Well, it's not. She wasn't going to do it anyway. And look, Millie, this is work. You can't afford to turn down work.'

'I know. I'm broke.'

'Work helps to get you through the days. Which helps to get you through the nights. Or so the theory goes.'

His hands went limp. 'And anyway, Millie, there's many a slip. We've all had jobs that looked as though they were in the bag and got away at the last minute.'

'Yes, counting my chickens. They probably won't offer it.' But I knew different; I was sure. 'I won't have to make a decision after all.'

'But if they offer it, Millie, you must accept.'

'Not a betrayal of her?'

'Never. See yourself as doing it for her sake.' His face was grey.

'You've given me your permission. It's what I wanted, I suppose. I don't know if it helps. I have to work this one out on my own.'

We both stared into space, inside and out. My stomach felt like lead.

'What will her mother think?' I asked.

He looked at me but didn't speak for a bit. Then: 'I don't think she knows Liza was offered it,' he said.

'Don't tell her, Paul.'

'I won't,' he said.

My agent rang at five o'clock. We were halfway down a bottle of Scotch by then and I can't handle alcohol.

'They want you for the part, Millie.'

She was wild with simple delight.

'I knew it,' I said. The producer had liked my reading then. They hadn't needed the weekend.

'I'm so pleased for you, darling, especially at this awful time.'

'Thanks, Dorothy,' I slurred. 'It's a bit difficult to take in. I'm afraid that I am rather drunk. I'll call you back on Monday when I've thought it through.'

'What is there to think through?'

I couldn't tell her that.

'Don't you want me to accept at once? It's not every day a part like this one comes your way.'

'I know that, Dorothy, but at the moment I'm in no fit state.'

'No darling, no, of course, if you – But we mustn't keep them waiting too long.'

She watched the job evaporate before her eyes. I could hear it in her voice.

'No, Dorothy. I'll call you on Monday at ten o'clock.'

'You got it,' Paul said with a thick tongue.

'Oh yes.'

'I'm glad, Millie. I'm really glad.'

We both sat and cried. For our different reasons.

Amazing, the healing power of alcohol. For an hour or two. It was the first drink I had had in ages. Paul too.

'I can't at home,' he said, 'because of Margaret.'

'Mrs Drew?' So she was Margaret now. 'Doesn't she approve?'

'It's not that.' He scratched his nose. 'It's just—'

'It's just you mustn't do anything to scandalise – Margaret. When did you start calling her that? Very chummy,' I said.

'It's just that she never touches the stuff herself and—'

'Of course she doesn't. The paragon of all the virtues might fall off her pedestal if she got a little tipsy and that wouldn't do at all.'

'At least she doesn't down half a bottle of whisky and start picking meaningless quarrels.' He was cold. 'And you don't understand.'

'What I'd give to see her tight.' I laughed.

'Don't, Millie,' he said.

His voice was angry; disappointed too.

'She's in love with you, you know.'

I said it because I was stung. His disapproval hurt. The woman caused devilry even when she wasn't there. It was a mean revenge to watch his face drop open like a fish's.

'Oh yes,' I said, 'I saw it on Saturday morning in her kitchen. I must say it came as a shock.'

'You're drunk, Millie, and trying to make mischief. Stop it now.'

'Okay,' I said. 'It was a bad-taste joke.'

But I could see him starting to see. He shook his head like a dog, to clear the pictures out.

'What do you two talk about at home?' I asked.

'Nothing,' he said. 'It's very quiet at home.'

'Come and see *me* more,' I said. 'Just think what fun.'

We smiled sadly at each other across the room.

'What does it feel like,' I asked, 'to be loved by all the world?'

'Great,' he said. 'Just great.'

We were silent for a while, then:

'Heard from—' I stopped. What was his real name? '—Detective Inspector John Bright at all?' I asked.

'No, someone else rang about the car.'

'He's been lying very low,' I said. 'Not a word from him'.

'I expect he's busy,' said Paul, 'up in Sheffield grilling all my friends. Poor Jane. She won't know what to say.'

I didn't speak my thoughts on the subject of 'poor' Jane.

'Or at the BBC,' I said, 'walking those circular corridors till he's dizzy, finding out if I was really there on Wednesday and for how long.'

Suddenly I decided to say it. 'We could all have done it, you know, you, me, Mrs Drew.'

'What?'

'Well, you didn't spend Tuesday night with whatsername. I know you talked to – Thing – in the bathroom quite early on Wednesday morning but you could have got to London on Tuesday night and back again. Sheffield's not the end of the earth.'

He looked as though I were accusing him.

'I'm just trying to think like John Bright,' I said. 'They don't know exactly what time on Wednesday morning it happened. It could have been the early hours. And as for Mrs Drew, her only witness is her cleaning lady. She could have picked up her bed and walked the minute the coast was clear on Tuesday, raced up to London, lured her daughter to the house etcetera etcetera and trotted back to her sickbed in Suffolk in time for the milkman on Wednesday morning. She didn't even have to rush. No one expects a sick person to answer the door.'

'Why on earth should a perfectly sane woman kill her only daughter whom she loved?'

'She's not perfectly sane, she's mad with love for you.'

'This isn't funny, Millie.' He was white around the mouth, but I had to go on.

'And as for me, I could have done it easiest of all, of course. I could have met Liza at the house at noon just as we arranged, polished her off and trotted round to the BBC to get interviewed. For her job. Which I've now actually been offered. Looks good, doesn't it? Wait till Mr Detective Inspector Bright finds out about the job. I'm the favourite in this race.'

There sat Paul, beautiful and distressed, my friend of – what? – ten years, as fond of me as anyone could be, trying not to show he had considered this before.

'Number one favourite,' I reiterated. 'Very short odds.'

He got up unsteadily and came to me. He cradled me in his arms.

'Don't do this to us, Millie. Don't do it to yourself.'

'I have to face the facts. It's between us whether we talk about it or not. It's better to talk about it.'

'It's not.'

'Not between us or not better?'

'Neither. Both.'

'Secret thoughts destroy.'

'Words destroy.'

'Had you really not thought any of that?'

'I haven't thought anything. I've been in a coma. It's easier. I'm not like you.'

'You're nicer than me. You're the nicest man I've ever known.'

'Yes. I was being nice to Jane Barnes while Liza was lying dead in an empty house in Belsize Lane. I'm a really nice guy. That's the only thought I've had in my head for the last week, Millie. That's the God's truth.'

'I shouldn't judge other people by myself,' I said.

What had I done? My mouth again.

He slopped a large drink into his glass and drank it fast and neat.

'I'd better get back,' he said, lurching onto the arm of a chair.

'Stay the night.'

'Got to go.'

What had I done?

'I'll get you a taxi,' I said. 'Neither of us is fit to drive.'

As I was piling him into the cab he said, 'I'm sorry to be leaving the car outside your place. But I can't touch it again. It gives me the horrors.'

'I'll try not to look at it,' I said. 'Take him to King Henry's Road.'

He rang the next morning, Saturday, very quiet, very flat.

'I'm going back to work,' he said. 'It's the only thing that will stop me having to think. They could replace me, there's over a week left to opening. But I'm going to go back.'

Someone had just announced the imminent amputation of one of my limbs.

'That makes two of us,' I said.

'You've decided to take the job then?'

'I just decided now.'

'I'll keep in touch.'

'Ring me as much as you can,' I said, 'if you can still bear to talk to me after last night.'

'I can bear it.'

'I'm sorry about the things I said.'

'Did me good.'

Silence.

'What about Mrs Drew?' I asked.

'She's staying on at the flat. Better than Suffolk for the time being. Keep in touch with her, Millie, she needs someone.'

'I'm not the someone.'

'Nonsense.'

'I'll do my best.'

'Thanks, and take care. Good luck with the job.'

'And you,' I said.

# CHAPTER TEN

What a morning after. I looked like hell. Goodbye Paul. What now? Suddenly I couldn't stand it any more, the misery. I did what I never do, except at work: looked in the mirror and slapped on the gunge, did the eyes, the mouth, the cheeks, the lot. Then I clapped on a pair of dark glasses and a woolly hat and went to do my shopping in Camden Town. They knew me in my local shops; for the time being I'd had enough of being known.

The market was full of people. There was colour, noise; the sun was shining, melting the snow. It hurt my eyes. This had all been going on in my absence? I was an alien from inner space, standing in a queue.

A man in a muffler and a hat with dachshund earflaps piled vegetables into my bag.

'One pound eighty-five, love.'

I stared at him, transported.

'You all right, love?'

'Oh yes.' I came back with an effort. 'How much did you say?'

'It's the cold.' He blew on purple fingers and stamped his feet. 'Slows your brains down a bit.'

I'd been far away: same place, different time. In the summer, in the market, with Liza, in the sun. Piles of pimentos, green and red, shiny aubergines, white-faced cauliflowers, crisp little apples, golden pears; the wild man on the fruit stall: 'Eachy peachy Don Ameche, come and get 'em while they're hot.' Liza laughing, reaching out to the rough dark-skinned avocado pears. 'Millie it's a – what do you call it – a cornucopia; and so cheap!' We'd stopped at the flower stall. 'Look, a white hydrangea. I must have it, Millie, it's beautiful; so pure.' Memory is a cruel gift, and not in our control.

I stopped at the same flower stall, the first daffodils, banked azaleas, primulas in pots, spring in winter, lighting up the street. And in the midst of the winter of Liza's death I felt the spring of my life and hope, the cruel exhilaration of the survivor, the power of life. I wanted to run, leap, fly. 'I am alive, I am alive!' I bought a huge bunch of daffodils, iris, white and blue, blood-striped pinks, tulips the colour of a setting sun.

'Lovely, aren't they, dear? Remind you of spring.'

I laughed. What if someone saw me now, laughing in the market with my arms full of flowers? I had to contain the riotousness, keep it to myself. People wouldn't like it, even those who had felt it themselves.

On the way up Chalk Farm Road to find my car, I passed a Frenchified bistro place I'd been in a few times and I decided to go in now. Their coffee was good. I had to push the door with my back because of the flowers. A waiter laughed. I laughed; I had forgotten my resolve. Then I saw them, in the corner, in the inner room: Mrs Drew and a man. I wanted to hide, to leave. The waiter had pulled out a chair near the door. I sat down.

'A cappuccino, please.'

She hadn't seen me, she didn't turn her head. The menu was large, I held it in front of my face and watched them over it. They were in profile against the wall, too engrossed to notice me. I started to relax. There was too much noise to hear their words, but my view was good. She was doing most of the talking, issuing instructions it seemed, in her usual style, stiff-backed. I concentrated my attention on the man. He was an incongruous type to see with her, though difficult to place. He was a big man with a handsome head, a mane of thick blue-grey hair and a small beard. His air of distinction sat strangely with his shabby clothes. He held himself proudly, like an actor of the old school; but he wasn't an actor, I was sure of that. He was doing the talking now. Vociferous, he used his hands a lot, small, delicate olive-coloured hands that reminded me of someone, I couldn't think who. He was trying to persuade her of something, or to something; she resisted with small emphatic shakes of the head.

I saw her say no, twice. The second time he took her hand with both of his. She left it there, unwillingly I thought. He tried to make her smile, looking at her from under his brows, flashing white teeth. She took her hand away and put it in her lap. His shoulders drooped. He shrugged. He poured wine from the bottle. Into both glasses. He had seemed to know her better than to offer her booze. She sipped from her glass. Well, well! She opened her handbag. He swallowed his wine in one draught. He turned his head and caught my eye. I was wearing dark glasses so he couldn't have known, but I looked away. When I looked back she was handing him money, and it wasn't to pay for the wine. It was a thickish wad of what looked like tenners. He was embarrassed; he stuffed them in his jacket pocket and he didn't count them first. She was aloof. He filled his glass again and lifted it to her before he drank. She didn't smile. Neither of them appeared to have any idea what to do or say next. I had a sudden sense that she was about to turn her face in my direction. I made use of the menu, my heart beating fast.

'Anything else, madam?'

'Oh. No, thanks.'

The waiter took the menu away. She was looking straight at me. My dark glasses were no match for her. But with no sign of recognition she looked away. My coffee was finished. I had no idea what I should do next. I found myself walking towards her, wishing I wasn't. The man looked at me when I stopped at their table; she did not.

'Hello,' I said.

She was slow to turn around.

'Oh.' A heavy pause. 'Millie.'

It didn't help the conversation along. I nodded at the man. He smiled at me. It was her cue to perform the introductions; she didn't take it up.

'You appear to be in some form of disguise, Millie. I did not recognise you.'

She was a cool liar.

'I am, in a way.'

I took off the black glasses.

'You are wearing make-up, Millie. How unusual.'

'Yes.'

'Your mascara has run.'

I put the glasses on again. The man was amused.

'Millie is an old friend of – my daughter's.'

'David Summers, glad to meet you,' he said. He was more leonine close up and younger than I had thought, ten years younger than her, with a voice like Jack Daniels on the rocks. What was he doing with her? I couldn't ask. David Summers: it rang no bells. Not in my belfry anyway. He drank, and heavily, you could see that, but was no alcoholic, I'd have guessed. He looked like a man who lived loose and used women as stepping stones when the waters rose high. He looked like the women wouldn't mind. But Mrs Drew?

'Join us,' he said, lifting the bottle. 'Have a drink.'

My eyes met hers. 'I'd better go,' I said.

'So sorry you are not able to stay.' She was magnificent. David Summers laughed; I didn't.

'Bye.' I nodded at him.

'Hope we meet again,' he said.

He waved as I negotiated the door with the flowers and the bulging bags. She sat like a stone looking at the wall.

The incident had left me feeling foolish and wild. I flung the shopping into the car and screeched off up Adelaide Road. A Jaguar was faffing about in front of me. I gave him a blast of my horn and felt a little better. I'd decided how to spend my weekend.

It took only a few minutes to dash up the stairs, stow a few things in the fridge, throw some clothes in a bag and race down again with a hunk of bread and cheese in my mouth. I hurled the bag onto the back seat with the flowers, and jumped in. I was off. Sun and the scent of flowers filled the car like a hothouse. When the traffic thinned I opened the window. The cold air cut my face, tore my hair; it was good. The horrors were sucked out with the scent and the heat. I breathed again.

The M11 is a decent road, empty of traffic on a Saturday afternoon; it gave me the illusion of speed, spanned by its beautiful bridges, each one a perfect ellipse. There were three horses on one of them; I flew under flying horses. The sky was getting bigger, clouds racing me, and I started to think about my encounter with Mrs Drew. Who was that man? An odd type for her to consort with, shabby, randy, insolent, but more cultured than he looked. How could she possibly ever have got to know him? Their air was intimate, or at least smacked of an earlier intimacy. He treated her like a *girl*, she who expected, and got, the deference due to a queen. Ex-lovers were they? Anyone but her and I'd have said yes, but the notion was unthinkable; I tried to think it and failed. I felt her cold green gaze on me; I'd shocked myself by trying. What was he then? Old family friend? Hardly. 'Mother has no friends,' Liza used to say. 'I wish she had.' A poor relation perhaps? Younger brother, black sheep? That was in the realms of Gothic romance, and his treatment of her wasn't brotherly. I kept seeing that money changing hands. Was he blackmailing her? Apart from her habitual minor cruelties, notably towards me, she lived a blameless life. How can you blackmail the blameless?

In contrast to the glassy blue air I was driving through, my mind was a fog. I knew three things: she had given the man a lot of money, in a manner that did not betoken generosity; she, who never drank, was drinking wine with him; and she was horrified that I had seen them together. Mrs Drew had a secret life. And I had discovered her secret. I shivered, and not from cold. It gave me a sort of hold on her; the idea wasn't pleasurable.

I shook it out of my head; I was at Bishop's Stortford; I had to get off the motorway, into the dull country, bungalows and DIY. Then I was through that, into the lusher meadows, horses and thatch. I passed the house named 'Live And Let Live'.

'Good advice!' I yelled, slinging the problem of Mrs Drew into the sky. I had made good time but Braintree slowed me down. The Braintrees were out in their thousands, Saturday shopping, driving like dogs. Just outside Woodbridge I went slow on purpose, past my favourite bit of landscape, a quarter of a mile of fir trees, gorse and heather, like a mirage, like Dunwich. I drank it in, and sped on. And the Dutch landscape of Suffolk appeared, a thin line of land, enormous empty sky, birds wheeling and swooping, like me. And then I was in the lanes, in the flat lands. There was the tower of Blythburgh Church; and there was the sea. I stopped the car, got out and looked. The water was silver and still, bird-call the only sound in the air. The bare earth lay in wait, brown ploughed oblongs, green fallow strips, corners where snow still lay, gleaming pools where the sun had melted it. And, standing up against the sky, one house, a grey wedge, a line-drawing in monochrome, small, isolated,

four blank windows and a door, a lane snaking down to it, nothing but
flat fields, stunted trees blown all one way by the same wind, between
it and the silver sea. I got back into the car and drove slowly down the
lane noting the small changes, green points pushing up through earth
made granite by the winter hard, the hedges bare. The car scrunched
over the gravel forecourt in front of the house; I got out and stretched,
feeling the familiar satisfactions and anticipations of the place, the grand
silence of the air.

The grand silence? I couldn't believe what I heard. Cars didn't come
here. The occasional tractor passed down the lane; no cars but mine. I
turned to look. A red Escort was bumping over the ruts. I watched it
sweep over the gravel towards me, a hard lump in my chest. Knife-blade
got out in one neat movement and leaned on the bonnet.

'Hands up, lady, I got you covered,' he said, and smiled. I didn't speak.

'You went quite fast for a 2CV.'

I didn't move. He looked around.

'Bit bleak round here, isn't it?'

No reply.

'Who does this belong to, then?' He indicated the house.

'Me.' My voice was black ice.

'You, eh? Interesting. In that case, I've come a long way, aren't you
going to invite me in?'

'No,' I said.

'Ah come on, Miss Hale, where has British hospitality gone? We'll
freeze to death out here.'

It was true. His appearance had shut out the sun. Now there was
no corner that couldn't be hurt; you can be spied on, followed, your
every movement watched and checked; there is no escape. I was locked
in a small cell with one rat watching me with its malevolent laughing
little eyes.

'It's not exactly what you think.' His words were thinned by the vast
space and the wind that always blows over that flat coast. 'I haven't been
spying on you.'

His claws picked over even my thoughts. I made a sound that could
have been called a laugh.

'It's true,' he said.

'You were just passing and thought you'd drop in.'

'Not exactly. I arrived at your flat just as you came racing down the path. You seemed in a great state; you were running from something. Or to something. *I* couldn't tell which; maybe both. I thought I'd tag along and see. You brought me a long way. I wasn't prepared; had to stop for petrol on the way. I only wanted a little chat. It's a long way to come for that.' He came close to me. 'Come on. I'm here; I'm like the toothache, Miss Hale. I'm not going to go away.'

I thought of getting back into my car and driving off. But the idea died. What did it matter now? My secret was blown. He picked up the flowers and the bags.

'That's my girl,' he said.

I opened the door of my house.

# CHAPTER ELEVEN

Other times, I'd always stood just here inside the door and looked. At the stone slab floor polished by generations of feet, the Kelim rug I had found filthy and frayed in the attic of a digs and had had cleaned, red, blue, green, gold; each chair, table, I had found somewhere for nothing or a few pence and stripped, polished, mended myself. And through the back window to the white stretch of sky and sea. Today I didn't stop. I plodded through to the kitchen at the back. It was he who stood looking. My first guest. He whistled with surprise.

'It's beautiful,' he said. 'I knew that dreary flat couldn't be all your life. I'm never wrong. Oh, there's a fire already laid.'

I never left without preparing for my return, though I never knew when the return might be. Like an addict trying to kick his drug I would put off and put off my next fix, saving it till I could resist it no more.

'Mind if I put a match to it?' he said.

I didn't bother to reply. He could set light to the whole place if he wanted to; he'd reduced it to ashes just by being there. I heard and smelt the logs begin to catch. He sighed with satisfaction.

'That's better,' he said. 'That's very nice.'

He sounded like a suburban husband home from work, ready to put his feet up on the hearth. I put the kettle on, little housewife preparing his tea; I wanted to vomit in the sink. He appeared in the arch; no doors in my little house, just space. He grinned, those surprising white teeth again.

'I'm bursting,' he said. 'Where's the loo?'

'Upstairs,' I said, my back to him. I remembered him running up the stairs in the house in Belsize Lane, weightless as a cat. No doubt he'd have a good look round, whiskers twitching, licking the corners clean.

The tea was ready when he came down, sleek.

'Loveliest place I've ever seen,' he said. 'You wouldn't think it from the outside. A bit forbidding outside. Like you.'

'Do you take sugar in this?'

'No, don't use it.'

'Pity. I haven't got any.'

He laughed. 'Where did you get the patchwork quilt?'

You had to walk through the bedroom to the bath.

'I made it,' I snapped.

'Like I said: more to you than meets the eye.'

I sat in the pine rocking chair.

'How long have you had this place?'

'Eight years.'

'Own it?'

'Yes.'

'Don't suppose it cost a lot.'

'No.'

'Had to do much to it?'

'Yes.'

'Roof looks quite new.'

'It had no roof.'

'When you bought it you mean?'

'Right.'

'You bought a house without a roof?'

I saw my house as I had seen it first. I was visiting Mrs Drew, just after Liza had met Paul. I went for a long, long walk and came across Blythburgh Church, all that white stone and the angels keeping watch from the roof. I left the church and stood in the dark trees outside. I saw this grey wedge standing alone in the fields, nothing between it and the sea. Where the roof should have been were blackened timbers; there were trees growing out of the walls. I didn't so much see it as recognise it; finding something I didn't know I'd lost.

'I hadn't seen you as a romantic, Miss Hale. Where did you find the money? Even ruins cost something.'

'Did a commercial.'

'A-ha. Do many of those?'

'Only one I've ever done.'

'I hear they pay well.'

'It was shown a hundred times; paid better than proper work.'

'You don't like doing commercials?'

'Not much.'

'But you got some good out of your ill-gotten gains.'

'It's a legitimate way for actors to earn a living. Art doesn't pay.'

'A-ha.'

Silence while we drank the hot tea.

'Earl Grey,' he said. He almost winked. I didn't respond. 'You didn't tell me about this place.'

'You're not alone in that.'

'Who knows about it, then?'

'Nobody,' I said.

'Nobody at all?'

I shook my head.

'Not Paul Mannon? Not Mrs Drew? Not Liza, your best friend?'

'Nobody but the man I bought it from.'

'Who's that?'

'Farmer who owns the land.'

'Why doesn't he live in it?'

'He was born in it. There was a fire in nineteen fifty-two. He lives in a neat bungalow about a mile away. He likes it. Not my idea of fun.'

'Well, you have odd ideas of fun, Miss Hale.'

'When I want your opinion I'll ask for it.'

I went upstairs. I hadn't meant to talk to him at all. He probed things out of me like a dentist's drill. I looked about. My beautiful bed, silver ash, the only thing I'd paid real money for, the quilt, the rugs, my little chest of drawers. His eyes had stroked everything like a greasy hand. And he'd moved things on the bathroom shelf.

He was helping himself to tea when I came down. I'd pulled myself together.

'You wanted to talk to me about something, you said. Will you say what you've come to say and then leave? I came here to be alone.'

'You don't have to go anywhere to be alone, Miss Hale.'

'Just get to the point.'

'Am I really the first visitor you've ever had here?'

'The first and the last.'

'You're a very peculiar girl.'

'Everyone is peculiar. What did you want to talk to me about?'

'Oh, this and that.'

He was driving me mad. 'You're just a nosey parker,' I said. 'You've elevated it into a profession, that's all. If you want to ask me questions then go ahead and ask but don't waste any more of my time.'

He was unperturbed. He leaned his elbows on my table and looked at me. I looked back. It took a long time.

'Stop it, Millie,' he said. It wasn't a threat.

I sat down, like a breath being let out.

'Now,' he said, 'this is how it is. Somebody kills this beautiful girl. Oh yes, she was killed all right. Beautiful, pregnant girl. They don't do it quietly, make it look natural or accidental; they go to some lengths to make it look violent. And they leave her in a place where she's going, sooner or later, to be found. Maybe they hoped that by the time she was found she'd be unrecognisable, maybe that's why they mutilated her face, but for various reasons I don't think so. It's an advertised killing. She didn't do it herself. Oh yes, we know that, but you never thought she did, did you? No, it's a peculiar killing, this, with a lot of hate in it. An unusual lot of hate. She had aroused in this person some extraordinary malevolence. This someone planned it, you see. People don't carry a little cache of, let's say, spirits of salt, shall we, on their person, have a little row and suddenly think, I'll just pour half a bottle of this down your beautiful throat. This person was prepared. The victim was lured. And that's a very nasty thing. Now, what I've got to find out is what caused this quite out-of-the-ordinary degree of hate, rage, call it what you will. We've got no clues to that. And the girl can't tell us much, lying with her guts spilled out on a slab in the morgue.'

He looked at me closely to see the effect. I didn't blink.

'What I've got to know, Millie, is what this girl was like. What was it in *her* that roused this fiend in somebody? See, my feeling is, if you advertise a killing as thoroughly as this, you're challenging me to pit my wits against yours, and find out. This person does really want to be found out. No other reason to leave her there to be found.'

'Not necessarily,' I said.

He thought a moment. 'No, not necessarily, you're right. This person could be a proud and mighty person, two fingers up to the lot of us, yah boo you can't catch me. Either way, you see, to me it's a bit of a challenge. And I'm not resisting the bait. Now—' He leaned back. '—I know it's probably hard for you to talk about her at the present time, but you've got to help me understand this girl; I've got to know everything about her that it's possible to know.'

I was confused for a second. Who was he talking about, what girl? My mind had got out. He appeared not to notice my momentary panic.

'It's the only way for me to get any idea what aroused this hate.'

He was talking about Liza, then.

'I see. All right. I don't mind talking about her. What does it matter now?'

'Oh! I must be more persuasive than I thought.'

I was without expression.

'Right,' he said. 'Now you met her at drama school. You were both eighteen, right? What was she like then?'

'Like a flower in the morning,' I said, 'with the dew on it.'

'My God,' he said.

'She was that beautiful I mean.'

'I got that, yes. But that was just her appearance.'

'Oh no. She was like that all through.'

'A bit dim you mean?'

'I mean innocent and open. I do not mean dim.'

'A-ha. What were her opinions on – things?'

'She didn't have opinions on things. She – responded to things.'

'How do you mean?'

'Well, she listened. Not just with her ears. Her whole self. Open. She heard what was underneath the words. She responded to that.'

'How?'

'With – love.'

'Sounds as though she didn't know how to take care of herself.'

'She didn't need to. Other people took care of her.'

'Felt protective you mean?'

'More than that. Devoted.'

'Everyone?'

'Everyone I ever knew.'

'You're sure? No one hiding some mean old feelings? No man she'd rejected? No somebody who'd wanted her and couldn't have her? No girl whose man she'd pinched?'

'I'm as sure as I can be.'

'That sort of beauty can rouse up some fair old desires and envies, you know.'

'I know. But not hers. It – dazzled. That's the only word. It dazzled people. They wanted to be near it, touch it. They wanted to watch it. There was a kind of shyness in it. On her part, I mean. No vanity.'

'Very beautiful people hide behind it – their beauty,' he said.

'They're hidden *by* it. People can't see them for it. They can't get through it to people. It comes between them.'

'But it didn't come between her and you?'

'No. I was lonely that first year, I told you. I had plenty of time to watch what was going on. I saw she was lonely because of what she looked like. Hidden behind it she was all alone. Once I realised that, I made an effort to see behind it, try to find out what was there.'

'And she responded to that?'

'Yes. With gratitude, with – love.' I stopped.

'A-ha. Was there anything erm . . .' He rubbed his squinting eye. 'Er, sexual in all this?'

'No.' I was scornful. 'This is *friendship* I'm talking about. Ever heard of it?'

'Okay. Important to know.'

'Yes.' I'd stopped fighting him for the moment, I didn't know why, and didn't care much. 'We went everywhere together; a lot of people might have thought – that. But it wasn't so.'

'What did her mother think?'

'She knew it for what it was.'

'Did she like it?'

'She liked it. She knew about Liza's loneliness.'

'She made you welcome, then?'

'More than that.' I swallowed. I couldn't go on.

'I see. Part of the family.'

'Yes.'

'A-ha. What about her dad?' I looked at him.

'There wasn't one.'

'Liza was a virgin birth? It wouldn't surprise me; hard to imagine anyone getting a leg over Mrs Drew.'

I looked my disgust.

'Vulgar?' he said. 'Yes, I am.'

'Her father died when she was very young. It may even have been before she was born. She never knew him. He was a something high up in the Royal Navy, I believe.'

'A-ha, Commander Drew,' he said. 'He wasn't her dad.'

'What? What do you mean?'

'We've looked him up. Mrs Drew was married to Commander Drew all right. But he was killed on active service in nineteen forty-five. Bit of a hero it seems. Liza was born in nineteen fifty-three. The certificate says "Father Unknown".'

'It can't be true.'

'It's true,' he said. There was a long pause. To break it I said:

'Have you asked Mrs Drew about this?'

'Not yet.' He smiled slightly. 'But it explains to some extent why she holds herself so stiff. Do you think Liza knew about this?'

'She didn't. I know she didn't.'

'How do you know?'

'The way she – her whole – She'd have told me if she had known. If she'd known and hadn't told, I'd still have known.' I was walking fast around the room. I touched the cold window with my hand. 'I'm certain,' I said; but there was no wind in my sails. Doubt walked over the sea.

'Okay,' he said, 'calm down. I knew from the start Mrs Drew was a woman with a secret to keep.'

'You leave her alone!' I turned on him. I saw her with the man in the café. I heard my own thoughts in the car on the way here. I even heard her say to me in her kitchen, 'Do you know if the child was Paul's?' What if the man – David Summers – were the father of *Liza's* child,

and she were paying him to keep quiet? I hadn't thought of that . . .
Whatever happened, Knife-blade mustn't know any of it. That part of
her secret was mine to keep. A sort of shiver ran over me.

'Were there any chaps around when Liza was growing up?' he said.

'No, there weren't.'

'Not perhaps one chap, a nice uncle on birthdays, bearing gifts?'

'Never. Liza worried about it. Her mother was always a beautiful
woman. Liza thought she should marry again. She thought her mother
sacrificed too much. For Liza's sake.'

'Yes. Other people's sacrifice is hard to take. Generally a bit too
much is required in return.'

'There speaks the fount of all wisdom,' I said.

'Yeah, I'm great on wisdom. Straight As.'

'Wrong in Liza's case. She didn't count up the price of things.'

'Liza sounds too good to be true,' he said. 'I've talked to all these
people. You, her mother, Paul Mannon, you three I'd expect to be – well
– the way you are about her. But the others, the actors, directors, even
the postman, the milkman, they all say the same. We're talking about
a woman without faults here, a living, breathing saint, a paragon. Now
come on, no such thing exists.'

'You've come across the one exception to prove your neat little rule.'

'Maybe. I didn't know her. To me it's hard to believe.'

'You have to believe it. It's the truth.'

'Well what was it in this paragon that somebody wanted to kill?'
He banged the table with his capable little hand. The flowers jumped.
He steadied the jug then rubbed his eyes. 'Now look,' he said, speeding
up, 'this Paul. She meets him, they fall in love; he's your fellah at the
time – no you didn't say so but don't interrupt. Mummy, the paragon
who has a secret, makes him very welcome. It's my belief she's got the
hots for him.'

'You pig,' I said. My face was hot like a twelve-year-old's.

'Yeah, I'm a pig, never mind. The young couple set up house, not
exactly poor – lovely flat, happy, successful, lots of friends, everything's
fine; but no kids. Eight or more years of more-or-less married bliss. But
no kids. Why was that?'

'Don't know,' I said.

'Come on, she told you everything.'

'Not that.'

'Why not?'

'It upset her. Wouldn't talk about it.'

'Not intentional, then? To be childless.'

'No.'

'Did they have any tests or anything?'

'No, Paul refused.' Why had I said that? He was going so fast.

'So, Paul refused. Who told you that?'

'Paul did.'

'He wanted kids?'

'Not passionately. He wouldn't have minded. He felt bad about it for Liza's sake.'

'But he wouldn't have the tests?'

'He didn't – he couldn't bear to know the details.'

'I see his point.'

'You would,' I said.

'We poor males have our weaknesses.' He grinned.

'Yes, I am aware of that.'

'Not much love lost on the male sex, Miss Hale?'

'With one or two exceptions.'

'Glad to hear it,' he said. 'I must meet one some time.'

'Keep to the point.'

'It may be a point. We never know.'

A chill ran down my back. I took a shawl from the back of a chair.

'That's nice,' he said, looking me over.

'Get on with it.'

'Okay.' He crossed his legs. 'So Mr Mannon is worried about his virility. Is that why he plays around?'

I closed my eyes. 'Virility and sterility are unconnected. I'd have expected a person of such wisdom as yourself to know a thing like that.'

'Tempting though, isn't it? If you can get another girl pregnant, any girl, it goes to show it's not your fault. Perhaps Mr Mannon was conducting his own set of tests.' He squinted up at me. 'Come on, Millie, admit it's possible.'

'I don't know.' Feeble it was.

'Got you on a sore point?'

'Paul's my friend.' My voice was a breath in a hollow reed; you find them in the marshes round here.

'Yeah.' He was gentler. 'I know you've got a soft spot there. Don't blame you; he's a handsome guy.'

I managed a disdainful look. 'Paul would never knowingly behave like that,' I said.

'I'm not suggesting he knew what he was up to. I imagine his behaviour is a mystery to him.'

'A degree in psychiatry as well, have you?'

'I've read a few books – I can read, believe it or not; and I've met some funny people in my time. In some funny situations; like this one.'

I looked away. I did not wish to discuss Paul with this sleek water rat in my living room.

'It's a theory,' he said. 'A working hypothesis. Admit it's possible.'

'It's possible,' I said, hardly opening my mouth.

'And is it also possible, when his girl gets pregnant, that having conducted all his tests and failed, he should consider the possibility that her little foetus just might not be his?'

'No!' The shout surprised us both. I got my breath back. 'No,' I said, quieter. 'Liza was absolutely faithful to Paul. He knew that. Everyone knew that. It was never even a question. For anyone.'

'No one will let this girl have a single fault.'

'Letting doesn't come into it.'

'I'll find out.'

'You'll be wasting your time.' I was out of breath, again.

'You sound as though you've just run a four-minute mile.'

'Congratulate yourself.'

'Not yet,' he said. 'There's a mile or two to go yet.'

'In that case we'll have some more tea.' I threw the things on the tray and escaped from the room.

Water squirted over the kitchen floor, tea leaves spattered, I caught a cup as it flew from my hand. The questions were circling round a terrible bull's-eye: Paul. Never, in the nightmare this man was spinning around me, never had I considered the implication of Paul. Paul had been in Sheffield, he was out of it. There had to be something incontrovertible I could say or do. The rat in there with his feet under my table got under my skin like nothing ever had; it seemed literally under the skin, scratching and tickling from inside. But he wasn't invincible; nothing was.

'Paul was in Sheffield,' I said.

'A-ha.'

'You must have questioned people there. Don't they say so?'

'A-ha.'

'Well then. Why are you making out he killed her?'

'I'm not.'

I put the tray on the table with a bang. 'Well what *are* you making out then?'

He smiled, saying nothing, looking at me.

'Well, what?'

'There are more ways than one of killing the cat.'

'I don't understand you.'

'You quoted Macbeth to me the other day.'

'Did I?'

'There were two Macbeths. One of them did it; the other one put him up to it. It can take more than one person to perpetrate a crime. In my experience.'

'What are you saying?'

'Would you say Lady Macbeth was in love with her husband?'

'Madly.'

'There are two women, to my knowledge, in love with Mr Mannon.'

'Who?'

'Mrs Drew. And you.' He looked almost sad. Like a dog hearing music.

'Me?'

'Aren't you?'

'I am not.' My heart was pile-driving against my ribs.

'You were once. Liza stole him from you. These things can flare up again. He plays around. Why not with you? What if—'

'What if, what if! I am not *in love,* as you put it, with Paul. I got over that many years ago. Paul is my friend. He is now probably my only friend. Are you trying to destroy that too?'

'Too? I'm not trying to destroy anything. On the contrary. Something has been destroyed. I'm trying to—' He thought better of what he had been going to say. '—to finish a jigsaw, let's say. Something like that. See the whole picture, you know. Shall I pour this tea?'

I rubbed my face all over, hard. 'Yes,' I said.

'Can you swear to me you're not in love with Paul Mannon?'

'I don't swear. I tell you categorically I'm not in love with him. But I do love him. Dearly. And I won't have you making insinuations against him.'

'So he didn't put you up to it?'

'Up to what?'

'Well, killing your friend.'

'Oh yes, he did. He came over one evening and said, "Hey, Millie, here's a spot of – what did you call it? – spirit of salts, which I happen to have about my person. How about you throwing it in Liza's face one day when I'm out of town, and you and me shacking up together after-wards, wouldn't that be nice?" And I said, "Gosh yes, Paul darling, what a great idea, I'll do it as soon as I have a free day."'

'Stranger things have happened.'

'To you maybe.'

'A-ha.'

'You soil everything.'

'Yeah.'

'And I'm not the kind of person who is "put up to" things. I'm pretty counter-suggestible, wouldn't you say?'

'Mmm. Oh yes.' He was thinking about something else. 'There's Mrs Drew,' he said.

I started to laugh; and stopped. I was glad I was able to stop.

'I see,' I said. 'Paul and Mrs Drew have this secret passion which can just no longer be denied. Liza stands between them and happiness, so they decide to bump her off. He's in Sheffield, she's supposed to be in bed with flu, but she sneaks up to London at dead of night and does in her only daughter, and Paul comes running to her loving arms: "At last, my darling, we are alone!" It's great. You accused *me* of being a romantic.'

'She'd like us to believe you did it.'

'I don't think so.' My chin was up.

'We'll see.'

'We will.'

'And did you, Millie?' He put down his cup.

'Yes,' I said. We looked at each other for some time.

'Tell me how,' he said.

'By not meeting her at the house.'

He leaned back, folded his arms and sighed. He closed his eyes. I poured more tea. I put more logs on the fire. When I turned round he was standing at the window.

'It's dark,' he said.

He drew the curtains, shutting me deeper in with him. He came and stood by me at the fire. His face was lit from below, from the lamp I'd lighted and the flames. The intimacy of it was horrible, repellant; but I didn't move away. We were tired, like two fighters after a long bout.

'So you've got no ideas?' he said.

'Fantasy's not my strong point. Unlike you. Sorry.' I spoke without rancour, tiredly.

'A-ha.' He stared into the fire. Then seemed to wake up. He looked around. 'It's cosy here,' he said. He looked at me. I didn't reply. 'I'd better go,' he said.

Just as he was about to get into his car, while I stood at the door not feeling the cold, he changed his mind, or seemed to, and walked back across the gravel to me.

'Just one thing,' he said. 'Who benefits from Liza's death?'

'Benefits?' My throat closed.

'Yes. Her money.'

'Money? She was an actress; we don't have money,' I said.

'She was a successful one.'

'Yes. But she worked for the BBC. Come off it,' I said.

'You don't know if she made a will?'

'Oh God,' I said. 'No, I don't.'

'A-ha.' He nodded into the night. 'By the way,' he said, 'congratulations on getting her job. That's nice.'

My mouth was open when I turned to him. I saw his white teeth in the dark.

'It's an ill wind,' he said. 'Goodnight.'

I stood watching his tail lights disappear up the lane.

# CHAPTER TWELVE

I lay that night flat on my back, arms at my sides, watching the moon travel across the sky. As it disappeared from the window I may have slept. Sunday was grey. In the afternoon I walked to Blythburgh. The earth round the church was hard, its moat-like river a steely snake, sluggish under ice. I read the familiar gravestones, Blois's, Fisks's and Dodds's. The bells rang mournfully, their sound emptying across the marsh. I went into the church, treading quietly over the brick floor the colour of sunlight round the font. The bell-ringers were in the tower, a small boy and five men swinging on the ropes. They practised on Sunday afternoons. Through the high windows white light met white stone. The protecting angels spread their wings down the centre of the roof. I touched one of the little carved figures on the pew ends. It was the reaper bending to a stook of corn. I stroked the folds in its long gown, its small hands, its rounded back. It had no head. I trod the stones in the centre aisle; 'Eliz. wife of William Maggs, daughter of Will Sparrow', and more of the baronets Blois. The place had always brought me peace. Not today. The bells grew exultant, mocking me. I went outside. Gulls were swinging over the lake, on the sound of the bells. I walked to Dunwich, through the gorse and pine trees to the sea. It was a long walk. The sea was the colour of oysters, smashing itself against the shore. I sat on the stones, back against the tufts of grass, deadening thought with the battering water and the cold. I walked back to my house. I lay watching the moon that night also.

On Monday I drove back to London down the A12, punishing myself. The A12 for all eternity is a pretty good paradigm for hell. It rained unceasingly; I was drowning all the way. The great trucks from Harwich roared over me like breakers on an angry sea. I laughed once, passing the board that said 'Netherland Dwarfs For Sale'. There was nothing else to laugh about.

There was a puzzling pile of mail on the mat, letters sent on by my agent from Liza's fans, pouring out sorrow and love. They see you on the telly and you become the repository of their grief. I decided to answer them some other time.

Robin Foxe Mills was pleased when I rang. 'Millie! Have you made up your mind?'

'Yes, Robin, I have. Of course I want to do it. Very much.'

'Oh good.'

'But I can only accept on one condition.'

'Yes, Millie, what's that?' Wariness in the voice – oh difficult actresses.

'That you don't make it public that you offered the part to Liza first. I don't think I could stand that. I feel bad enough knowing it myself.'

'Oh, Millie,' – relief – she's not asking for champagne at rehearsals or her own caravan on location, 'of course!'

'It would make a good story for the press,' I said.

'Not at all, Millie; she turned us down, you know.'

'Did she?'

'Oh yes. On the Tuesday afternoon; that's why we were interviewing again on the Wednesday.'

'Oh.'

'You mustn't give it another thought, Millie. Everyone who knows will be sworn to secrecy.'

Tell a secret to one, you've told it to the world, I thought.

'At least it won't get out to the press,' he said.

I wanted to know how Knife-blade had found out, but I didn't ask. I said, 'Thank you, Robin, I'm more grateful than I can say,' in Liza's best vulnerable style.

The phone rang all afternoon: could I come for a costume discussion tomorrow? A make-up conference on Wednesday? Lunch with the writer on Thursday?

My agent was like a child at Christmas.

'It's good money,' she said. 'For the BBC,' she added, 'considering that you haven't worked for them before.'

I wasn't arguing. 'It's fine, Dorothy, it's fine.'

'Shall I accept then, darling?'

'Yes, Dorothy, just go ahead.'

I let her run with the excitement I didn't feel.

When I was four years old they took me to have my photograph taken in the back of a camera shop in South Norwood high street. I was not pleased. The man gave me a doll to hold to cheer me up. I liked the doll and did cheer up, I held it tight and smiled. When they put on my coat to leave I still had hold of the doll. It had been given to me; I was taking it home. 'No, dear, it's not for you to keep.' They had to prise it out of my hands.

So even when the scripts arrived by special messenger at three o'clock and I smiled at the cabman and signed for them, I was just waiting for them to take it all away. Catch me getting excited before the contract was signed.

But it was Knife-blade who scared me to death. You're in a strange state after two sleepless nights. The outlines of things get very clear. Each night without sleep makes you lighter by pounds; you move in slow motion, you float. So, sipping tea at the window, watching a sleek black cat wash himself on the garden wall, I floated on fear. He wasn't a net that entangled me; he was a knife that slid into me. It was he that frightened me, not just his job. He threatened me with an invasion I couldn't control, couldn't tolerate, and couldn't escape. Other people who threatened to invade me I could walk away from; he had squatter's rights; there was nowhere I could walk. And worst of all, there was a part of me that didn't want to walk; the battle exhilarated me; there was an uncontrollable excitement in it like nothing I had known before. The black cat lifted his hind leg and licked himself luxuriously. I shuddered. Humiliation flooded me. The man was small, seedy, unprepossessing. I despised myself. He crept through every part of me, like the blood in my veins. Something in me liked it. I wanted no part of it. The cat settled himself on the cold wall, drawing his legs under him, wrapping his tail around. I didn't want to see Knife-blade again. I couldn't wait to see him again. The battle was on. One of us had to win. For once in my life I couldn't predict which of us it might be. I closed the curtains. As I did so, the cat turned his head. I shut him out in the cold. I swallowed three Valium with the tea. I was going to sleep tonight.

Next morning I was normal again, not trembling in suspension over a floorless world. Full of energy, I cantered through the scripts. Even on one swift skim I could see it was the role of a lifetime, and that the writer was no slouch.

Fortified, I answered the pathetic letters: retired colonels in Sussex, teenage boys in Scarborough, middle-aged housewives, aspiring girls; I parcelled them in their envelopes, banged on the stamps. Strange feeling; touched by strangers. I shoved them in my bag.

The costume lady at Television Centre – 'Hello, I'm Diana' – treated me with a kind of hushed respect. It was embarrassing. She was a kindly soul, bespectacled and overweight; you wouldn't pick her out in a hundred as a costume designer. We walked down miles of narrow paths between rails, wrestling skirts, sweaters, coats, boots from the forest of clothes. She was apologetic.

'I think, if we can, we ought to dress you from stock. It's not a question of money, the budget's good; it's just I think your things ought to look old and worn.'

'I agree,' I said.

'Oh good!' She was relieved to the point of incredulity; had she expected me to snarl and bite? She cheered up and told me who my fellow actors were: a respectable list of people, none of whom I personally knew. I was glad of that; I wanted to start my new life among strangers. But I acted apprehensive.

'Oh! Nobody you know?' She commiserated.

'No.' I smiled ruefully.

'Never mind. Everyone is very nice.' She was mothering me. I encouraged her.

'I hope so, Diana.'

'You'll be fine.' She squeezed my arm.

When I did my Liza act, sweet and soft, this was what happened to me. It was a great lesson in cause and effect. It held a certain interest now, while I was trying it out, but I could see it might get tedious in time.

When I left the Centre at six I was glad to be leaving it behind, the performance, not the place. Turning the key in the ignition restored me to myself; the growl of my own engine made me feel I could escape from anything. After years of doing my own make-up in the theatre it would be odd to have a stranger messing with my face. The make-up supervisor wore none at all herself. I decided this was an encouraging sign. She was a pale natural blonde called Celia. She sat me in the dentist's chair, wrapped me in a blue cotton gown, and chatted softly to put me at my ease. She was like a gentle nurse softening me up before the operation, with the same cool hands.

'You've got marvellous bones,' she said. 'No, you have.'

They were all so nice to me. I wasn't used to it.

'Is there anything you're allergic to?'

A certain squinting policeman, I thought.

'Not that I know of,' I said. 'I hardly use the stuff except at work.'

'You don't need to,' she said. 'Marvellous skin.'

Everything about me was marvellous today.

'But we'll have to use a light base, just for the lights, you know. You won't mind that, will you?'

Everyone round here was so considerate I wondered if the word had gone out – dangerous lunatic on the loose, handle with care.

'I'll be doing your make-up myself,' she said.

I gathered this was a privilege. 'Oh good,' I said.

'Marvellous eyes,' she sighed. 'We won't need much on them.' She stood back and regarded my marvellous reflection, but a note of worry had crept in. She'd come across something that wasn't marvellous?

'Now what about the hair?' she said.

'What about it?' I asked nervously.

'Well, it's a marvellous colour, and really thick, but I think we'll have to get it off your face a bit.'

'Oh fine,' I said.

She let out a sort of moan of relief. 'Oh thank heaven! Some actresses just can't bear that; they always want their hair the same, no matter what. Even in period things.'

'Good heavens,' I said.

As I was about to leave, feeling marvellous, she said awkwardly, 'I'm awfully sorry about – you know. You were very close to her, weren't you?'

'Yes.'

'It must be awful. I can't stop thinking about it myself. She was such a lovely person.'

'Yes.'

'I always made her up, you know. The last five series. Yes.'

A shiver travelled through me. Those cool hands. There were too many mirrors in the clinical room. I had to get out. I nodded dumbly.

'Well, you don't want to talk about it, I can see. No wonder: it's so terrible there's really nothing to say. I just hope they find out what happened, that's all.'

'Yes.'

'Oh, I'm so sorry, I didn't mean to upset you. I'm awfully sorry. Here.'

It was strange; I hadn't cried since Friday, the night I got drunk with Paul. She pushed a bouquet of tissues into my hand and brought a paper cup of water.

She didn't know. My tears were not for Liza. They were for me. I had been feeling so good: pampered, important, relaxed, at ease. She'd taken my doll away. I wanted a make-up girl who'd never heard of Liza Drew, a make-up girl of my own. The tears were tears of childish rage and though I was ashamed of them I made no effort to stop the flow. She was alarmed, enough, I hoped, to deter her the next time. There are people, though, who unfailingly hit the mark, even aiming blind; I feared she was one of them. I hoped I was wrong; I had to spend months being stroked by those cool, scented hands.

'I shouldn't have mentioned it,' she said, her own eyes wet. 'I never will again, honestly I won't.'

'It's all right,' I said. 'It's just—'

'I know, I know.'

She didn't know the half of it. She was like a new-born kitten blinking its eyes.

'Not your fault. Really,' I said. 'It's okay. I'm all right now.'

Brave Millie pulled herself together with a watery smile and turned shakily to go, the kitten bobbing and diving around all the way to the lifts. We smiled desperately at each other as I got in.

'See you at the first rehearsal,' she called. Her words jammed in the closing doors. I cried all the way home.

And when I got there I felt worse. The flat was empty, impersonal and cold. The phone didn't ring, there were no letters on the mat. That served to remind me I still had a bagful of commiseratory notes to Liza's fans; I wanted to be shot of them and walked to the postbox, largely to get me out of the flat.

When I got back nothing had changed, but I had pulled myself together a bit. I lit the gas fire, ate some food, and settled down with the scripts. They, like the make-up girl, the fan mail, were not mine by right; they were second-hand.

Paul didn't ring. I needed to hear his voice, so badly I picked up the phone five times in the course of the evening to call Mrs Drew and get his Sheffield number and five times lacked the courage to go through with it. Knife-blade's nasty voice saying, 'She has a secret life', and her cold stare in the café last Saturday seized my resolve. So I returned to the scripts, pretended they were mine, and worked till late.

So at least I was ready for the meeting next day with Robin and the writer, in an Italian restaurant at Shepherd's Bush Green.

'You remember Joe,' said Robin, 'from the interview.'

He was wrong there. I had no recollection of him. He was surprisingly young, tall and gangling, with glasses too big for his face. He thrust a large bony hand into mine, tentative and over-eager at the same time.

The costume and make-up consultations got us through the first course. No problems there. We kept the scripts for the main course. I had a lot of questions to ask. Joe was touchingly pleased – someone taking his work seriously perhaps? Robin, also, was impressed.

'You've done a lot of work already, Millie,' he said, making short work himself of an overweight Dover sole. I started to feel good. It wasn't the wine (I went easy on that, I wanted my wits about me), it was their courteous respect. They both *deferred* to me. I started to get the faintest whiff of an inkling of what it might feel like to be a star. I decided I could take to it. Carefully, no one had mentioned Liza at all. We were almost into dessert. My courage was up.

'Work's been the only thing to turn to,' I said.

'Yes,' Robin said quietly, touching my hand.

The subject having been introduced, my having given permission as it were, Joe hesitantly said:

'I'm sorry parts of the script might be painful to you. Erm, when the child – erm – dies and so on.'

'It is painful; it's beautifully written, that's why.'

'I hope not too painful for you at this present time.'

'I can cope,' I said. 'You use your pain, you know, as an actor; you adapt it to the job. Sounds ruthless, but you might as well put it to use. It's something to do with it. Artists are lucky that way.'

Joe eagerly agreed. Nearer to the knuckle was that Jackie, my character in the story, is suspected of killing her child and gets extensively questioned by the police. It is this that drives her ultimately to breakdown and attempted suicide. I didn't want to dwell on that.

Joe looked at me owlishly through his spectacles. 'You're very brave,' he said. I looked back, vulnerable, Liza-like, afraid I might have sounded a little tough. 'She's perfect for the part,' Joe said to Robin earnestly. 'Just how I imagined it.'

'I know. I'm clever, aren't I?' Robin preened. 'As soon as I saw her I knew.'

Nobody mentioned that he had offered it to Liza first.

Over the brandies they toasted me.

'To you and to Jackie,' they said. I sipped my mineral water and blushed.

'Everyone's so sweet to me,' I said. 'I just hope I shan't let any of you down.'

'Not a chance of it.' Robin was emphatic. 'And I'm here to help, you know.'

'You do,' I said.

Joe loped off to the gents just then, stepping among the tables like a bewildered giraffe. A look of embarrassment came over Robin's face. He leaned closer to me.

'Millie.'

'Yes?'

'A police inspector rang me to ask who we were offering the part to. I'm afraid I had to tell him.'

'I know,' I said. 'He told me. Sort of. It's all right, don't worry.'

'I hope it really is all right.'

'Oh yes.' I was very positive and lying through my teeth. 'It's just the press I was worried about. And, well – people. You know.'

'I haven't told another soul.'

'Thanks. It's awfully good of you.'

'Not at all. You have enough to worry about.'

I smiled pathetically. 'Yes.'

Then Joe came back, and we lurched out into the shabby dusk of Shepherd's Bush to say our euphoric goodbyes.

There was still no word from Paul that night. I wasn't just missing him by now; I was seriously disturbed. After all, I convinced myself, the scripts were all the company I needed. They would keep me warm. But the thought of Knife-blade hovered uneasily. What was he up to? Who was he questioning now? Why was he leaving me alone? Had he taken Paul in for questioning? Even his absence was a threat. His shadow lurked behind every page.

Next morning I still couldn't concentrate. I ached to hear a word from Paul, knew if the phone rang it wouldn't be Paul. I had to know something, I was desperate. I decided to visit Mrs Drew.

## CHAPTER THIRTEEN

But I didn't get there till it was nearly dark. I hadn't been abducted on the way. I made King Henry's Road all right. I parked and got out of the car. Then I walked straight past the gateposts of Paul and Liza's place and round the corner. I couldn't go in.

It was the first time I had set eyes on the house since the fatal Friday when I had rushed round there to fetch Paul. That was bad. And the thought of facing Mrs Drew was, if possible, worse. An hour later I was still wandering over Primrose Hill among the frozen dog-walkers and tramps. I sat on a bench arguing with myself but received no influx of courage from the bare brown trees and crisscrossing paths.

When I returned to King Henry's Road, again I went straight past the house and got back into my car. I sat behind the wheel freezing to death. In the end I had to drive if only to engender some heat. I parked in a street off Finchley Road to get myself some hot tea and food. In the event I found I couldn't eat. I did some desultory shopping, even bought a bunch of daffodils. I still felt pretty bad. I decided to give the whole thing up, and set off for my place. I couldn't go on like this. I did a fast about-turn and made for King Henry's Road again. My resolve lasted long enough for me to find myself at the top of the steps with my hand on the bell.

There were no lights on in the flat. I hoped she was out. Then I heard footsteps in the hall.

She looked blind when she opened the door. It took time for her to focus on me. When she managed it she wasn't pleased.

'Hello,' I said.

She walked away from me down the hall. I shut the front door and followed her into the flat. She switched on the lights. She had been sitting in the half-dark.

I had an illogical idea that with Liza's absence the flat would have changed. It hadn't. The light bathed the pale carpets and the Dufy-like paintings on the walls with the same soft glow as before. I thrust the daffodils into her hands. She regarded them with distaste.

'I had forgotten daffodils smelt so strong,' she said faintly, turning her face away. She handed them back to me and wiped her hands down the sides of her skirt. 'Thank you. How kind. Could you, do you think?' She indicated the kitchen. I took them and went to find a vase. Liza was even more present in there than in the living room. I was having a bad time.

Mrs Drew was standing at the empty fireplace with her back to me when I carried the flowers in.

'Where shall I put them?' I asked.

She waved a hand without turning round. I couldn't tell whether her air of deep reverie were real, or just a great way of freezing me out. Whatever it might be, I'd had enough of it.

'I'd love a cup of coffee,' I heard myself say.

She turned fast, focussing. After several insolent seconds she said, 'Of course. How rude of me. Do sit down.'

I didn't.

I listened to her in the kitchen. She seemed to be clattering a lot, for her. The coffee was a long time coming. She brought it in two cups. If I wanted a second I should have to ask for it. We drank standing at the long window in a rocky silence. Sparrows pecked at the curving stone steps outside, getting the last of the light. Snowdrops shone dimly in the grass. Her hand shook a little. She smelled of toothpaste.

'I wanted to know if you were all right,' I said.

Silence again. The dark was falling fast outside. The sparrows had gone. The coffee seemed to revive her a little.

'Millie,' she said.

I waited for her to go on.

In vain.

'Yes?' I said.

Whatever she had been going to say, she changed her mind.

'I have been attempting to go through Liza's things. It has to be done. You are almost the same size, I believe. Would you care to have some of them? So many lovely clothes.'

There were simpler ways, surely, of getting rid of me; she could have just told me to leave. She could have just poisoned the coffee, if she had to get complicated about it.

'No,' I said. 'No,' I said. 'No.'

I moved away.

'Ah well,' she hummed to the window, 'never mind.'

I did mind. I sat down. I wasn't leaving now till I had got what I came for. There was an eternal pause. Even the bird-song had ceased outside.

'Have you heard from Paul?' I said.

She walked slowly to the other side of the dead fire.

'No.'

'Not a word? Since last weekend?'

'No,' she said.

'That's a bit odd, isn't it?'

'Do you think so?'

'He told me he would phone you every day.'

'Then I dare say he has had more important things on his mind.'

'Aren't you worried about him?'

'He will be working very hard.'

'Even so.'

'If you are so concerned, you should telephone him yourself, perhaps.'

That put me in my place.

'Yes,' I said.

Silence again. My coffee was nearly finished. I could be said to have got what I came for. In a manner of speaking. I had no excuse to stay. I stood and picked up the empty cups.

In the kitchen the waste bin was open. In it was a whisky bottle, half full, surrounded by moulding bread and coffee grounds. Her empty cup smelt more of alcohol than coffee. I rinsed the cups under the tap. I rinsed my face at the same time.

She was in the doorway when I took the towel from my face. She was looking at the waste bin. I was looking at her.

'I'd better go then.' It wasn't what I had meant to say.

She looked at me straight for the first time.

'What did you come for, Millie?'

There was little point in lying now. About anything.

'To find out if you had heard from Paul.'

'I see. It took you a long time. But then I dare say you have been rather busy,' she said.

Her voice was like a diamond cutter on glass. She knew, then. About the job. She was blocking the doorway and made no attempt to move. We stood.

'Inspector Bright was here today,' she said.

'I see.' I learned from her example: attack was the only defence. 'He visited me too,' I said. 'On Saturday evening. After I had seen you in the café.'

She took that in. Her eyes sharpened to pencil points.

'He is an unpleasant little man,' she said.

'He is a rodent,' I said.

At last a subject we could agree upon. But dangerous ground to tread. He had told her my secret. Did it follow that he had told me hers? Or that I had told him about the café? I watched her thinking, not knowing how many steps to risk.

'His method is superb,' I said.

'What do you mean?'

'Dissension in the ranks, divide and rule, sowing suspicion like bloody seeds. And never on stony ground either. I loathe the man, he makes me ill.'

'Yes,' her voice was faint. 'I see.'

'He told you about the job, then?' I said.

'He told me you had been offered a role that was to have been Liza's, if that is what you mean.'

'And what did you say to that?'

'I told him it was my opinion you would refuse to accept such a role.'

'I accepted it,' I said.

'A decision, if I may so, that appears to me to be somewhat lacking in – taste.'

'I have to eat. When you're hungry the taste doesn't seem to matter very much.'

She looked the disgust my remark deserved.

'I'm sorry,' I said. 'But I have to work. It's horrible, I know, but I have to do it. I couldn't turn it down. I wanted to but I couldn't. I am truly sorry. I am.'

She still said nothing.

'Liza had turned it down, you know. Before—' I stopped.

'Did she tell you that?' Sharp as a cat's claws at a bird.

'No, I didn't know about Liza's connection at all till the producer told me. Then the director said she had turned it down. That's when I accepted the part.'

She was struggling.

'I'm sorry,' I said. 'I wanted to tell you. I didn't dare.'

'Did you tell Paul?'

'Yes. Before I decided. I asked his advice.'

'And what was his opinion?'

'He thought I should do it, for Liza's sake.'

She made a sound betokening violent distaste.

'You swore Paul to secrecy, I suppose?' she said.

'Yes.'

I saw her swallow that. Which was more palatable? That Paul had kept a secret from her of his own accord, or at my instigation? She didn't like it either way.

'You realise, I suppose, that this – engagement – might do you harm?'

'It's fuel for Inspector Bright, yes,' I said.

'And that doesn't inhibit you from going on with it?'

'It can't.'

'You are in great danger, Millie.'

She tried to put concern into the words. They sounded what they were – a threat.

'We are all in that,' I said.

She walked in a rather reedy way into the other room. I followed her.

'So what else did he tell you about me?' I said.

'I have no intention of lowering myself to the level of repeating his degrading insinuations.'

I could imagine. He'd tried the two ladies in love with Paul ploy. She wouldn't get into that. Her words sank into the silence, deep.

'I didn't tell him I had seen you on Saturday in the café,' I said.

'Why ever not?'

That shook me a bit.

'I didn't think it was any of his business,' I said.

'He appears to think everything is his business.'

'I got the impression you thought it was none of mine.'

Cold green flames flickered in her eyes; the blind look had gone by now.

'Nor it was. If I choose to lunch with an old friend, it is nobody's concern but my own.'

She couldn't be allowed to get away with that. Not now we'd come this far.

'An old friend?' I said.

I watched her while she considered that. She sat down, deliberately, back straight, hands in her lap. Was there nothing that could make her lose her air of retaining the whip hand?

'Sit down, Millie,' she said, giving the whip a crack. I sat. She looked at her locked hands for a bit, then at me.

'I assume Inspector Bright told you,' she said, 'that Liza was not my husband's child.'

Her voice was firm.

'Yes,' I said.

'And you believed him, naturally.'

'Not at first.'

'I am sure he furnished you with incontrovertible proof.'

I said nothing. She said, 'It is true, of course.'

'Yes.' What else could I say?

Her hands had started to tremble slightly. She needed a drink. I thought of offering her one, but I didn't have the nerve. She clenched her fingers to stop the tremor. It didn't work.

'You must have been considerably shocked,' she said.

'Not in the sense I think you mean.'

It was true. I felt more outrage at the whisky hidden in the waste bin and the pathetic toothpaste on the breath. But we weren't talking about that. It was easier to talk about her illegitimate child.

'It didn't change my opinion of you. I admire you for keeping it to yourself for so long,' I said. 'And nothing that man said could shock me. He tries too hard.'

'I had to keep it to myself. He was an impossible father for Liza to have. I could not allow him to be part of her life.' She spoke with more feeling than I had ever heard from her. She controlled herself. 'It was in London, after the war. I worked, part time, for the Society of Authors as a sort of secretary-cum-dogsbody. I had no need of the money; my husband's pension was adequate and as you know I have a small income of my own; I simply needed – an occupation. I—' She stopped. She heard the loneliness in her words as clearly as I. I looked blank. She went on.

'I met him in 1950. He was a writer. Of sorts. Extremely wild. Irresponsible. Younger than I. He was a totally unsuitable father for any child. When I learned that – when I knew . . . I did not tell him. I told nobody. I bought the house in Suffolk and moved there as the widow of Commander Drew. Which of course I was. I never actually lied, even to Liza. There was never any cause. Now, I have no doubt, it will all come out. I have told you for the simple reason that I prefer you to hear the truth from me.'

And to put me off the track of something else, I thought.

'What was the man in the café to do with all this?' I said.

'Why should he be anything to do with it?'

'I saw you giving him money,' I said.

Her body fell into fragments for a moment. She gathered it together again. It didn't take her long.

'He was Liza's father. The man in the café.'

She spoke with weary contempt. I was fairly shaken. Though not surprised. His hands had reminded me of Liza. They were Liza's hands. She went on. 'He saw my picture in the papers in connection with Liza's – death. You know how I have kept out of her publicity all my life. But it is not difficult to trace a murder victim's mother, especially for a person who has connections with the gutter press. He insisted on a meeting and made it quite clear that he would accept payment to keep the story of her parentage to himself.'

'What a bastard,' I said.

'As I have said. An unsuitable father for a child.'

'But that,' I said, 'was before you knew that Kni – that John Bright knew. If you tell him, he will stop this man.'

'It is the press that concerns me. He assures me that if the police get in touch with him the story will be released.'

'Oh my God,' I said. Her face was like tissue paper in a breeze.

'There must be a way to stop him,' I said. 'John Bright is unspeakable but he is a clever little rat. He will find a way to stop him, you've got to let him know. Oh, I'm so sorry.' I found my hand reaching out to her. She flinched, and my hand withdrew.

'I told you this in order to satisfy your curiosity. I have no desire for your pity; nor do I wish for your advice. I will deal with this matter in my own way.'

'But he will want more money. Those people always do, don't they? You're not rich enough to go on paying him.'

'You will kindly leave me to be the best judge of that.'

She stood up, steadying herself with a hand on the mantelpiece. 'I should like to be alone now, Millie. If you would be so good.'

'But—'

She moved to the door. She was desperate for a drink and I knew she would never have one while I was there. And there was nothing more I had the nerve to say. I got up.

At the front door I said, 'Will you let me come and see you again?'

'You will be far too busy with your new engagement, my dear, I am sure.'

She managed to put a fair amount of venom into that.

'Will you be staying on in London?' I said.

'For the time being, I believe. I have made no plans.'

'Well, then—'

'Millie, it is extremely cold in the hall. You must forgive those of us who are not so warmly clad as yourself for wishing to return to a less arctic atmosphere. Goodbye.'

I sat in the car with the engine running for ten minutes before I was in a fit state to drive. Even then there was sweat on the steering wheel, and my foot trembled on the clutch.

I had to phone Paul.

# CHAPTER FOURTEEN

Paul wasn't at the theatre. They gave me the number of his digs. He wasn't there either. I asked for Jane Barnes's number and tried him there.

'Jane Barnes speaking.'

A voice like velvet, husky and warm.

'He isn't here, I'm afraid.'

I told her who I was.

'Oh, Millie Hale! He's talked about you a lot.'

'Have you any idea where he might be?'

'I'm afraid he might be anywhere.'

'What do you mean?'

'Well – I might as well tell you: he's being very – odd. Well, you can't wonder, can you, with this awful thing?'

'What sort of odd?'

'Well . . . Oh lord.'

'I'm very worried about him,' I said, to help her out.

'Well, he – Oh, Millie, it's awful, he's just drunk all the time, well, not when he's working of course, he's working like a maniac, he's going to be absolutely brilliant in this play, but as soon as rehearsal's over he's – oh dear –. And it's not just the drink, it's the way he's behaving with – well there was this party on Wednesday and it took three of the actors to drag him off Alison – she's the ASM – and this was in the middle of the floor! Rolling about on top of her. And she's not the only one! You know what he's normally like, very shy and reserved and – oh you know – so nice! It's really horrible, honestly!'

She paused for breath. I didn't know how to put it.

'And what about . . . er . . . him and you?' I said.

'Oh that's all over I'm afraid. Won't look at me, speak to me, anything. I've been terribly upset. Not for myself so much, you know, as him. I just can't help him at all.'

'I see'

'We'd all like to help him if we could. Everyone's worried about him, but you can't even mention – you know – the – her. And everything. Nobody can. He hasn't mentioned it himself. To anyone. He won't say a word about it, not a word. People have tried but he just chokes them off. With *jokes*. He keeps making these weird *jokes*. It's terrible, Millie, it really is.'

'Where is he likely to be later on tonight?'

'I just couldn't say.'

'Isn't he even sleeping at his digs?'

'I don't know, Millie, I really don't. He arrives at rehearsal in the morning looking absolutely terrible, as though he hasn't slept, shaved, combed his hair, anything. He looks wonderful of course, you can imagine, those blue shadows under the eyes. Isn't he the most gorgeous man you've ever seen?'

I treated the question as rhetorical.

'I'll have to get him at the theatre tomorrow,' I said.

'Yes, I think that's the only thing. He doesn't go to the theatre bar any more. No one sees him at all. Alan and Pete tried to stay with him one night, but he just got rid of them.'

'How?'

'Left out the back door of the pub. Said he was going to the loo and never came back.'

'Well, thanks.' I didn't need to hear any more.

'Anything I can do,' she said. 'In a funny way it's been good to talk about it. The police came to ask me questions, you know? Before I knew what had happened. I thought it was about an accident or a divorce or something, so I said he wasn't with me on the Wednesday night. Anyway, you know how secretive he is, I thought he wouldn't want anyone to know. Of course when I saw the papers, I realised. I had to ring them up and tell them the truth. It sounded so feeble, but they believed me I think. I hope they did. I mean, it was the truth. Oh sorry, I don't know if he'd want anyone to know about that.'

'He told me himself,' I said.

'Oh yes, well he'd have to really, wouldn't he? Oh that sounds awful but you know what I mean.'

'Yes, I know.' I lacked Mrs Drew's dismissive qualities.

'I feel so awful about it, I really do.'

'Yes,' I said.

I gave her my number, 'Just in case.' Of what, I didn't know.

'Ring me whenever you like, Millie. He's close to you, I know.'

'Thanks,' I said. 'Goodbye.'

A girl with her heart in the right place; shame about the brains. I saw her as large and dark with strong round legs like a Samurai. So Paul didn't like her now. It was a crumb of comfort; an ill wind, as Knife-blade would have said.

Crumbs of comfort were needed. Paul and Mrs Drew. Grief takes people funny ways. Something had to be done, and I was powerless; I was also unnecessary, which was harder to take. But surely tomorrow I should be in touch with Paul?

I leapt into the scripts to take my mind off its circular track. They did. I was up and down the room for hours, kicking the walls, mouthing the words, writing questions in the margin. It was a hell of a lot easier to be someone else than it was just then to be me. And for the first time since the horror began, in spite of everything, it was excitement that threatened to keep me awake.

I woke at three a.m. with the light still on and the script on my face. I turned off the lamp and slept again, heavily. It seemed like hours later that I woke with a bang. Liza's face was staring at me in the dark next to my bed. I lay rigid. There was an ambulance bell ringing, loud. I scrabbled for the light switch. She wasn't there. It was three-thirty a.m. The phone was ringing.

'Millie, Millie!' He was shouting.

'Paul!'

'Oh Millie.' He was very drunk.

'Paul, where have you been?'

'I'm sorry, is it very late?'

'It's late, it's early, what the hell, it's you!'

'I'm sorry, I'm so sorry, Millie.'

'Paul, what for?'

'Oh you know . . .' He mumbled somewhere; not into the phone.

'Paul, are you all right?'

'I'm not, Millie, I'm not. I don't know what to do.'

'Jane says you're wonderful in the play.'

'Oh that.'

'I've missed you, Paul.'

'I'm going out of my head, Millie. It's the loneliness.'

'Why didn't you call me?'

'I can't talk to anyone. I'm shot.'

'Do you want me to come up for the opening night?'

'No, no . . .' His mumbling missed the phone again.

'I saw Mrs Drew today. Yesterday.'

'Oh God.'

'Paul, it's horrible. She's started to drink.'

'Who hasn't?' he said. 'Poor old thing.'

'You must call her.'

'Oh yes, yes.'

'Paul, you've got to let someone help you. They're worried about you at the theatre.' I was trying everything.

'Not to worry, not to worry. I'll be all right on the night.' He laughed. Not a pleasant sound.

'Not about your performance. About you.'

'Oh that,' he said again. 'I've been behaving like a shit. Liza, Liza, Liza.' He was crying now. I was badly scared.

'Paul, I'm coming up to see you.'

'No!' He shouted it. 'Don't want to see you. Don't want to see . . .' He mumbled to the end of a sentence that I couldn't hear, though I imagined I had got the gist.

'Paul, I love you.' I was desperate.

'Love. Bloody meaning of the word. Anything. Love and bloody death.'

'Where are you speaking from?'

'I don't know. Sheffield, I think.'

'Where in Sheffield?'

'I don't know.'

'Are you at your digs?'

'Don't know.' There was a sodden silence. Everywhere.

'Paul?'

'Mmm?' He must have gone to sleep for a second or two.

'If there's a bed there, you're to lie down in it and go to sleep.'

'Sleep!' He gave a snorting laugh. 'That'll be the night.'

'You must go to a doctor and get something to make you sleep. You can't go on like this.'

'What d'you bet?'

'Paul.'

'Going now.'

'Paul.'

'Bye, Millie.' So he still knew who he was talking to.

'Don't phone me,' he said.

'Paul.'

'Going now.'

There was a clatter as the phone fell back into place. I listened to nothing for some time. Then I walked round the room hitting things. I was screaming, inside my head, 'I won't let anything take Paul away. Not now.' And I wasn't just angry. I was afraid.

It was a bright night with a big moon. It got light as I approached Sheffield. The dawn was a fitting finale to the night, a pale camellia spreading across the sky, and the ground silver with frost. I drove in the direction of the theatre, it being the way I knew best, and the first place to look. I got breakfast at the little Italian place up the road. Many a poached egg on toast I had eaten there, five o'clock, before the show, putting a lining on the stomach nerves. It had changed hands, nobody knew me there, but the breakfast was still as good. I dawdled over a second coffee till ten to ten. Then I went to the stage door.

Jack was still there, four hairs carefully arranged on top of his head, fewer teeth.

'Hello, Millie! Nice to see you! How are you, love? Come to see

Paul? Oh, love, he's in a bad way. No wonder, is it? Poor lad.'

'Is he in yet, Jack?'

'Don't think they're rehearsing this morning, love, it's the get-in, you see. Let me have a look.'

He consulted his list.

'No, that's right. He might be in for a costume fitting though, let's see. Aye, he is. Due in for wardrobe at ten-fifteen. Any minute now.'

'Will he be on time, do you think?'

'Oh aye. He's never *late*.' Jack leaned confidentially on his counter, settling in for a chat. The stage door was flung open. In came a tiny creature in a short black dress. She had a very pale face and a mass of dyed black back-combed hair.

'Oh Jack, I'm late for my costume fitting. Is Paul in yet?'

I thought I recognised the voice, but the appearance was at such odds with it, I couldn't be sure.

'No, love, not yet.'

The girl nodded at me.

'Do you know Millie?' Jack said.

'Millie! Millie *Hale*! Oh I'm sorry, I'm Jane Barnes.'

'Yes,' I said.

She gave a wide anxious smile.

'He'll be in soon,' she said. 'At least he's never *late*.'

I smiled at Jack.

'I've got to go, Millie. I'm *always* late. I shouldn't be more than half an hour. I could meet you in the green room after. If you like, I mean.'

'Yes,' I said. 'Fine.'

The skinny legs flashed down the corridor. I regretted having agreed; the green room might be full of people I knew and I hadn't come for a social visit. Showbiz reunions are not my line at the best of times.

'How are you then, Millie?' Jack took up where he had left off. 'Saw you on the telly. Terrible business isn't it?'

'Not too pleasant, Jack, no. I'm okay, thanks.'

'That lovely girl. She was up here visiting Paul during his last show. Lovely girl.'

I wanted to escape. But this was my best chance of waylaying Paul.

I had to stay. People came crashing through the doors, in and out, strangers to me.

'Hi, Jack!'

'Morning, Charlie, morning, Pete, morning, Prue.'

They took his mind off Liza and off me. Each time the door swung open my stomach lurched. Then he came in.

If I hadn't stepped into his path and put both hands on his chest, he'd have walked past without seeing me. It took time for his eyes to focus. When they did, like Mrs Drew, he wasn't glad.

'What are you doing here?' he said.

He smelt bad. Paul the fastidious; you'd have taken him for a tramp. I wasn't able to answer him.

'I need some coffee,' he said.

Jack shook his head with big eyes as I followed Paul.

The green room was just the same. Yesterday's newspapers littered the tables. One or two people looked up from their bacon sandwiches as we came in, watching Paul warily, me with interest. No one I knew.

'Coffee, Mary,' he muttered. She nodded. It was obvious no one dared to speak to him.

'Hello, Millie, nice to see you love,' Mary said. She looked more, but in his presence bit her lip.

Paul grabbed his coffee and walked off, fast. I followed like a dog at his heels. He opened a dressing-room door. There were purple curtains and a matching chair. The same room had been my second home once, for three months. One of the happier times. Not to be dwelt on now. He drank the coffee like a starving man. I gave him mine.

'You shouldn't have come,' he said.

'I couldn't help it.'

'I've nothing to say. To anyone.'

'You need a shower,' I said. 'You smell.'

That stopped him short.

'Do I?' he said.

'Yes.'

'Who cares?'

'The wardrobe lady will. Have you got a towel?'

I found one under a pile of stuff on the floor, pushed it into his hands with the soap.

'Go on,' I bossed. 'Go and do it now. You've plenty of time. Jane Barnes was late for her fitting. Go.'

Puzzled but obedient, he went. The room had an animal stench. I tidied it up a bit, opened the window and let in the traffic fumes; they were preferable. And I waited, uneasily, wondering if I ought to leave. I'd had a lot of practice at biding my time, but biding isn't always best. Somewhere inside that smelly wreck, Paul still was. My Paul. If he went on like this, there'd be no Paul there to reach; for me, or anyone. I stayed.

He came back with the towel round his waist. He'd got thin. My heart turned over. His hair was wet.

'These stink,' he said, holding his clothes helplessly in one hand.

'I'll get them washed while you're in wardrobe; here's your dressing gown.'

It had been a posh white towelling affair. It was filthy, caked with make-up round the neck from the last show. He put it on.

'Go on, it's time for your fitting. Don't be late.'

He went without a word. I made my way to the laundry room and piled the clothes into the machine.

I watched them go round with the concentration of a snake watching its prey; and I thought. I thought about Jane Barnes. So that was what Paul went for when Liza wasn't around: a black and white grasshopper with legs like sticks and nothing above the neck but a lot of hair. She was kind, I supposed, and no doubt mothered him; people did. Liza did. I did. I got up and walked around; my thoughts had been lurching towards Mrs Drew. I wondered if Knife-blade had followed me here. I felt – not just watched, actors are used to being watched, though normally we're paid for it – but *stalked*, holding my breath at every crack of a twig in the undergrowth. It kept me on my mettle; no bad thing.

'Oh Millie!'

The shaggy black mane fell round the door just above waist height. Her little white face looked up at me.

'Jane. Sorry I didn't come to the green room. I decided to wash his clothes; he stinks.'

'Yes. He said. Hope you don't mind me coming down.'

'No,' I lied.

'He's been dreadfully smelly for days. No one dared to tell him.'

'I don't think he bites.'

'No. But we've all got so frightened about – what he might do.'

'Does he eat?'

'Not as far as I know. Just drinks. Alcohol and coffee, that's all.'

'What I thought.'

'You can't speak to him, he just pushes you away from him; he's so alone.'

'Yes,' was all I could say.

She burst into loud tears. There was a towel on the table. I gave it to her.

'I'm sorry, oh I am, only . . . Well you're the only one who knows I was – what was going on – between him and me – no one else does. He made it a secret; he was so scared of Liza finding out. So I couldn't tell anybody and – and – I – miss him so much. It's awful, it's really awful, you just don't know.'

The wash cycle conveniently reached its end.

'Sorry, Jane. I'll just shove these in the dryer if you don't mind.'

'He's never looked at me since. Not that I'd expect . . . Only I want to help him so much; I'd be happy just to look after him.'

'How does this thing work?'

She helped me, mopping at her face with the bath towel, tripping over it.

'Thanks,' I said.

'I'm in love with him, Millie.' She lowered the towel dramatically. Her big round eyes were ringed with black. So was the newly washed towel.

'I'd wait forever,' she said, 'if I thought there was hope.'

'There isn't any.'

'What?'

'Hope.'

I felt as though I'd kicked a puppy.

'Oh God, I shouldn't have told you. I thought you'd sympathise.'

'I do.'

She didn't know how much.

'I just don't see any point in . . . And anyway I could be wrong,' I said.

'No. You're not wrong.'

She sat on an upturned laundry basket with the towel up to her face. Even a grasshopper could feel despair.

One death. So many waves. Moving outwards, lapping over people you hadn't so much as heard of before. The ground seemed to rock under my feet. It was the dryer juddering to a halt. Maybe.

'You'll have to give it another go,' she sniffed, lowering the towel. 'It's very old.'

'How's the play going?'

'Oh it's marvellous,' she said sadly.

'That's something.'

'I suppose so, yes.'

The door opened. It was Paul, his eyes like holes in a mask. He saw her and left.

'Oh God,' she wailed. 'You see! That's what it's like all the time, at rehearsals and everything. It's unbearable.'

I wanted to say, You'll get over it. I said nothing.

'I'd better go,' she sniffed.

'I'm sorry not to have been more help.'

'No. I've just got to get on with it. I just wish this play was over, now. There's four whole weeks to go! And I was enjoying it so much, more than I've ever enjoyed anything before. And now it's . . . At least there won't be rehearsals after Wednesday. I'll only have to see him during the show; that's something, I suppose.'

She gave a down-cornered smile. You could see how attractive she might be, happy.

'Good luck with the opening anyway,' I said.

'Oh that,' she echoed Paul. 'Oh thanks.' She folded the towel carefully, looking down. 'Are you staying up for it?'

'I don't know yet. I might.'

'See you round then perhaps?'

'Yes.'

She was a person who found it hard to leave. She'd always be there at the end of your party when you were dying to go to bed, offering to wash up. The dryer stopped.

'Will this be cooked now?' I asked.

'I should think so, yes.'

'I'll get it out then. See you.'

I held out my hand. She put hers in it. It was like a little dry leaf. She got out quickly when she went, with a sort of speedy shuffle on her backless shoes. I liked her. I was glad she'd gone.

# CHAPTER FIFTEEN

That night began the descent into Hades. Paul walked ahead oblivious and I followed behind. All I could do was keep him in my sights. He behaved as though I wasn't there. I opened my own doors after he had swept through them. I bought my own drinks after he had bought his. I drank on average one mineral water to his five vodkas. When the pubs closed he made for a café near the station and fell asleep over a coffee, dark head in the breadcrumbs and spilt tea. When we were turned out of there he walked the black streets. I wondered how long I could go on with this. I had started to feel insane.

'Where do you live, Paul?'

Nothing.

'If you're not going back to your digs again, can you give me the key so that I can go there and get some rest?'

Nothing.

It must have been three a.m., the deadly hour of the night. The cold was frightful, he was in a light jacket. I couldn't afford a hotel.

'Paul! Stop!'

He stopped and waited with his back to me.

'Please let me go back to your flat and sleep. Just give me the key and tell me where it is, please.'

Without a word he turned round and strode back the way we had come. Perhaps an hour later we entered a suburban gate and a substantial front door. He proceeded up the stairs.

It was a big room. He flung open another door, to a large kitchen, and indicated a sofa. I threw myself onto it boots and all. A blanket was hurled at me and the door closed.

My sleep was not profound, I heard him walking up and down all night; but in the morning when I woke there was silence from his room. I opened his door like a thief. He was fully clothed flat on his back on top of the bed. He was snoring. I crept close to him. He didn't stir. I covered him with my blanket and watched him. He looked as though someone had knocked him out.

I closed the door silently, cleaned up the kitchen as quietly as I could, made some instant coffee from greyish granules set hard in the jar, threw away some milk with a half inch of green growth on top and some bread looking much the same. I took him the coffee. He had stopped snoring. For a horrible moment I thought . . . but he was breathing softly like a baby in its crib. I went back to the kitchen and sat.

When I went out he hadn't stirred. I knew he wasn't rehearsing today, the last Sunday before the opening night; I nearly locked him in, but didn't. I thought I could find an Indian shop open but not in this area. The sun was shining, the air was crisp. Day did still exist then. I was high on one of Sheffield's seven hills. Solid citizens walked their dogs. They bade me good morning when our paths crossed; I had forgotten how unlike London it was.

I found my Indian shop, bought milk, eggs, bread. I was closer to my car than to Paul's digs. I got the car and drove back. It was midday when I silently let myself in. He was as I had left him, still concussed. I shut myself in the kitchen and ate, ravenously, reading through a pile of newspapers dating from before Liza's death. There was a picture of her in one of them. 'Liza Drew in Sheffield' was the caption. 'No, I have no plans to work here at the moment,' said the TV star. 'I've just come to see the show. But I'd love to work here one day, it's a marvellous theatre.' I put it in the waste bin with the mouldy food.

He didn't come into the kitchen until after dark. He made himself some coffee, ignoring me.

'I'll get you something to eat,' I said.

He shrugged. But he ate, standing up staring at the window, sightless. Then we set off again, he in front, I behind, pub after pub, silently. I had caught the disease, I didn't dare to speak to him. Sunday night we were in his digs by two a.m. but he didn't sleep. Nor did I; I listened all night to him bumping into things as though he really had gone blind.

Monday morning I followed him to the theatre, dead on time to rehearse at ten. I found the phone, told my agent where I was and said I'd be back on Thursday unless something urgent came up. I spent the day in the car on the Derbyshire Hills among the dead bracken and the birds, studying my scripts and dozing and breathing the air.

That was the crazy pattern of each day, each night. But Tuesday night, after the dress rehearsal, he led the way back to his digs. No booze. Things were looking up. I made boiled eggs and toast. We did not speak. He fell on his bed face down and was unconscious instantly.

On Wednesday, during the afternoon dress rehearsal, I phoned my agent again.

'You've got a costume fitting tomorrow,' she said, 'and the first reading is at ten-thirty on Monday at Acton Rehearsal Rooms.'

'Okay, Dorothy.'

'You all right, Millie?'

'Yes.'

'You sound strange.'

'I'm fine.'

It was weird to enter the theatre by the front of house on Wednesday evening and find the foyers upstairs and down milling with people and brightly lit. There was a group playing in the bar, excited conversation. On the way to my seat I heard a middle-aged Sheffield lady say, 'I haven't been to this theatre since Richard Todd was here in *Seagulls Over Sorrento*; it was lovely, it really was.' I wondered why on earth she had come tonight until, sitting just behind her, I heard.

'This Paul – Thing – lived with Liza Drew, you know,' in a thrilled whisper.

Perhaps that was why the place was packed.

The house lights went down. I was more sick with nerves than if I had been appearing myself. It was a good play, I gathered. Not that I was conscious of much that was going on till Paul appeared; and after that I was conscious of little else.

From the moment he came on he never touched the ground. His energy was frightening, magnificent, he bounced off the walls, he flew, he soared. I stayed in my seat in the interval unable to move. In the second act there was a violent fight: three young actors playing skin-heads, against Paul. Chains and knives. It was a brilliantly directed sequence, but we all knew that in Paul we were watching a man who didn't care if he got killed there and then in front of us all. The audience did not breathe. At the end there was a moving scene between Paul and Grasshopper (who was not bad at all) during which he wept.

When the final blackout came, thirteen hundred people sat in silence, stunned. The Richard Todd lady sobbed audibly into her frilly handkerchief; she was not alone. Then the applause broke out, people stood and shouted, banged their feet. The actors were visibly shaken by the response.

I bumped into Peter Grant in the foyer. He was the local critic who also did the northern reviews for the *Guardian*.

'My God, Millie,' he said, 'I've never seen anything like that.'

I noticed three national critics in the bar. Nothing like a connection with a violent death to arouse interest in an actor, even if he's working in the provinces. Even if he's not working at all; like me.

Then I saw Knife-blade. I was on the stairs; he stood in the foyer looking up at me. I don't know how long we stood, looking. Then I went on down.

'The lad's an actor,' he said. 'I might go to the theatre more often from now on.'

'You won't see a performance like that more than once in ten years,' I said. 'What are you doing here, need I ask?'

'Just keeping an eye on things.'

'When did you arrive?'

'In time for the show. You've been here a few days, Millie. Staying in his flat.'

I ignored that.

'And when are you leaving?' I asked.

'I'll stick around for a bit.'

A group of people pushed between us, putting on their coats. When they disappeared, so had he. I searched the crowd with my eyes. I wondered if I had hallucinated him.

I pushed through the pass door to the green room. People were opening bottles of wine and squealing. Paul wasn't there. I made my way through them to his dressing room. He was sitting at the dressing table looking washed out. I stood not knowing what to say. 'Marvellous, darling' was hardly appropriate.

Alan Draper, the director came in, very high.

'Paul! Oh, Millie, hello, you were in tonight? Wasn't he wonderful?'

'Yes,' I said.

'There's drinks in the green room, come along.'

'Thanks, I will.'

'Paul,' he said, 'for Christ's sake come and have a drink with us all tonight.'

Paul gave him a smile, of singular sweetness. It was a shock. Like a sunrise in the middle of the night.

'Don't worry, Alan,' he said, 'I'll be there.'

Alan hugged him from behind the chair awkwardly.

'That's my lad,' he said; and went.

There were screams of congratulation in the corridor as the door opened. I was unwilling to leave Paul alone. That smile had worried me. I felt more than ever like a guide dog to the blind. I handed him his clothes. He put them on, even combed his hair. He held the door politely for me as we left the room. Except for the matter of not speaking a word to me, he was behaving like Paul.

The euphoria of the first night had lifted the rest of the cast out of their dread of him. The moment we entered the green room he was covered with clinging bodies. The noise was deafening. Everybody was drunk without the help of alcohol. I noticed from my corner that Paul, though almost silent, kept giving that piercing smile like the smile of the dead.

Grasshopper flew up to me.

'You were terrific,' I said.

'I was shaking all through.'

'You couldn't tell.'

'Couldn't you? Oh good! But wasn't he wonderful?'

'Yes.'

'There were lots of critics in tonight, you know.'

'Yes, I saw them.'

'Did you?' Big round eyes. 'Did they seem impressed?'

'How can you tell with those guys?'

'Oh they must have been!'

'Don't bank on it. They don't have the same responses as human beings, you know.'

'Well, I just know they must have been. If they don't give Paul great reviews I'll write letters to them all. I will.'

Paul was in the corner by the bar in conversation with a man much smaller than himself whom he was regarding with the same sweet smile he bestowed on everyone tonight. I recognised the brown leather jacket and the sleek hair. Knife-blade was talking earnestly. I reached them fast, all cylinders on high-octane rage.

'It's a very interesting play,' he was saying. 'I like the way good and evil are turned on end, the way your character embodies pure goodness and turns out to have caused nothing but harm. A monster of goodness. It's an interesting idea.'

Paul looked at me. That made a change. Then back at Knife-blade.

'I'm glad you saw that,' he said. 'It's what I wanted to convey. It's not overstated in the play.'

The polite actor in interview. Perfect. Always be nice to the discerning punter.

'You conveyed it all right,' said Knife-blade. 'I am very impressed. I was saying so to Millie here, earlier.'

Paul turned his eyes on me again.

'You didn't tell me,' he said charmingly, 'that you'd brought a friend.'

Icy, it was.

'No friend of mine,' I said.

'Interesting atmosphere, this,' said Knife-blade. 'I've never been backstage before. Everyone gets more excited than I would have imagined.'

'The release of nervous tension,' said Paul.

'Everything seems "interesting" to you tonight,' I said.

'Don't be rude to the policeman, Millie,' said Paul.

'I apologise for the paucity of my vocabulary, "Miss" Hale,' said Knife-blade.

'But not for your presence,' I said.

'The spectre at the feast,' he gleamed. 'I'm used to that.'

'What's one more or less?' said Paul. 'Have another drink.'

He slopped white wine into our polystyrene cups.

'Excuse me,' said Knife-blade, and he edged himself through the crowd, in the direction of the Grasshopper, I thought.

Paul's hand caught me by the neck, not gently, and pulled me close to him.

'Now look, Millie,' he said, still smiling that awful smile, 'you have to listen to me. I don't want you here. I don't want to see you, I don't want to speak to you. Don't interrupt. That man has put unspeakable thoughts into my mind. No, not tonight, days ago, before you arrived. Not just about you. He has made everything – untouchable – leprous to me. I won't go into details, it all makes me sick; there's nowhere I can look that isn't crawling with snakes. It isn't your fault; but I don't want you around me. Go away.'

He let go of my neck. To the assembled multitude the gesture may have looked like one of affection.

'Paul, he has done the same thing to me. But you can't let him win. It's his method, can't you see that? He wants to splinter us off, you, me, Mrs Drew.'

He made a face as if the mention of her name had soured the wine.

'Are you abandoning her, too?' I asked.

'Yes.'

'She's desperate to hear from you. She's started drinking. Paul. I went to see her. She was drunk and—'

'I can't have anything to do with her. He's poisoned everything I trusted. He's the nightmare man.'

'You've got to fight him, Paul, or there'll be nothing left. He wants just this. Don't give him what he wants. It's easy to give in. You have to fight as hard as you can.'

'What for?'

You can't answer 'Life' to a man who wants to be dead. I didn't answer at all. But he saw my thoughts.

'Don't worry,' he said, 'I'm not going to kill myself. Yes, I know it's what everybody thinks. You've been a great guard dog the last few days.

I assure you it isn't necessary. I'll be alive until that man finds out what happened to Liza. Then we'll see. That's all I'm living for. So set your mind at rest. I'll still be here amusing the public with my antics every night. But I don't want you around. I'm saying it for the last time, Millie. Stay away from me.'

And he walked away. The music had got louder, people were dancing. He grabbed a little blonde girl in jeans and a paint-stained shirt, and started whirling her about.

I went to the ladies and threw up. Then I found my car.

# CHAPTER SIXTEEN

I don't know how I got back to London that night because I drove blind. But I had a lot of hours on the road to drive out the rage. The 2CV almost fell apart, it rattled and shook and vibrated and banged. It hadn't been driven quite like that before. It slid about a fair bit, too. There was black ice on the road; I steered out of a few interesting skids.

Black ice described my state when I arrived. The anger had congealed into a stony resolve. So I had lost something, but I sure as hell hadn't lost everything; I had the job, my chance; and that was not going to be taken away from me. By anyone. From now on I would concentrate exclusively on that.

I needed sleep. There hadn't been a lot of it lately. I took a few pills and threw myself into bed, set the alarm for the costume fitting and got up for it. No dreams.

The fitting was satisfactory. We did a kind of costume parade for Robin. He was pleased. Afterwards I had a drink with him.

'Here's to us, Millie,' he said, lifting a large vodka and something. 'This is the worst time for me, just before kick-off, hoping I've put it together right.'

'I'm sure you have. The cast is great.'

'Butterflies till after the first reading,' he said. 'But one thing I know I've got right, and that's you.'

'I hope so, Robin.'

'I know so, Millie. No worries there.'

Oh yes, the job would do.

I bought the papers in West End Lane. Rave reviews for Paul and for the play in the *Guardian*, the *Telegraph* and *The Times*.

'A Young Peter O'Toole Back Amongst Us?' was the *Telegraph* headline. I read them in the car and threw them on the back seat. Outside the flat I had an impulse, did a fairly dangerous U-turn before it had time to die, and went to King Henry's Road.

Mrs Drew looked the worse for – something. There was an impression of a hair or two out of place. She let me in. I thrust the papers folded to the relevant pages into her hands. She sat, gradually, as she read. She read slowly. Then she said:

'I wish I had been there.'

'I was,' I said.

She gave me one of her whiplash looks.

'Oh?'

'It was better than they say.'

She nodded. 'And how is Paul himself?'

It cost her a lot to ask it.

'He's terrible. I've come to tell you because it's best you should be warned.'

'What? What?'

A rare spontaneous reaction and as such to be treasured in the memory.

'Inspector Bright has done his work well. Paul will not speak to me and he will not speak to you. He'll have nothing to do with either of us until Liza's death is . . . sorted out. He may kill himself then, he says, but not before.'

'He could not have known what he was saying.'

'He did. It was the only thing he said to me in three days. He is consuming a lot of alcohol but it wasn't that that was talking, it was him.'

She got up slowly and, tottered is the word, to the mantelpiece. Her hand felt vaguely along its surface. She looked, for the first time, old. In the days since I had seen her last her back had assumed a curve and even seemed to have thickened between the shoulder blades.

Her searching hand found what it was looking for: a glass, but it was empty. She handed it to me.

'Would you be so kind, Millie? The bottle is in the kitchen. Thank you.'

'Is that wise?'

'Do as I say!' It rang out like a gun shot, hit the wall behind my head.

'All right.'

'Thank you.'

She took the Scotch in a slightly vibrating hand. There was a lot of water in it. She noticed but didn't say. She drank half of it in one gulp.

'You were not aware that I – drank?' she said.

'You didn't,' I replied.

She ignored this.

'It started after the death of my husband. I do not offer that as an excuse.'

Not much, I thought.

'And stopped when I knew I was to have a child.'

'And started again, when?'

She smiled and swallowed the other half. I recalled Paul's embarrassment on the subject. 'I'd give a lot to see her tipsy,' I had said. I was regretting that. Paul knew then. A secret had been kept from me.

'Paul tried to tell me once. Or rather tried not to,' I said when I saw her face.

'Paul appears to have told you many things. I refused, by the way, to listen to melodramatic messages relayed through you.'

'I only came to warn you. I was trying to help.'

'Were you.'

It wasn't a question, the way she said it. I answered anyway:

'Inspector Bright has filled his mind with hideous suspicions. He's tried to do it to me, he has tried to do it to you; with Paul it has worked, that's all. Go up and see him if you don't believe me. Follow him round Sheffield night after night like I did, from pub to pub. You never know, you might succeed where I failed. It's possible.'

I was angry to find myself on the point of breaking down. I believed I had put it in a place where it couldn't hurt. I was wrong.

She watched me, leisurely. 'He has upset you, Millie,' she said.

'Yes. I didn't want the same thing to happen to you. Perhaps I shouldn't have bothered. Mr Bright has done his work brilliantly. With everyone except me.'

She considered me quietly and intently, still supported by the fireplace.

Eventually she said, 'Yes. Nothing can be the same again.'

'We have to fight to—'

'No, Millie. We simply have to wait. Paul has had the courage to admit that. So must we.'

I felt as though a hundred white mice had escaped all over the room. If only I could bundle them all back inside the cage. I couldn't catch one.

'We can do nothing for one another,' she said, sucking the last drop from the glass and placing it on the mantelpiece in a full stop.

'I need you both,' I whispered.

It was a fair throw but the game was over.

'Yes, Millie, I am afraid you do.'

A red film shot across my eyes, so hot it might have been visible.

'What will you do about David Summers?' I asked.

'That, as I have said before, I believe, is my own affair.'

'Well then . . . I'll go . . .'

No reply.

She gazed out of the window as I picked up my things. Until I laid my hand on the newspapers I had brought. She shot round then.

'Don't take those!'

I looked at her.

'Please,' she added reluctantly.

I slowly put them down.

'Thank you.' She forced it through her teeth.

'Don't mention it,' I said.

I let myself out.


Friday, I slept.

Saturday, I went down to Covent Garden to buy clothes, working clothes. I'd got shabby in the last few years, and I wanted to look good. I was broke, but there'd be money soon; I reckoned I was good for an overdraft.

Covent Garden was carnival. Again it was a shock to see the ordinary world enjoying itself in the winter sun. One of these days I might find myself a place in it.

Sunday, I soaked in the bath. I peeled my legs, washed my hair, wrapped in a cloud of expensive bath oil and unguents. Until the woman on my landing started beating on the door.

In my room I painted my toenails, caked my face with a face-pack and my hands with hand cream, plucked my eyebrows and brushed my hair till it mirrored the mirror. I put on my new suit and the smart swinging greatcoat and went for a walk on the Heath. The North London dogs were in good form, out for their weekly exercise; they know how to have a good time, dogs.

I sat down in the Dome in the High Street with the Sunday papers to have a leisurely meal. It gave me a strange turn to see Paul's face, large, staring at me from the review page. More raves. I didn't take those to Mrs Drew.

The evening I spent in bed with the scripts. I was going to be prepared. The phone rang at ten o'clock. The nasal tree-saw said, 'Good luck for tomorrow, Millie.'

I wondered if I hallucinated once more. I put the phone down without a word. It didn't ring again.


The Acton Rehearsal Rooms aren't much to look at. Acton's not much to look at, at least not the part that surrounds the rehearsal rooms; worse than South Norwood on a bad day. They call the building the Acton Hilton, because it's high. Well, in Acton it looks high. I rattled into the car park at ten-fifteen. I was wound tight, but not with fear. With readiness. I strode in and announced myself to the uniformed commissionaire.

'You're going to be with us for a bit, dear,' he said. 'You're on the third floor.'

There it was on the noticeboard, the title of our show and Room 302. I don't think I believed it till I saw that, large as life, white on black.

I got into an empty lift. I could have flown up without its help. There are three rehearsal rooms on each floor. 302 was the middle one. I pushed open the double swing doors.

It was a big room, windows all down one side showing the light industry of Acton; you wouldn't be much tempted to look out. There were more than twenty people dotted about in small groups in subdued conversation, lost in the space.

Robin came to meet me at the door. He put an arm round my shoulders. I looked scared and shy. He looked fine, but his hand left a damp patch on the top of my sleeve.

'How are you feeling, Millie?'

'Scared,' I said. 'How about you, Robin?'

'Don't ask,' he said. 'One hour's sleep last night; it gets worse as I get older, the first day.'

He left me to Brian, the Assistant Floor Manager, as someone else arrived. Brian took me to the tray of coffee.

'This is a first-day luxury,' he said. 'It'll never happen again.'

We took our coffee to the huge table, set around with chairs. Robin started by introducing everyone to everyone else. No wonder he was scared. It was not a small cast. I knew them all by sight and reputation. No one knew me by either. Yet. I was just dead Liza's best friend. But I was satisfied; they'd know me soon.

'Bill Warren, playing Jackie's husband.'

He was on my right, a burly chap, ugly and attractive; usually played foreign heavies in movies. This part was a change for him.

'Nigel Ward who plays the police inspector.'

Opposite me, he was small, dark and wiry, but without further resemblance to my friend the rat.

'Marjorie Dobbs, Jackie's mother.'

She sat farther down the table, a short flabby woman with a broad smile.

'Yes, it's mums now for me, dear!'

She usually played comedy and it got a laugh. I didn't think much of Robin's choice there; but if it was a mistake, it was the only one. The thing was well cast.

'And Millie Hale who is playing Jackie.'

I lowered my eyes modestly. Joe, the writer, gave an encouraging nudge on my left, and the reading began.

You know when you've read well. You know when people are impressed. I had, and they were. Bill Warren squeezed my shoulders in his big arm.

'You're going to be great, kid,' he said into my ear.

No one mentioned Liza all day. Perhaps Robin had warned them off. But they showed their sympathy with speaking looks, treated me with solicitude. I reciprocated with wide, soft smiles and modest gratitude.

Lunchtime was daunting. The canteen was packed with actors, dancers, comedians. Paul Daniels sat at one table surrounded by little dancers laughing at his jokes; the two Ronnies at another in serious conversation. Again, there was no one I knew, or who knew me, and I was thankful for that.

In the afternoon we started to rehearse, just Bill Warren and I, in little sets marked out on the floor with coloured tape and furnished with battered old things which seemed to have been stored in the BBC attics for some years and kicked a lot. Just like theatre props. I felt at home.

We stopped at five. Robin's nerves had exhausted him. The commissionaire said, 'Goodnight, dear. Had a good day?'

'The best,' I replied. 'Thanks.'


Next morning my bell rang at seven-thirty. Knife-blade, I thought, come to spoil the fun. I almost didn't go down to answer it. Two reporters stood there.

'Hi, Millie, hear you've landed this great part, that's nice. How do you feel?'

I stopped myself beaming.

'It's helping to take my mind off – things,' I said.

It went on till I left for work. They rang the bell two by two, their cameras flashed; they must have been short of news. Robin had been true to his word. None of them knew it had been Liza's part.

For the second time I was on the front of the *Standard* on my doorstep in a dressing gown. 'Millie Hale to star in new serial. "It's a wonderful part," says Millie', and a small paragraph adding that there were still no clues to the death of my friend.

It was a fast fiery week. It flew, and so did I. Knife-blade never put his nose in it, though I expected him hourly and was on my guard. The most extraordinary thing was that the consideration with which I had been treated the first day, due, as I thought, to my mourning state, went on. And on.

'Have a chair, Millie.' 'Can I get you a coffee, Millie?' 'Do you feel like having another go at this scene, Millie, or shall we stop?'

If someone had offered to throw their coat over a puddle, Millie, in case your shoes get wet, I could hardly have been more surprised. It dawned only gradually that all this attention was because I was the star. Not *a* star, like some of the others, but *the* star, of this show. It was heady stuff, being surrounded by love. So it was temporary love. So what love isn't? As I had learned. It would do. It was fine. I received it sweetly, with Liza's big soft eyes. They thought I was a darling girl. They couldn't do enough. If anyone mentioned Liza, which they all did, of course, as the week went on, the big soft eyes filled with tears, and the word went round, 'Don't talk about Liza to Millie, it upsets her too much.'

I refused to think about Paul, about Liza, about Mrs Drew. I didn't think about Knife-blade much, though I kept myself in readiness everywhere. Even in the rehearsal room, I gave a swift look round each morning to see if he was there; it would be just his style.

A week after the start of rehearsals the papers showed a blurred picture of a bespectacled little man with a bewildered stare. 'Drew Fan Questioned By Police.' He had written Liza some odd letters, had been seen hanging round her house, and now, it appeared, had confessed. Then there was no further news of him. No arrest was made.

The following week I read in Sunday's *Observer* that Paul's play was coming into town, to the Almeida Theatre in Islington. So he would be in London again. I wondered if Mrs Drew had gone back to Suffolk yet. I even rang the flat, but there was no reply. I thought about going round there. I didn't go. I had lunch with some old friends who'd read of my good news. Old friends were coming out of the woodwork now. That's what it's like being a star. It was pleasant. And it took my mind off Paul and Mrs Drew.

In the middle of the third week we had the technicians' run. Innumerable men with big paper plans came in and followed us from set to set as we performed, plunging into deep discussion between scenes, talking a language I didn't understand, composed of initials rather than words. The next day was the producer's run. After it Donald, the small fat producer, took my hands in his podgy ones.

'Very good, Millie, I am most impressed; delighted. Thank you. Most moving.'

Then we all filed out tactfully to the canteen, leaving him to tell Robin what was wrong with the show. Nothing much was, it appeared. We could look forward to the studio days without a qualm.

It was, naturally, the night before the first studio day that Knife-blade appeared.

# CHAPTER SEVENTEEN

I knew it was he before I opened the door. I was in a dressing gown, wet hair wrapped in a towel. He ran his eyes over me from head to foot, and grinned.

'You were expecting me I see.'

'As always,' I said.

'You look good like that.'

'As you can see, I'm busy. What do you want?'

'It won't take long.'

He walked past me into the hall. I had no choice but to lead the way upstairs.

In the room he sat down. At the table by the window.

'Got a cup of Earl Grey by any chance?'

'You said it wouldn't take long.'

'It'll take that long.'

I put the kettle on. 'Well?' I said.

He sighed. 'We're not getting on very well.'

'You and I?'

He half smiled. 'The investigation, "Miss" Hale.'

'I thought some fan had confessed.'

'Oh. Yeah.'

'No good?'

'This turned out to be the fifteenth murder he'd confessed to. He just wanted to talk about her and cry.'

'So what's new?'

'Several things are new. There are some puzzling facts. Liza was seen leaving her flat on the Wednesday morning. The neighbour upstairs. That doesn't quite fit in with what the doc thinks about the time of death. But the neighbour is certain so we're going along with it.'

He looked at me narrowly. I looked back.

'The neighbour's only just come out with this?'

'Oh no, we've known it from the start. That's not what's new. Be patient, Miss Hale. Liza walked round the corner, presumably to where her car was parked. Nobody saw her get into her car or drive off. For such a recognisable girl she was remarkably invisible.'

'What time was this?'

'Ten to twelve. About. The neighbour's not sure. Naturally. Next thing we know, Liza picks up the keys from the estate agent, quarter past twelve. About. They're not sure either. Only the receptionist remembers her. She was wearing the fur jacket, dark glasses; wonder what happened to them? She spoke very soft, the girl said. Just asked for the keys, got them and left.'

'And then?'

'Ten minutes later someone sees a blonde girl in dark glasses drive a silver Alfa Romeo into the courtyard of the house in Belsize Lane. A passer-by. A man who doesn't watch television, would you believe? Never heard of Liza Drew. Just got in touch with us. That's what's new.'

'And then?'

'Then nothing.'

'The passer-by didn't see anyone else go in?'

'No. He passed by.' He raised his eyebrows. '*No one* saw anyone else go in. Or come out. Nothing.'

'She didn't take the keys back?'

'The estate agents found them on the mat the next morning. They'd been put through their letter box by hand.'

'She wasn't seen doing that?'

'Who?'

I sighed.

'No one was seen doing that,' he said.

'So why are you telling me all this?'

'Thought you might help me out.'

'How?'

'We want to do a re-enactment,' he said.

'Oh yeah?'

'It might throw up something. They often do.'

'And where do I come in?' I turned away to make the tea.

'Could you be her?'

His voice was cool enough to freeze the blood.

'What?'

'Would you be Liza? For me?'

I was standing with the teapot in my hand. I only slowly became aware that the handle was hot. I put it down. Carefully.

'I thought policewomen normally did that sort of thing.'

'You've been watching too much television. A-ha. They do. But you're an actress. And you knew her well. You'd do it better.'

'That Irene at the police station looks more like her than I do. She's blonde.'

'We'll get you a wig.'

I shivered.

'Or maybe you've got one?'

'No.'

'I thought actresses had that sort of thing.'

'Not a blonde one. You'd have found it when you looked.'

'A-ha.'

He was smiling. I poured the tea, sat down.

'Please don't ask me to do this,' I said.

'Why not?'

'It's awful. Ghoulish. I can't.' I looked at him helplessly. 'I can't.'

'Don't you want me to get any further with this case?'

'I don't see how it can help.'

'People get reminded of things. They see a girl who looks the same, doing the same things, they might notice something they missed before.'

'I understand the principle, thanks.'

'You'd have to wear her clothes, of course.'

A drop of tea splashed onto my hand. 'I'd have to wear her clothes?'

'A-ha.'

'Oh no.' I stood up. 'I won't. I can't.'

I was shaking. I had no control.

'Take it easy, Millie. It's not that bad.'

'It is, it's just that bad, it's awful. Don't make me do it.'

'There's no compulsion, of course.'

'Like hell.'

'Seriously. Your own free will.'

'I've heard of helping the police with their enquiries but this—'

'You'd be doing it for her.'

'She'd understand why I can't.'

'The point, surely, is that she's not here to ask.'

'Oh God.'

I put my face in my hands. He pulled my hands away.

'Here, drink some tea.'

I did.

'It's okay. If you can't you can't. Never mind.' He sighed. 'How's the job going?'

'The job's great.' I spoke bitterly.

'Heard from Paul Mannon at all?' he said. He knew.

'Yes, sure, every evening before his show he rings me up, we have long jolly chats about this and that, holidays in Bermuda, the weather, the latest line in Gucci handbags, you know the sort of thing, it's great.'

'And Mrs Drew?' he said.

'The same. Cosy teas alternate afternoons, one day her place, one day mine. We lace the tea with a little alcohol, of course. That's nice. About half a bottle of Scotch per cup. You bastard,' I said.

'Me?'

'She's drinking. Directly down to you.'

'Directly, is it? Now why would you think that?'

'You started dripping your nasty insinuations into Paul's ears, you found very fertile ground. He's abandoned her.'

'A-ha. Well, it had to work with someone, didn't it? Mrs Drew now, easy to turn her against you, she was already nine tenths there; but nothing would turn her against him. Can't turn *you* against anyone, can I, Millie? Stoniest ground I ever came across.'

'Why do it?'

'Got to see people clear. That means alone. Then they're vulnerable and might just start to crack. A solid phalanx of three locked in loyalty – no good at all. You'd never crack that.'

'Those two are cracking all right; they're cracking up. What's the use? They didn't kill Liza.'

'No?'

'No.'

'I'd like to be as sure as you are, Millie.' He said this slowly, watching me with eyebrows raised. 'I really would.'

'Well, get a few drinks inside her, take the bottle away and when she breaks down and confesses –' I laughed ' – you can offer her a little nip as a reward.'

'Mrs Drew was in London on the Tuesday night.'

I stopped laughing, suddenly.

'The night before Liza was found. She was in town. A-ha, she lied to us.'

There were black specks in front of my eyes. I could hardly see, and I could not speak.

'I told you she had a secret,' the voice went on. 'And I knew we had to look in the past. A nice old lady who used to work at the Society of Authors helped us out. Does the name David Summers mean anything to you?'

I did not speak.

'A-ha, I see it does. Well, well, withholding information from me, Millie. Met him, have you then?'

I said nothing, again.

'He's been squeezing money out of her for years, a monthly stipend for staying away from Liza and keeping his mouth shut.'

'It's not true!' I blurted out. 'It was only that once.'

'Just that once, was it? And which once would that be?'

'No,' I said. 'No. I didn't – it was – Oh Christ!'

'See them together, did you? When was this?'

'No . . . She told me about him. Of her own accord.'

'A-ha. And *what* did she tell you? Of her own accord?'

I remembered at the time thinking how odd it was, her coming out with all that, sensing that the story was camouflage. She, who couldn't wish you good morning without striking a bargain first. I had chosen to believe her, so as not to have to think? I had to believe

Knife-blade now. He was making too much sense. But I had to protect her too.

'She said he got in touch with her after Liza's death, after the news came out. That's how he traced her. He threatened to sell the story of Liza's parentage to the gutter press if she didn't give him money. That's all. I told her to tell you so that you could stop him. She said if the police got in touch with him the story would be released.'

'It's a good tale.'

'I believe her,' I said.

'No you don't, Millie, you believe me.'

'How did you find out all this?'

'He's told us everything. He's an easy guy to threaten.'

'To bully,' I said.

'If you like.'

'He could just be trying to make trouble for her. Have you questioned her?'

'We have them both in for questioning.'

He watched my white face.

'And what does she say?'

'She makes no attempt to deny it. Apparently since the murder he had upped the price. He's not a fool. He realised what the implications were.'

'Oh God.'

'She thinks you told us about him.'

'You bastard,' I said.

'I told her you didn't. She didn't believe me though.'

'How convincing you must have been.'

I got up and walked about the room a bit. I had to think. He sat calmly sipping his tea, his air of private amusement deepening. I came back to the table and sat again.

'But you *can't* believe she killed Liza,' I said.

'She was here in town when Liza was killed. And she told us she was in bed with flu.' He shrugged.

'But it must have been true about the flu. Liza knew about it days before.'

'Yes,' he said. 'It was a pretty well-set-up story for a person who needed an alibi. Wasn't it?'

I had no answer.

'She had the flu all right,' he said. 'Summers confirms it.'

'There you are then. She wasn't planning anything.'

I couldn't help wondering why, if she was sick, she had come all the way to London to see the man. Surely she could have simply *sent* the money to him? I wasn't about to put that thought into Knife-blade's head. I didn't need to:

'You're wondering why she left her sick bed to come and see him, aren't you, Millie?'

'No,' I said.

'It wouldn't do, from his point of view, for her to know where he hung out – dangerous for him. So they always met in cafés after a phone call from him. I gather as well that he was fond of his pound of flesh, liked to see her crawl to him. Not a pleasant character. No wonder she didn't relish the idea of letting him loose on Liza.'

'Why don't you suspect him of killing her?'

'Too fond of the golden eggs to kill the goose. Anyway he has an alibi for the whole night. They were seen in the café where they met, then he went on to his Soho club where he flashed his money around till the early hours. He was poured into a cab by a marginally less paralytic friend at three a.m. and they both spent the rest of the night at his place sloshing more booze down their throats. She says she went back to Suffolk on the eight-thirty train.'

'Well, she must have been seen at the station,' I said.

'Sorry, Millie, no good. She says there was no one at the station when she arrived. The man who was supposed to be on duty says he was there and that no one got off that train.'

'The bloody police station is right opposite the railway station; you mean to say that team of dynamic Suffolk bobbies missed her as well?'

He looked interested for a second.

'We're making enquiries,' he said.

'Anyway, what's all this about Tuesday night? I thought Wednesday morning was when she was killed.'

'Ah. Wondered when you'd ask me that.'

He raised an eyebrow and assumed his expression of amused inquiry.

'We are having some second thoughts about the time,' he said. 'Keeping our options open a bit.'

'Surely your forensic wizards are better than that?' I said.

'We'll see.'

'I talked to Liz on Wednesday morning.'

'Mmm.'

'So what happens now?'

'We keep them both for questioning a while.'

I tried to imagine Mrs Drew held for questioning at the police station. Sitting in the dog-smelling room, or in a cell even. I put my hand over my eyes.

'How long will you keep her there?'

'Until she cracks; or until we get some solid information that she went back to Suffolk when she says she did.'

'Does that mean you have arrested her?'

'Not enough evidence. Yet. No, she's—'

'Helping you with your enquiries, yes.'

'That's right,' he said.

'What can I do? To help her?' I asked.

'You could do this re-enactment for us, Millie. As I said, you never know what it might throw up.'

I gave him a long steady look.

'There's more than one kind of blackmail,' I said. 'You and David Summers must get on just fine.'

'Yeah, that's right. Can you do it on Sunday, then?'

'Of course I can't bloody do it on Sunday. I am in the studio on Sunday from nine a.m. till ten p.m. Since you appear to know every time I cough at any hour of the day or night, you presumably know that. Sunday! Of course I can't.'

'Okay, okay. Slip of the mind.'

'I bet.'

'How about Monday, then?'

'The same thing applies. Tuesday is my one day off before rehearsals for the next episode. I need it to rest and to work on the script.'

'It wouldn't take long.'

'Where have I heard that before? It won't hurt either. I suppose; just open wide.'

'We'd do it actual time; you could lie-in till ten to twelve.'

'Oh yes? What about the dressing up for this pantomime?'

'Do that here at say eleven-fifteen. Time enough?'

I sighed. 'We're discussing this as though it's going to happen,' I said.

'Well it is, isn't it, Millie?'

I sighed again, dry throat. 'I loathe it, it's a loathsome idea. You don't understand how actors work; if you did you'd never suggest it.'

'That's one of the things I'm trying to understand. I've had some surprises already.'

I didn't ask him what they were. He stood up and stretched. A good day's work done.

'I'd like to know why you really want me to do this,' I said.

'Let's say I like putting people on the spot.'

'What do you expect to happen that wouldn't happen with a police-woman doing it?'

He said nothing.

'Oh I see! The idea is that in the middle of this comic opera Millie breaks down and, sobbing, confesses to the murder of her best friend. You are incredible, Mr Bright.'

'Inspector Bright to you.'

'Oh sorry, Mr *Inspector* Bright.'

'A different kind of policeman would have done you for impertinence by now, Millie.'

'A different kind of policeman wouldn't induce impertinence.'

He laughed. 'Actually,' he said, 'this whole thing wasn't my idea.'

'Ha.'

'True. My superiors are chaffing a bit at the slowness of the pace; they like to see something happening.'

'Haven't they got enough with Mrs Drew?'

'That happened after I agreed to this.'

'So I am playing this stupid charade to make you look good in the eyes of some fat detective superintendent or whatever he is.'

'I thought we agreed you were doing it to help Mrs Drew.'

'Oh God,' I said. I gave up. Sat with my head leaning on my hand. He stared at me in silence for a while. I stared back wearily. He suddenly seemed to shake himself.

'I'll see myself out,' he said. 'Don't want you catching cold before the big day.'

I didn't ask which big day he was referring to.

'You should always wear a towel round your head,' he said. 'It suits you.'

Then he left.

## CHAPTER EIGHTEEN

Next morning, the shock of the studio drove out the other shocks. You have spent three weeks in a bleak room in Acton which has become cosy through familiarity and use. You've been working hard there, getting it right, the director increasingly pretending to be a camera, which seems rather a joke. Then, wham, the studio. All of a sudden you're a parcel, shuttled from make-up to wardrobe to the studio floor to go through the motions for the cameras, five or six massive monsters on wheels. Daddy Director disappears, ingested into a laboratory upstairs. He communicates by remote control, through the floor manager, his representative on earth. It shakes you a bit. After lunch I started to get my concentration back, get the pace right. There was an exhilaration in getting on top of it. The second day, when we started to put it in the can, a sense of euphoria flooded me; I was lifted, carried, in love; nothing could touch me here, I couldn't be caught; not even by Knife-blade. I was out of reach. As the second day was better than the first, so was the third better than the second; I floated home and into sleep and out of it again on a wave. Millie Hale triumphant. At last.

'Is that you, Miss Hale? This is Constable Baxter. A policewoman will be coming round to you in thirty minutes if that's all right. She'll be there to help you. Thanks.'

My Tuesday costume and make-up call.

I tried to clothe myself in a padded cover of indifference to the occasion, impermeable. It didn't work.

It was the pleasant Irene who turned up, laden with polythene bags on hangers containing familiar clothes. '*Oh I'll wash you in milk and I'll clothe you in silk.*'

I pleaded with her. 'Not the underwear.'

'I'm sorry,' she said.

Knife-blade was having his money's worth.

When I was dressed I said, 'I don't want to look in a mirror. Can you fix the wig?'

My voice shook a little; a lot. But the actor's instinct dies hard. I had to look.

'Oh God,' I said, and covered my face.

'Yes,' she agreed in an awed whisper. 'It's awfully like.'

It was an understatement.

'Do you feel all right?' she asked.

'Faint,' I said. 'And the shoes are too tight.'

I had the horrible feel of a bride being dressed for her wedding, all the guests hushed in the church and will the groom turn up on time? Only worse.

'We'd better go now,' Irene said. 'Oh. You have to wear these.'

She handed me a pair of dark glasses. I put them on.

My legs shook as I went downstairs. A police car stood at the gate. Irene helped me in. There was a young policeman in the driving seat. He turned round to look at me.

'Christ,' he said.

She sat beside me in the back. She was the bride's father, coming to give me away. Great expression that; I had always thought so.

We pulled up in King Henry's Road. Liza's front door was open. Irene held my arm up the steps.

'Christ,' another voice said as I went in. I couldn't see who because I couldn't see. I was blind with terror. A camera flashed. Then Knife-blade came out of Liza's living room and beckoned me in.

'Now,' he said, 'it's nearly ten to twelve; here are the car keys.'

He didn't look at me. His hand was cold.

'The car is in Elsworthy Rise. Go round there, get in, drive slowly up to Hampstead Village. Park as near to the estate agent as you can get – ' he half smiled, ' – without breaking the law. Go in. Say, "Liza Drew. I've come for the keys." I'll tell you what to do after that. Good luck.'

I didn't speak. He looked at his watch.

'Right. In one minute.'

He went out with Irene, closing the door.

I looked round the room. There was no sign of Mrs Drew or of her presence there. Was she in Suffolk or in jail? I was doing this for her. Wasn't I? I looked in the mirror and closed my eyes.

Liza left the flat. I closed the door behind me; with an effort I walked down the path, moving as little like Liza as possible, aware of the neighbour's eyes on me at the window upstairs. I turned the corner. The car was there. I fumbled with the keys, not too much. I had some trouble with the dashboard and pedals, also not too much. Two police cars moved off in my wake. I parked in the High Street outside the pub, almost exactly where I had parked my own car that terrible Friday morning.

Outside the estate agent's I hesitated. I really considered for a second making a run for it. A police car was parked on the pavement, breaking the law. I went in.

The same girl on the desk. The place was expectant. Phones were being answered in hushed voices, all the self-important young men on the watch.

'Liza Drew,' I said, in my own voice, flat. 'I've come for the keys.'

The girl's eyes were round. She handed me the huge jangling bunch. 'Thanks,' I said.

Knife-blade appeared from the back.

'Could you try imitating Liza's voice?' he said. 'Would you mind?' Very formal in front of all the minor public school boys in their smart suits; it was the most attention they had paid to a customer in a long time. His question wasn't worth a reply. I handed back the keys. I said, 'Liza Drew. I've come for the keys,' exaggeratedly soft and sweet, an amateur's approximation of her tone. The girl handed me the keys again. This time she stood up to do so. As I opened the door she said suddenly:

'Different shoes!'

I turned, looked at Knife-blade.

'A-ha,' he said. 'What were they like?'

'I'm not sure,' she said. 'But I think they were boots.'

'What kind?'

She thought hard, then shook her head. 'Sorry, I just can't remember, but I'm sure they were boots. That's all.'

I looked enquiringly at Knife-blade again. He nodded. 'Carry on.'

At the house in Belsize Lane I again had trouble with the keys. I remembered the bent one had got me in but had difficulty even with that. Not deliberate: my hand shook.

I opened the big wooden gates, drove in the car. Then I stood. After a bit, Knife-blade appeared.

'What is it?' he said.

'Should I close the gates? Or leave them?'

'I should close them,' he said. I did, in the faces of a small group of people standing outside. I didn't even glance at them.

I had more trouble with the front door. Eventually it opened onto the same dusty little hall, empty now.

Knife-blade came in behind me.

'And what did you do then?' he said.

'Me?' I said. 'I wasn't here.'

'Sorry. I meant you in the character of Liza. What did you do then?'

'I got killed,' I said.

'I wonder.' He gazed at me.

'Is that it? Can I get out of all this lot now?'

'You see,' he went on uninterrupted, 'someone could have brought her here already dead. Somebody got up to look like her: a wig – her hair was distinctive, people don't look close. I've wondered about the dark glasses; it would explain them, you see. And the boots: that's new; maybe Liza's shoes were too small, or too big, for whoever it was. It would all fit. Do you think it could have happened like that, Miss Hale?'

Irene looked impressed. I didn't.

'It's possible, I suppose, but crazy. Can I please get out of these things?'

'Shoes pinching a bit?' he said.

'Yes. They are.'

He looked at me, waiting. I looked at him. It was a strange moment. Once, my first time abroad, on a school trip to Paris with the sixth form, I'd stayed awake all night, boat and train; when we arrived at the Gard du Nord, French spoken all round, crush of people, smells of coffee and bread, I came out of my body. That cliché is the only way I have of describing it – out of my own body and into the atmosphere. I came back to myself with a jolt to hear someone talking to me. I didn't know how long I had been 'away', a minute perhaps? The moment was outside time. This is what happened to me now with Knife-blade. I say with Knife-blade because it seemed to me we were together somewhere, in another element.

No one was talking when I came back to myself; Irene looked embarrassed but that was nothing new. Knife-blade took a breath.

'Okay,' he said. 'Take her home please, Constable.'

'You were great,' Irene said, back in my flat. 'It must have been hard.'

'I've got to have a bath,' I said.

I left her methodically pushing the things back into their polythene containers one by one.

When I came back, partially cleansed, she had gone.

It was over, then. I went to work next day, and the next. That was fine; better all the time.

Constable Baxter rang to ask if someone could come and pick up my boots.

'Sure,' I said.

He and Irene came that evening, hunted in obscure places while I read my script. They took two pairs of boots from the wardrobe, the last place they looked. They were my only two pairs.

'Thank you very much, Miss Hale.'

'Not at all,' I said.

They left.

Knife-blade rang the next day. 'Sorry about purloining the boots; we're running a few tests.'

'Oh really? I thought you wanted them for sentimental reasons.'

'Not my line, Miss Hale. They'll be returned to you when forensic have finished with them.'

'Soon, I hope. My feet are cold.'

'Can't see you getting cold feet.'

'Ha ha,' I said.

A week later I arrived home about six-thirty, pretty tired, to find a police car parked outside.

## CHAPTER NINETEEN

A sandy young policeman got out of the car as I reached the gate.

'Excuse me. Miss Hale?'

'Yes?'

'Could you come with us, please?'

'Where to?'

Irene got out. 'The station,' she said.

'What for?'

'Well . . .'

'Right now?'

Irene looked apologetic. 'Detective Inspector Bright would like to see you right away.'

I got into the car without a word.

They kept me waiting in the tiny vestibule, Irene at my side. In case I made a run for it, I supposed.

The door into that terrible little room opened. A shirtsleeved policeman said, 'Could you come in, Miss Hale?'

He sat me down on a chewed chair and left by the inner door. I waited, probably ten minutes – it seemed more. I decided not to be angry. I kept calm, breathed slow on purpose. You can control anything.

The inner door opened again. Paul came in, behind the shirtsleeved policeman. He was pale. He stopped in shock when he saw me. It was a while since we had been in this room together the first time; another life. I stood up. Paul had to squeeze by me to get out. Shirtsleeves held the door for him.

'Thank you, Mr Mannon,' he said.

Paul left without another look.

That bastard, Knife-blade. You can control *almost* anything.

Shirtsleeves held open the inner door. 'This way please, Miss Hale.'

He was giving me no time to recover. Very clever stuff. We went upstairs. 'In here, please.'

An office. A desk. Three chairs. Shirtsleeves sat himself in one, against the wall. Guess-who was already in the one behind the desk.

'Miss Hale,' he said. 'Thank you for coming in.'

'Don't mention it.'

'Just a few questions we'd like to ask—'

We?

'Some things we have to get absolutely straight. Will you take notes, Constable? You won't mind that, will you, Miss Hale?'

I raised an eyebrow. I was still trying to get my breathing straight. I sat down facing him.

'Right. Now. Tuesday. I know you have told us what you did on the Tuesday before Miss Drew was found, but I wonder if you would mind going over it again?'

My breathing was coming fine, in – one, out – two three four, in – one; imperceptible too, even to him.

'All day?' I said.

'All day.'

'I got up quite late, read in bed till about noon—'

'Remember what you were reading by any chance?'

'*The Memoirs of Alfieri*,' I said.

There was a momentary glint in his eye.

'Got that, Constable?' he said.

'Think so, sir.'

'Till noon. And then?'

'Long bath, got dressed, went out shopping around – I don't know – three perhaps.'

'What did you buy?'

'Just food. A piece of fish for dinner, things like that.'

'A-ha. Then?'

'Went back to the flat—'

'One moment, sorry. Was this on foot or by car?'

'On foot. I only went down West End Lane.'

'A-ha. Right. Carry on.'

'Put the things in the fridge. Decided to go down Mill Lane and look in the antique shops, so I went out again. On foot.'

'What time was this?'

'I don't know, but it was getting dark. Half past four maybe?'

'A-ha.'

Shirtsleeves was dutifully scribbling all this nonsense down.

'I wandered down Mill Lane and back again. I suppose I got in about six – yes, because I listened to the news on the radio while I cooked supper. I ate grilled plaice, broccoli and salad.'

He wanted detail; he was getting it.

'And then?'

'Nothing. Washed up, tidied the flat, read a bit. Went to bed. Read some more. Went to sleep.'

'You rang no one?'

'I rang no one.'

'And no one rang you?'

'And no one rang me.'

'Would you say this was a usual or an unusual day?'

'When you're out of work, usual. Pathetic, isn't it?'

'Yes,' he said. Seriously. He did it to sting me. I was stung. 'Now. You are quite sure you spoke to no one?'

'Yes. Quite sure.'

'You didn't speak to Liza Drew?'

'No.'

'You were close friends. If you were feeling lonely and had nothing particular to do, why not ring her, go round and spend the evening, have a chat?'

'I didn't say I was feeling lonely,' I said.

'Sounds a pretty lonely day to me, Miss Hale.'

'I don't suffer from loneliness.'

'You are a monster of self-sufficiency.'

'Yeah.'

'Sounds to me the sort of day when most people would call for help.'

'Not me.'

'If there's someone to call, Liza was only five minutes' drive away. Why not give her a ring? Had you quarrelled? Had a bit of a tiff?'

'We never quarrelled.'

'In my experience, close friends quarrel. From time to time. Some coldness between you, perhaps, for some reason? Something you haven't mentioned to us?'

'No.'

He was like a road drill.

'Come on, Miss Hale. Don't be afraid to admit it: a little quarrel between friends? I'm got going to jump to the conclusion that you bumped her off just because of a little disagreement. Come on.'

'I was not lonely, we did not quarrel, and anyway I'd only seen her the day before.'

I stopped. The room became very still.

'Oh,' he said. 'You never mentioned this. Why?'

He might well ask. Why on earth had I mentioned it now? Because he was trying to make me appear pathetic? Was I really as vulnerable as that?

'I wasn't asked,' I said.

He sighed.

'This was the Monday, right?'

'Monday night, yes. Paul had gone back to Sheffield. She rang me. I went over for tea.'

'Did you now?'

'Yes I did.'

'And how long did you stay?'

'All evening. I left about eleven.'

'Monday night?'

'Monday night, yes.'

He shook his head in wonderment from side to side.

'What did you talk about?' he asked.

'All sorts of things. Work. Paul. The fact that she was looking for a house.'

'And, of course, she told you she was pregnant.'

'She didn't tell me that.'

'You were there a whole evening alone with her and she didn't tell you her big news?'

'That's right. I knew she had a secret. She said she had, but she wasn't going to tell. She was very happy. I thought she was up for a very special job and she wouldn't tell until it was confirmed. Actors are superstitious like that; don't tell till the contract's in your hand.'

'And you didn't try to make her tell.'

'No.'

'Come on, Miss Hale.'

'I didn't. There was no point. She'd tell me in her own good time. There was no point in pressing.'

'I don't believe you, Miss Hale.'

He looked at me long and steady without a blink.

'Well, you have only my word for it,' I said.

'I put it to you that she did tell you she was pregnant and that the news made you depressed and jealous.'

'Depressed and jealous? Why? She'd been trying to have a baby for years. I'd have been extremely happy for her.'

'She told you on the Monday. You pretended to be pleased; in fact, you were in a terrible state. You brooded about it on Tuesday; you had nothing else to do all day. Why didn't you tell us about seeing her on Monday? Why should you keep quiet about that? Why?'

The bastard.

'I told you, nobody asked. I saw Liza every other day when we weren't working. It wasn't significant, it was like any other day.'

'No, Miss Hale. It was the last time you saw her alive. Maybe. That makes it significant. It makes you the last person who knew her to see her alive. Maybe. As you knew. But you told nobody: not me, not Mrs Drew, not even Paul Mannon. Why?'

I started to cry.

'I don't know.'

'I think you know very well. I think she told you she was pregnant. I think it was too much for you.' His voice went very soft, even gentle. 'This was a friendship that had to stand very many tests. She stole Paul Mannon from you – years ago, yes, but you were in love with him at the time. I believe you still are. I believe you tried your best to forgive her for that, but it still hurt. And she had become a more successful actress than you; that must have rankled all the time. But at least she couldn't have a child by Mannon; that was the one respect in which you could pity her, in which you didn't have to feel inferior; it was a flaw in their relationship that gave you a spark of hope, even. I suggest to you she told you she was expecting his child and you decided you couldn't take any more. I don't say you decided to kill her there and then, but after a black day on Tuesday with nothing to think about but how lonely you were, how out of work you were, how she had everything you wanted and couldn't have, it got too much for you. At some point on Tuesday night or early Wednesday morning you killed her.'

He stopped. I was crying, but silently.

'What do you say, Miss Hale?'

I shook my head, tears dropping into my lap.

'I will even tell you how you did it,' he went on. 'You had plenty of time to plan. It's easy for you to look like her. We've proved that, haven't we? You're much of a size; in a blonde wig like her hair, anyone would take you for her, at a distance. On Wednesday morning, after you had killed her, after you had been seen by your bathroom-sharing neighbour, you went round to Liza's flat. Maybe you were already disguised as her so that if anyone saw you they'd think it was Liza going in. You had a key; you still have a key; Mannon and Mrs Drew are certain on that point. Did you wear her outer clothes? You must have done. You don't own a fur jacket as far as we know. Yes, but her shoes were too tight for you so you wore your own boots; we've more or less proved that too, haven't we?'

My tears had stopped by this time; I simply stared at him, entranced.

'You left her flat and drove to the estate agent in her car, all that, just as we did it the other day. *Only Liza's dead body was in the back of the car.* That's why you drove in through the big gate and closed it behind you. You needed privacy. You put her in the house, replacing her outer clothes on her. You drove out of there, still in the wig and dark glasses. Or perhaps you'd removed them by then. Had you?'

He waited. I simply went on staring at him, fascinated.

'I hope you won't mind my saying this, but you'd be less likely to be noticed as yourself than disguised as her.'

He watched me closely; I didn't rise to that.

'However, you might not have thought of that. Anyway, let's say that without the wig, etcetera, you drove out into Belsize Lane. You waited till there was nobody about; you got out of the car and left it there. Then you walked to wherever you had left your own car and drove – where? Back to your place? Or possibly straight to your interview at Television Centre? Yes, I imagine that's what you did; the fewer comings and goings the better.'

He paused, looking at me. 'What do you say, Miss Hale?'

I shook my head. When my dry voice came, it was a whisper. I cleared my throat.

'It's a story you've – made up. It's a – fairy tale. You know it – didn't happen.'

'I think it did. Your account of your movements on Tuesday night; on Wednesday morning. None of it can be proved apart from the phone call from your agent at eleven a.m. on Wednesday and the bathroom encounter soon after, both of which we have checked, of course. You're not seen again on Wednesday till three p.m. at your interview. You cannot prove you were at home on Wednesday morning except at those specific times.'

'But I rang Liza back on Wednesday to tell her I couldn't meet her,' I said.

'Ah, Miss Hale, we have only your word for that.'

'But—' I stopped. 'But it can't be proved that I was not in my flat all that time, because that is where I was. I know you've only got my word. I can't do anything about that because that is where I was.'

I ended on a helpless note, close to tears again. I lifted my hands in a vague gesture and dropped them. I looked at him and said feebly:

'I don't know what else I can say.'

'You could just admit that it happened as I said. You could even put me right on the odd detail I might have got wrong. I'd like to know, for instance, where and how you got rid of the wig.'

I had started to pull myself together but my voice was not quite steady.

'It's an outlandish story. Why would anyone go to all that trouble, the disguise and everything? It's crazy. Whoever killed her could have just left her – wherever she was; why all that nonsense, the disguise and putting her in the house? It doesn't make any sense.'

'I don't know why. You tell me.'

'I can't tell you. It's your story, not mine. I don't even believe it.'

'Putting her in the house, that's easy: it disconnects her from anyone she knew. If she'd been found in her flat, say, it might have connected to you; you were the one person in London at the time who knew her *and had a key*. So you put her in a place that connects to nobody; a neutral place.'

'But the house did connect her with me. She'd asked me to meet her there.'

'So you say.'

'And I was the one who found her there. If I'd done it, if I put her there, in this neutral place, why not just leave her? Why should I go and deliberately draw attention to it? It seems mad.'

'Yes, it's odd.'

'It's odder than odd.'

'Yes. But you had expected her to be discovered earlier. People go to see houses that are for sale. You imagined some nice yuppie house-hunting couple finding her there. But you're an impatient girl, Miss Hale; when nothing happened you had to go and see for yourself. Maybe you even thought it would divert suspicion from you, get things moving. Who would ever suspect that the person who had killed her would draw attention to themselves by finding her? That's what you thought. It certainly diverted me for a while, but that was before I knew what an actress you are. You played the scene of shocked discoverer very well.'

'Played!' I took a breath. 'I went to see the house because when I told Liza on the Wednesday morning that I couldn't go with her, she asked if I would go another day and tell her what I thought. It was just chance I chose the Friday morning. I wish I'd never gone.'

'I bet you do. It was your mistake.'

I said nothing to that. He shifted in his seat.

'And then there's the job,' he said.

He put his fingertips together and looked at them. He let the words hang.

'The job,' he said again. 'You inherited, as it were, Liza Drew's job.' He looked at me and then at Shirtsleeves. 'A marvellous part, as you have said yourself, an enviable part. I think she told you about it, maybe on the Monday. She may even have showed you the scripts. You may have seen that this was a perfect part for you, only it had been offered to her. I suggest that this was the final straw.'

'I told you I knew nothing about her connection with the job then. And if you think I decided to kill her in order to put her out of the running for a job you must really think I'm crazy. There must be something like a thousand actresses who could play that part, many of them more likely to be chosen than me.'

'Until you got all the publicity as the grieving friend who found her dead. That drew people's attention to you, didn't it?'

'You horrify me.'

'That's the reason you went to the house and "found" the body, isn't it? There was no other way you could achieve that amount of free publicity so fast.'

'You are suggesting that I killed my best friend for a publicity stunt?'

'That is precisely what I am suggesting. Yes.'

'Then I think you are insane.'

'It looks bad for you, don't you think, that you got that job?'

'If this is the way it is interpreted, yes, it certainly does look bad. I had an interview for that job before—'

'Before you "discovered" the body, not before she was dead. You had the interview immediately after she was dead. That was cool, to go straight to the interview afterwards; that shows amazing cool. But I have conceived a great respect for your cool, Miss Hale. I believe you to be capable of all that, playing it to the hilt. You brought it off.'

'This is the flattery bit, is it? I'm supposed to flutter my eyelashes and say thank you, Officer, how sweet of you to notice, yes I am rather clever, I think. I am getting angry. This whole thing is a fabrication out of your perverted head, and if you're going to try to take it any further, I want to get out of here and phone a lawyer—'

'You are not under arrest.'

'You could have fooled me.'

'Do you think my fabrication, as you call it, would be generally believed?'

'I believe you could make people believe it, if that's what you mean.'

'Now *you* are flattering *me*.'

There was a short silence. I glared at him. He touched the pen on his desk, with the tips of his fingers. He said slowly, 'Paul Mannon thinks you did it.'

I was at the bottom of the well where the words had fallen. There was a pause.

'Did he tell you that?' I said.

'No.'

If he had said 'Yes' I shouldn't have believed him. He knew that.

'I see.' I put as much scepticism into the words as I could manage, but I did see. I saw why he had contrived the meeting with Paul downstairs in the dog room; he wanted the wound fresh. It was a perfectly aimed blow. It knocked the stuffing out of me; I felt defeat; a sort of lassitude.

'But he believes you did it.' He pursued his advantage. 'I am sure of that.'

'Yes,' I said, 'I'm sure you're right. And it's your doing. And if you can convince my best friend you can convince anyone. So why don't you just arrest me now and set about convincing everybody else?'

'You know why.'

'I don't.'

'We have no evidence.'

'Of course you have no evidence because I didn't do it, but I don't see why that should stop you.'

'It generally does.'

He sounded weary. His heart had gone out of it. Somewhere it had gone wrong. Telling me about Paul; he regretted that? I couldn't understand. He had suddenly got – bored, was it? He rubbed his eyes, his familiar gesture.

I was tired, too, to death. I had again the impression I'd got in Suffolk of two fighters worn out. Again it was a moment of appalling intimacy; Shirtsleeves might not have been in the room. There was a long silence.

His hand was still over his eyes. He said, 'Did you do it, Millie?'

My eyes filled with involuntary tears.

'No,' I said. 'I don't know how you could think—' The emotion was getting out of control. 'I can never, never forgive – convincing Paul that I – I can never – never—'

I fumbled for a tissue in my bag. He regarded me speculatively and with – sadness? – in his face. There were lines of tiredness down to the corners of the wide thin mouth.

'Okay,' he said on a breath. 'Okay. Have her taken home, Constable.'

He stood up and opened the door. I stumbled past him in the doorway, mopping my eyes. He said, 'Thank you for coming in, Miss Hale.'

I stopped and turned my wet eyes on him full of rage. He pressed his lips together, tightening the corners of his mouth. He shrugged slightly. It was an apology. Or something. He turned away.

The Sandy One took me back. No Irene. I sat in the front with him. We didn't speak. I got out at my door without a word.

## CHAPTER TWENTY

After that night, during which I did not sleep, but watched the window change from red night to white dawn, I did not think about the 'Interview' again. I put it away. It was in its box. I closed the lid on it. I got on with my work. I lived for that. I gave it everything.

The word started to get round that we had a good show on our hands; in the bar after the studio days our group was the one to be attached to; there was a buzz. It was a good feeling. Reporters called me regularly to ask how it was going; there were constant little bits in the papers with a picture: 'Millie Hale who stars in new series. "It's most exciting," she says. Is this the series the BBC needs? Producer Donald Etheridge says, "It has everything. We are very optimistic. Millie is marvellous." ' And so on.

My first cheque arrived. Not before time. It wasn't a fortune – this was the BBC – but it paid off the overdraft.

As I passed it over the counter at the bank I imagined I was pushing it down Knife-blade's throat. It felt good.

During the three recording days for the second episode, I read that Paul's play was to open at the Almeida Theatre in three weeks. That was quick. 'Booking opens tomorrow,' it said. There was a picture of him and quotes from the Sheffield reviews: 'Paul Mannon . . . A performance of rare intensity, power and passion . . . *Observer*.' That sort of thing.

So he was back in London now. Nothing I could do. Except wait. I could wait for a long time, no one better. But for what? Waiting was a habit I couldn't kick, however; though I waited without hope.

I wondered where Mrs Drew was now. Buried in Suffolk again? Sober? Drunk? Still being questioned by Knife-blade as to her movements on the Tuesday night? I had no one to ask. Except Knife-blade. I was in the dark.

Irene returned the boots one evening in the polythene bag labelled with my name. Knife-blade rang.

'You got your boots back?' he said.

'Yes.'

They'd had them three weeks.

'Find anything interesting?' I asked. I tried to resist the question but couldn't.

'Nothing at all,' he said.

'What a surprise.'

'A-ha.'

'Perhaps you should test some other people's boots.'

'We've done that.'

'Oh?'

'Her mother's. A few of her other friends.'

'Find anything?'

'Nope.'

'So you're no further on?'

'That's my business, "Miss" Hale.'

I did resist asking him about Mrs Drew.

The third episode was recorded, in which Jackie's baby is found dead. Make-up girls were found in floods of tears, Donald Etheridge was steamed up behind his spectacles. People treated me with a sort of friendly awe, though it wasn't tough to do. I floated into work and home again and to work again on a wave.

Paul opened at the Almeida. The reviews were, if anything, better than before. The advertisements said, 'The hottest seat in town.' Too hot for me. I didn't go.

He was in the papers a lot, mostly in the gossip columns, staring into flashbulbs with a succession of beautiful girls at nightclub tables. It was quite a nasty press: 'Paul Mannon whose constant companion Liza Drew, etcetera, with yet another lovely blonde on his arm . . .' I didn't care for the tone, but there was nothing I could do.

Then one night Knife-blade appeared at the door of my room. The woman downstairs had let him in.

'It's over, Millie,' he said.

'What is?'

'We're closing the case.'

'What?'

'No evidence. Nothing we can hang on anyone. We can't go any further. Waste of police time, public funds, all that stuff. It's closed.'

'I thought cases were never closed.'

'Officially, they're not.'

There was a long silence.

'What happens now then?' I asked.

'Hand it back to the coroner. It's off our hands.'

I sat down.

'Like to go out and celebrate?' he said.

I gasped. 'Celebrate what? That you can't find out who killed my friend?'

He jingled the loose change in his pocket. He did that when he was ill at ease.

'Got any booze?' he said. 'I'm not on duty now.'

I poured a mean Scotch.

'Come on, Millie, I need a drink, not a dab behind the ears.'

I filled it up.

'Don't do things by halves, do you?' he said.

'Why have you come to tell me?' I asked.

He shrugged. 'Didn't want to drown my sorrows alone.'

'Why me?'

'I like you, Millie.'

We looked at each other. I turned away.

'Have a drink with me,' he said. 'Come on.'

I poured a finger of Scotch, added water from the tap.

'That's better,' he said. 'Cheers.'

I didn't respond.

'And *you* like *me*,' he said.

I sighed.

'You think you don't but you do.'

'I wish you'd go,' I said.

'Okay. When I've finished this.'

'I suppose it won't take long.'

'No.' He grinned. 'It won't take long.' He rubbed his eyes. 'Don't like failure,' he said. 'They wouldn't give me any more time. Time was all I had. Even I knew it was getting cold. Cold, cold. Never mind.'

He took a gulp of undiluted Scotch.

'Mind you don't get breathalised,' I said.

He laughed. 'Drunk in charge of unsolved murder case. Yeah.'

He groaned. 'What do you think happened, Millie?'

'I don't know.'

'No guesses?'

'I have taken care not to guess.'

'My money was on Mrs Drew,' he said.

'And?' I sounded casual.

'You cleared her, Millie.'

'I cleared her?'

'If you want to know the time, ask a policeman. We asked around at the police station, which, as you pointed out, is opposite the railway station.'

'You mean one of them actually saw her?'

'Nobody saw her.'

'So?'

'After three days' prodding about, a sheepish bobby admitted to being in the pub, which as you may recollect is next door to the station, at the time her train would have arrived, with the guy who was supposed to be on duty on the station platform punching Mrs Drew's ticket. So there's another thing we'll never know.'

I felt hysterical laughter welling up, but I didn't laugh. He finished his drink.

'Going to offer me another, Millie? No? Okay.'

'I have to work,' I said.

'A-ha.' He stood up. 'It's going well, I hear.'

'What don't you hear?'

'Not much. Paul Mannon hasn't been in touch?'

I didn't reply.

'A-ha,' he said.

'You've seen the press; it's done him a lot of harm, all this.'

'It hasn't done any of us much good.'

'Some of us can take care of ourselves.'

'Not as well as we think we can.' He gave me one of his cross-eyed looks.

'See you at the inquest,' he said. 'You'll have to attend.'

'When?'

'Soon. Three days' time or so.'

'Okay.'

There was an awkward pause. I said quickly, 'What did you hope to find on the boots?'

'The boots? Oh. Well, you never know, something to match up in her car, the dust in the hall of the house, anything.'

'But I've been in her car in those boots many times; I went to the house on the Friday in one of those pairs of boots.'

'We realised that. It wasn't only yours we tested. Nothing anywhere.'

I looked at him.

'Okay,' he said. 'So it was mainly to scare you. Had to keep you on your toes, Millie.'

'I thought as much.'

'Yeah, well . . . '

We stood irresolute, he at the door, I in the middle of the room. He gave a sort of awkward salute. I nodded. Then he left.

I poured my Scotch down the sink. I was shaking, had to press my hands between my knees. I sat like that for a long time, and at some point I started to cry. It was startling. It went on and on. I was truly saying Goodbye to Liza. I was lonelier than I had ever been.

The next day the notice came instructing me to attend the inquest at St Pancras coroner's court on Thursday at nine a.m. I asked Robin for the morning off.

'Of course, Millie,' he said and then, hesitating, 'What will the verdict be, do you think?'

'I just don't know, Robin.'

'I hope it's all right, darling. Do take care of yourself.'

We didn't go into what he meant by that.

'Oh, I'll be okay,' I said. 'Thanks.'

Nobody knew about my questioning at the police station. I had said nothing, and the press had not got onto it. Odd; Paul was there and I was there and we were both 'news'. I reluctantly admitted to myself that Knife-blade had kept it quiet. Why? The man was a mystery.

# CHAPTER TWENTY-ONE

The inquest was an ordeal. I arrived insanely early again, about a quarter
past eight. No one else was there. The place was closed. Having learned
from the last time, I drove in through the main gates and left the car
behind the court building. I wasn't sure it was legal and I didn't care. I
walked stiffly round the cemetery-garden in the rain. Groups of nurses,
heads down, cloaks flying, crossed the yard of the Hospital for Tropical
Diseases over the way. The stone dogs guarding the war memorial sat
with that mixture of patience and eagerness that real dogs have, waiting
for their master to come out. These two would have a long wait. I looked
at a tree with stone roots, reading all the inscriptions on the stones. The
place was surreal. I felt like a character in a Russian film – woman with
an umbrella. There was even a man with a little dog. He stood getting
wet, watching it lift its leg against a stone sarcophagus only big enough
for a child. I shivered; I had become really chilled. I sat in the car for a
while. It was worse than walking in the rain. I got out again. The man
and his little dog had gone. It was ten to nine. I gave it five more
minutes. They passed like an hour.

The entrance of the court was packed with reporters. Paul had just
reached the top of the steps. It was a shock. People were crowded behind
him, policemen holding them back. Cameras flashed. He looked dazed.
I slipped inside while they spouted questions at him.

Identifying myself at the office counter, I caught a glimpse of Mrs
Drew sitting upright in black in the waiting room. I went into the
ladies' instead. It was a large broom cupboard, a pile of mops in one
corner, red carbolic soap, no mirror, just a paler oblong on the wall
above the sink where a mirror had once been. And the door didn't lock.
I didn't stay long. No one can say I lack courage. I needed it to enter
that waiting room.

'Hello,' I said.

'Millie.' She gave a stiff nod.

I sat down. For minutes no one spoke. I had no more nerve and she no inclination. Then, without looking at me, 'Appalling weather,' she said. I was too surprised to answer more than 'Yes'.

'It goes on and on,' she said.

'It's the longest winter on record.'

'It will never end.' She stopped, said, 'April,' and stopped again.

Then Paul came in, also in black. He saw me and looked away; nodded to Mrs Drew but sat on the other side of the room. We stared at the walls.

The big man with the moustache came to the door: 'Will you go into the court now, please.'

There was a crush of people in the small lobby. Cameras blinded us. And reporters sat close-packed round the table under the dais inside the court. We three sat in the front pew with the silver-haired inspector who had been at the house in Belsize Lane. The red-haired policeman stood at the side, as before, with his list. It was cold in there.

At ten past nine Red-head stepped forward and said, 'Will the court rise please be seated,' in his unpunctuated monotone. The small grey coroner came in from his door and sat on his throne, the lion and the unicorn, Dieu Et Mon Droit. We rose. We sat. We shifted. The reporters took out their tiny recorders and held them lovingly like so many black packets of cigarettes. The little coroner coughed. Silence fell.

'This inquest,' he began, 'is in regard to the death of Elizabeth known as Liza Drew . . .' The gentle voice droned on, his breath misting the air in front of his face. Certain phrases prodded their way into my frozen brain: 'The deceased being a person in the public eye . . . Great deal of media attention . . . influenced by what they have read and heard . . . therefore not to call a jury, it being within my discretion so to do . . . mysterious circumstances . . . Extensive police enquiries . . . I have deliberately delayed this inquiry in the hope of something more concrete emerging.' He stopped speaking. The heat from the bodies packing the room had begun to take the chill off the air. It was a full house.

Silver-hair was called first, very smart in his uniform. He was sworn in, asked permission to refer to his 'contemporaneous notes' and began to recite:

'At eleven-fifteen on the morning of Friday January the tenth, Mr Paul Mannon arrived at Rosslyn Hill Station and reported that his common law wife Miss Liza Drew was lying dead in an empty house in Belsize Lane. Mr Mannon appeared confused and incoherent. I called my colleague Sergeant Henry Cole to accompany myself and Mr Mannon to the scene. The sergeant drove the car in which Mr Mannon had arrived at the station and I followed in a police vehicle. When we arrived at the scene the body was lying a few feet inside the door. Miss Hale was sitting on the stairs. The body appeared undisturbed. As far as we could ascertain, nothing had been touched. Miss Hale confirmed Mr Mannon's identification of the deceased. I thought the circumstances sufficiently suspicious to call in the divisional surgeon, Dr Robert Biggs, and my colleagues in CID. Detective Inspector John Bright arrived at the scene in less than ten minutes accompanied by Dectective Sergeant Haines. I also informed the scenes of crime officer and the coroner's officer who all arrived within ten minutes with the photographer and the lab liaison officer. Immediate investigations were conducted at the scene in the hall of the house. Then Mr Mannon and Miss Hale were taken by Detective Sergeant Haines to Rosslyn Hill Station to fill out a nine nine one.'

'Excuse me, Inspector. For our information, this is a simple statement of the facts of the case as they knew them. They were not being arrested or suspected of having behaved in any way suspiciously in this matter?'

'That is correct, sir.'

'Thank you, Inspector.'

Suddenly I heard, 'Amelia Hale, please repeat after me' and I found myself facing the packed room, swearing on the book, thankful that my shaking legs were hidden by the box. He asked me the questions he had asked me three months ago in the same conversational tone. All I had to answer was Yes and I heard myself saying it over and over, 'Yes, Yes, Yes,' and explaining what I had been doing at the house that day. Then I heard him say:

'Now, Miss Hale, when did you last see Miss Drew alive?'

'Monday. The Monday before—'

I saw Paul and Mrs Drew lift their heads and sniff the air. They looked at each other for the first time. So Knife-blade had not told them that.

'Yes?' The soothing voice encouraged me, 'And will you tell us about that occasion?'

I did. As I had told it to Knife-blade. More or less.

'And she was in no way depressed or – afraid – at all, would you say?'

'No. Happy and excited, as I said.'

'I see. And I believe you also spoke to her on the telephone on the Wednesday morning?'

'Yes. Twice.' I told him about the calls.

'Yes . . .' he smiled. 'Your reporting of these phone calls alone would of course not in itself prove that she was alive on the Wednesday morning, but I believe she was also seen . . . Yes . . . Miss Hale, have you, had you at the time, any reason for thinking that Miss Drew might wish to – take her own life?'

'No. On the contrary.'

'Thank you, Miss Hale.'

That was all. I had no recollection of getting back to my seat.

Through a fog I saw that the next person in the box was a tiny mouse-like woman who twitched her nose and patted it with a small gloved hand. She whispered that, yes, she lived upstairs from Liza and, yes, she had seen her leave the house between half-past eleven and twelve on Wednesday morning, and no, she didn't know the deceased well, just to pass the time of day, but she could swear that the person leaving the flat was she.

The mouse was followed by the estate agent's receptionist who said she would know Liza Drew anywhere, she watched all her series on TV, and it was definitely Liza who had picked up her keys at about ten to twelve. She was asked about the re-enactment and answered, 'Oh no, the other lady was nothing like!'

Then Paul was called. Yes, he knew she was pregnant, yes, they were both delighted, he had last seen her alive before returning to Sheffield early on Monday morning when she was fine . . .

'And you were in Sheffield from then until late on Thursday night, I believe.'

Paul agreed.

'And do you know of anyone who might have reason to wish her harm?'

The silence went on forever. Thirty seconds, perhaps. He became, if possible, paler, his knuckles white, gripping the edge of the box. Then he shook his head, looking down at his hands. 'No,' he said. 'Nobody.'

Mrs Drew came next. She approached the box with dignity. She spoke clearly. He asked when she had last seen Liza, 'Alive, that is.' She answered coolly. This was the woman who had been in London on the Tuesday night and possibly on the Wednesday, who had lied to the police about it, who a few weeks ago had appeared to be a shaking alcoholic. It was impressive.

'I am told you were in London on the Tuesday night.'

'That is not so. I returned to Suffolk by the eight-thirty train.'

'Ah yes, I apologise, I should not have said night. Evening is what I meant to say.'

She gave an imperious nod, 'Early on Tuesday evening I was in London on business. I did not see my daughter or get in touch with her. I thought I should be seeing her very soon.'

He did not pursue the subject. There was a momentary silence. He asked her, too, if she knew of anyone who might wish her daughter harm.

I stared hard at her, daring her to look at me. She did not. Her eyes were on the coroner. Her silence, too, seemed endless.

'No,' she said.

The coroner looked down.

'Thank you, Mrs Drew.'

He continued to look at his clasped hands. We watched him. He raised his head. He seemed surprised to see her still in the box.

'Whoever it was who was responsible for my daughter's death must have hated her exceedingly. I hope that this person will be found and brought to justice.' Her limpid tones filled the room. The coroner, who seemed a little at a loss, thanked her again and gave her permission to stand down. A stir had been created.

'Yes . . .' said the coroner reflectively. 'Er . . . Doctor Biggs, may I trouble you please? Thank you.'

The little doctor who had been 'at the scene' approached the box looking flustered and was sworn in. He told what he had found when he was called to the house, handing over photographs of the position of the body, passed to him by the police photographer. At one of the pictures the coroner winced.

'Yes . . .' he said. 'Apart from the face, you found no marks of violence on the body?'

'None.'

It was the first mention of the face. The reporters sat up. The atmosphere in the court had crisped like a washed lettuce. 'I believe, Doctor, that at one point in your examination of the body, you turned the head so that the face became visible to those present.'

The doctor looked puzzled: 'Yes, that is so.'

'What was the reaction of Mr Mannon and Miss Hale to the sight, would you say?'

'They seemed completely horrified.'

'Will you describe their behaviour?'

'Yes. Mr Mannon turned his face to the wall. His body became rigid, he was difficult to move and was unable to speak. Miss Hale became hysterical, a sort of wailing, the body convulsed. I had to sedate her. The face of the deceased was not a pretty sight.'

'Thank you, Doctor Biggs.'

The little man got out of the box. The audience was on its hind legs. The coroner had become greyer.

The next person to enter the box was an elegant willowy man expensively tailored, with greying blond hair. He was told that he was James Hadfield, a Home Office pathologist, to which he agreed.

'And you performed the autopsy on the deceased?'

'I did.'

He answered the questions in a cool, held-back voice, no surplus energy in his manner, economical: no, there was no alcohol in the body, a small amount of barbiturate, not enough to cause death, he thought. To induce heavy sleep? Yes, in certain circumstances. Apart from the face, which had been mentioned, 'This was the body of a healthy young woman in her early thirties in the ninth week of a perfectly normal pregnancy.'

'Mr Hadfield, the disfiguration of the face has been mentioned. Can you enlarge on that?'

'Certainly.'

He proceeded detachedly to describe the appearance of Liza's ruined face, while next to me tears ran down Paul's, and not a muscle moved in her mother's stony mask.

'A certain amount of disfigurement around and within the mouth; the tissue in this area whiter than is normal even in death. Or perhaps greyer would be more correct. The lips bleached and shrunk back, as it were, revealing gums and inside of the mouth, similarly whitened and shrunk.'

'You have an opinion as to what caused this?'

'My initial impression was that a corrosive substance had been poured into the mouth and this was confirmed by my tests.'

'Can you tell us, in layman's language if possible, what the substance was?'

'Oh yes. It proved to be a solution of hydrochloric acid commonly known as spirits of salts.'

'I understand that this is quite easy for the public to get hold of.'

'Oh yes.'

'Pity.'

'It is only thirty-two per cent hydrochloric acid, less corrosive even than household bleach. Though the average member of the public would be unlikely to know that.'

'I see. Are you saying that the substance was not strong enough to cause death?'

'I am saying it did not cause this death.'

There was a rustling of reporters round the table.

'Will you tell us your reasons for that conclusion?'

'Yes. Of course this substance could cause death if administered while the victim was still alive, but it would be a slow death taking perhaps as much as two weeks. In this case the substance was poured into the mouth after death.'

Subdued commotion in court.

'Quiet please.'

Hadfield waited calmly for the tumult to die before continuing. 'Had it been poured into the mouth before death, the internal organs would have shown some damage; as it was, only the mouth and the area around the mouth were affected. There is of course no swallowing mechanism after death, thus confining the damage to the mouth and the surrounding skin of the face, where we assume some of the substance was spilt in the act of pouring. Also, of course, live tissue would react to the application of a corrosive substance. This tissue showed no reaction; only corrosion.'

'So you are saying that the spirits of salts was administered after death?'

'Undoubtedly, yes.'

'How long after death? Can you say?'

'Not with perfect accuracy. The body, according to *my* findings, would seem to have been dead between, say, sixty and seventy-two hours when it was found. The amount of corrosion of the tissue would seem to suggest that the substance was administered no more than forty-eight hours before the body was found.'

'There is a great discrepancy between the earliest and latest estimated times of death.'

'Oh yes. Place of death is not established, therefore I cannot calculate the ambient temperature in which the body was lying.'

'I believe also that police theories with regard to time of death differ somewhat from your original findings.'

'So I believe.' His face was expressionless.

'We will go into this later. For the moment, what in your opinion was the cause of death?'

'I found some congestion of the lungs which would indicate suffocation.'

'Do I detect a note of doubt?'

'A person being suffocated puts up quite a fight. I should expect to find the marks of such a violent struggle on the body and in the surroundings. There were none.'

'Are there any circumstances in which a person could die by suffocation and no marks be left?'

'There are two possibilities, in my experience. You remember I found barbiturate in the body. If sleeping pills are administered beforehand the act of suffocation becomes easier.'

'Much easier?'

'Oh yes. It would then be possible for a person using their whole weight and, say, a pillow or some such object, to kill without inflicting or receiving bruises or scratches.'

'You found traces of fibres to suggest the use of a pillow or something of the sort?'

'No. The corrosion of the mouth area made things difficult here.'

'You found nothing?'

'I found no fibres.'

'I see . . . This would give us a picture of an ingenious and know ledgeable person who had planned in advance?'

Hadfield said nothing.

The coroner made a note, and continued, 'You mentioned a second possibility.'

'A common method of – assisted – suicide, which is the taking of sleeping pills and the placing of a plastic bag over the head after the pills have taken effect.'

'The accepted – if we can use the word – method of euthanasia?'

'Yes.'

'But you have doubts of this also?'

Hadfield gave his weary elegant smile as if to say, in forensic medicine, as in life, there were no certainties. 'The corrosion . . .' he said.

'Ah yes. If it were not for the disfiguring of the face, the, er, assisted suicide would be your favoured theory?'

'Not necessarily. I should expect to find larger quantities of barbiturate in that circumstance.'

The coroner sighed. 'You say you found no signs of struggle in the surroundings. You mean the place where the body was found?'

'Yes.'

'Did you find such signs anywhere? Miss Drew's flat for instance?'

'Not there either, no.'

'Her car?'

'No.'

'So you have no opinion as to where the death took place?'

'The body when found in the house had an – arranged – look about it. But snow had fallen and been trodden on; there were no marks of a heavy object, such as a drugged or lifeless body, having been dragged into the house. The hallway where the body was found was dusty but there were so many footprints by the time my assistants arrived that it would be impossible to say for certain if anyone but the deceased had been there before us or if a struggle had taken place.'

'But the already dead body could have been brought there?'

'With great difficulty by only one person, but yes.'

'Do you have an opinion as to where the corrosive substance was administered?'

'There was one small discoloured spot on the floor close to the left side of the head which would indicate that the substance had been poured in that place and just one drop spilt.'

The coroner looked tired. 'We have established, then, that death was caused by suffocation and that the corrosive substance was likely to have been poured in the place where the body was found.'

'Yes.'

'Thank you, Mr Hadfield.'

Hadfield gave a kind of vestigial bow indicative of sorrow, pride and modest regret, and glided out of the box.

There was a general exhalation of breath. I closed my eyes. When I opened them Knife-blade was in front of me swearing that he was Dectective Inspector John Bright and that he was the investigating officer in charge of the case.

'Did your findings agree with those of Mr Hadfield?'

'We had a problem about times.'

'Times . . . Yes, this seems to be an area of some doubt?'

'Mr Hadfield believed death to have occurred sixty hours or more before the body was found. My investigations seem to show that Liza Drew was still alive at least until noon on Wednesday.'

'Which would make it – what – forty-eight hours or less?'

'Yes, sir.'

'And we have heard from witnesses who are quite clear about having seen Miss Drew alive . . .' Knife-blade agreed. 'I understand you and your team ruled out assisted suicide early on in the course of your investigations.'

'Yes, the pregnancy and so on. There was no evidence that she was considering such an act, and we have found no one as yet who might have agreed to, er, help her in such a way.'

'We have heard from Mr Hadfield that the corrosive substance was given about forty-eight hours before the body was found. According to your investigations this would be shortly after death occurred. You have been looking for a person or persons responsible for both the killing and the disfigurement?'

'Eventually, yes.'

'The possibility of a random, er, vandal, as it were, mutilating the corpse seeming too much of a coincidence?'

Knife-blade's squint became momentarily more pronounced. 'Yes,' he said.

'Did you at any point consider a random killing?'

'A lot of our questioning was to that end; it can't be ruled out. But the death followed no known pattern. And the house was not broken into.'

'The estate agent presumably had a list of those issued with keys.'

'Yes. They were followed up. And the owner also showed people over the property.'

'The owner was questioned?'

'Yes, sir. He was in the United States during the crucial period and had no connection with the deceased.'

'I see . . . Do you consider that the disfigurement of the face was in order to disguise the identity of the body?'

'No.'

The reporters turned their heads.

'Why not?'

'The clothes, and in particular the hair, were easily identifiable. It would be easy to disguise the body more thoroughly or even lose it altogether. I worked on the lines that it was an act of spite or revenge. Either that or just intended to confuse.'

'It has certainly confused.'

'Yes, sir.' Again the glint in the eye.

'I understand, Dectective Inspector, that you and your team have interviewed over two hundred witnesses in the course of your investigation of this matter.'

'Yes, sir.'

'And none of them showed bruising or scratches such as might result from a struggle with the deceased in the act of suffocation?'

'None.'

'And all those questioned have been totally eliminated from your inquiries?'

'Yes, sir.'

'Thank you.'

Looking dapper and incongruous in a dark suit, Knife-blade left the box.

The coroner poured himself a glass of water from his carafe and drank it slowly. The reporters in front of us scratched themselves and shifted on their chairs. People behind us whispered and coughed. I had no idea what would happen next. Perhaps he would call one of us up to be questioned again? The room had reached its maximum heat which, even helped by all those bodies, was not great. A cold sweat ran down my inner arms and I shivered. Mrs Drew's hands clutched her bag as though she feared it might run away. Paul sat with his head hanging, staring, fascinated, at the splintery floor. The little coroner read through his notes with his left eye while he rubbed the right with his fist. He sighed heavily from time to time. Perhaps only a minute passed. It felt like an hour. At last the coroner stopped screwing his fist into his eye. He looked up and cleared his throat. In an instant the court became silent. People sat up.

'Ye – es . . .' he said sadly. 'Having received evidence from those closest to the deceased, from the investigating officer in charge of the case and from the forensic pathologist who performed the post-mortem examination, I am sorry to say that the picture that emerges is still a confused one. The cause of death is suffocation but the time and even place of death are not yet established. No matter how we look at it, however, another hand than that of the victim appears to have been involved in her death. On the evidence I have received, therefore, I have no alternative but to record a verdict that Elizabeth known as Liza Drew who last lived at King Henry's Road, London NW3, who was born on the twelfth of May nineteen fifty-three, occupation, actress, was unlawfully killed by person or persons unknown. After three months of enquiries I am releasing the body to you—' He looked from Paul to Mrs Drew—'for burial.'

The laconic voice ceased; he got up. Redhead intoned, 'Thank you sir will the court rise please.' We did. The coroner went out. The inquest was over.

The reporters looked to be closing in. They were prevented by Redhead, his large moustached friend who had appeared from nowhere, and Silver-hair. The little doctor nodded awkwardly to us and left. We stood, not knowing what to do.

Silver-hair said, 'I'll accompany you outside if you'd like. It might prevent the gentlemen of the press from getting too obtrusive.'

'Contemporaneous' began to seem a less outlandish word. He spoke chiefly to Mrs Drew, who did affect people's vocabulary.

'Thank you, Inspector,' she said.

As we turned I saw Knife-blade slip out from the back of the court.

We followed Silver-hair out like lambs. The crows were roosting on the steps. He led the way in that direction; I dashed the opposite way to my car. Two or three noticed, but too late. They flapped against my windows as I revved up and got away. I felt pursued, though I don't believe I was. I panicked. I drove towards Camden Town intending to go to Chalk Farm and thence to my flat; then I remembered I should be at work, turned up towards Regent's Park to get to the west. Then I knew the crows would be at Acton, waiting, beaks thrusting. I did a U-turn in the park nearly causing an accident, thinking I could go to

Suffolk. But I couldn't go there; my house had been violated once. I should be leading the flock straight to it to violate it again. I had to pull in and stop in the Park. I could not think and was shivering with what felt like cold though the car heater was working, for once. Wherever I went, there they would be. Should I say, 'No comment,' or feed them some scraps? If I didn't turn up for work they would be cawing round Acton annoying my friends. I was trying to think straight, but filling up my brain and crowding out everything else were the stony faces of Paul and Mrs Drew. Neither of them had looked at me once during their evidence. Why had they not spoken against me?

I knew for myself what they thought. Or had Knife-blade lied to me? I knew he had not. Perhaps he had instructed them that as there was no evidence against anyone they should not voice suspicions. But why should he do that? He had put them through the same interrogation process as he had put me; were they simply frightened, then, that if they spoke against me I might speak against them? There was no reason, after all, to suspect me more than them. Paul's 'playing around' had not been mentioned; neither had the strange behaviour of Mrs Drew. Had they more to lose than I by flinging accusations publicly around? There was no-one I could ask. I was alone. I felt it, too, sitting there in my little tin box on wheels in Regent's Park. Hail started smashing against the windows, onto the roof. I felt battered from every side. I hadn't come to any decision. I just drove to the Acton Rehearsal Rooms, to work. It was where I was meant to be.

# CHAPTER TWENTY-TWO

They were there, of course, the crows, clambering over each other in their eagerness to get at the carrion, clustered around the entrance to the building. To my astonishment it was Paul they asked me about.

'Do you think he did it, Millie?'

'Paul? You must be mad. He was crazy about her; he still is.'

'Are you sure about that?'

'As certain as I've ever been about anything in my life. There's no way he could have done it.'

'We heard there was a bit of hanky-panky up North.'

'Nonsense,' I said.

'What do you think of the verdict, Millie?'

'Horrible.'

They are never satisfied, but I was able to get into the building at last, claiming I was late for work.

The commissionaire fed me brandy in a little room next to the ground-floor lavatory; I felt too faint to protest that it made me sick.

'Terrible people, aren't they, Millie? Never mind, they'll be on to something else tomorrow. You drink that up, it'll do you good.'

I swallowed it with difficulty, thanked him, went up to the third-floor loo and threw up.

My friends in the rehearsal room were almost as bad as the crows, though from a different motive. I think. They buzzed at me like flies.

'How did it go, Millie?'

'Was it terrible?'

'It must have been an ordeal.'

'What was the verdict?'

'Are they going to prosecute anyone?'

'Millie, what's the *matter* with you?'

'Can I get you anything?'

'She's in a frightful state.'

Bill Warren, husband in the show, protector in life, loosed me from the net; 'Leave her alone,' he said. 'Sit there, kid, and recover yourself, you're in a bad way. Leave her alone.' He shepherded them away.

Robin sat next to me. 'We're in the middle of scene twelve, Millie darling, so you're not needed yet. Sit quietly and get your breath back. See how you feel in half an hour. You don't have to work at all if you don't want to; we can do other scenes, it's entirely up to you. Brian, get her some tea.'

Tea restores some people, work others. In an hour I was deep into the controllable problems of drama; unruly life was of secondary importance. But in the afternoon Brian, the AFM, brought the nurse down from the first-aid room.

'You look a sight, dear,' she said cheerfully. She gave me a sedative and some more to take that night.

Bill drove me home. I left my car in the car park.

'You can come by taxi in the morning,' he said. 'You're rich now,' and laughed.

Five of the black birds were roosting round the door of the house where I lived.

'Give us your key,' Bill said. Bill is a big man. He pushed them off with one huge arm and held me tight with the other. He spoke quietly.

'Push off now, fellers, you can see she's had it. Come on, hop it, there's good chaps.'

He got me inside. 'Don't take a taxi in the morning. I'll come and pick you up. You're in need of care and protection. See you, kid.'

He squeezed out of the door and shut it. I heard them flapping and squawking outside, Bill's amiable voice calming them down. I heard them fading away.

I fed myself the sedatives, took the phone off the hook, and the faces of Paul, Mrs Drew, Knife-blade and the coroner revolved around me all night. Liza wasn't there.

Next day Bill threw me a newspaper. 'You've escaped,' he said. 'An aeroplane blew up, lots of people killed. Beat you to the front page.'

He was right: we were on page five. There were pictures, and a lot of words which I didn't read, but we weren't the hot news.

'It's an ill wind,' I said.

Bill laughed. He didn't know whom I was quoting.

'You can start getting over it now,' he said. 'Put it behind you, start living again.'

I wondered.

That night, late, the doorbell rang. I didn't answer it. It rang again and didn't stop. Paul stood on the step, looking wild. He pushed past me up the stairs, waited for me to enter my room and slammed the door. He stood with his back to it. He was breathing hard.

'This is the last time I'll see you,' he said. 'But I have to tell you this, just so's you will always know that I know. You killed her, Millie. You did it. I am certain of it to the marrow of my bones. The more I have thought about it, and God knows I've thought about it, the more certain I have become. I'm here to warn you, Millie, that you had better keep out of my sight, because I would like to kill you myself and one of these days when it gets too much for me I might find myself doing it. I dream of it every night. I'd like to—'

He turned and put his face against the door and hit the wood with his fist. I watched him with a detachment that felt curious, even to me. He turned back.

'How could you do that, Millie? She showed nothing but kindness to you always, nothing but kindness to anyone, she never harmed—'

He was drunk but controlling it.

'What did you hope to get out of it, Millie? Me, was it? Think I'd come running back to your loving arms? Let me tell you this – I couldn't wait to get out of them eight years ago. You're the coldest bitch I ever met, Millie. You couldn't even bear me to touch you, could you? You pretended all right, you were good at that. It took me in for a while, but not for long. That's something you can't fake, Millie, no matter how many times you see it on the movies. Just don't ever think I didn't know, that's all. I was ready to pull out of that, way before Liza ever appeared on the scene, believe me. I should have had the courage to tell you before she did appear. If I had, all this might not have happened. I'm to blame. I'm to blame for the whole sorry mess, in my inimitable fashion; I'm a coward and I'm a liar, always take the easy way out. I tell you this: Liza was the best thing that ever happened to me. I didn't deserve her, couldn't even give her . . . And you robbed me of her, Millie. You might as well have pulled my heart out of my body; you've killed us both. Perhaps that's what you wanted. What *did* you want, Millie? What did you do it *for*?'

He lurched towards me. He looked dangerous. I still didn't speak; I sat, limp, deliberately relaxing each muscle, one by one, breathing slow. He got quieter.

'Tell me, Millie. That's really what I've come here for. You've got to tell me why.'

I dropped my face onto my hands and stayed like that for some time. He said at last, 'Well?'

I lifted my head. 'Oh Paul,' I said. I stopped and got up. I turned back to him.

'I thought it was you,' I said.

'What?'

'I thought it was you. Who had done it. That it wasn't your child and that – Oh God.' I put my face back in my hands. 'Oh God!'

'Come off it, Millie. I know you well, don't forget. I didn't come here for the touching reconciliation scene. I know what an actress you are – better than me and Liza put together. It never stops with you; you have no other life, no real life. I don't think you can tell the difference any more, I don't know if you ever could.'

My voice came out hard. 'I thought it was you,' I said. 'John Bright convinced me it was. I tried not to believe it; I never admitted to him that I did; but I was convinced. I realise now that it's not true. And in spite of everything, I'm glad. You want to blame someone because you feel guilty, for playing around. I wish you hadn't picked on me, that's all. And I'd like you to go now, it's late.'

He found this tone more convincing. I knew he would. I said, 'Will you go now please.'

He looked at me as intently as his eyes would focus, a dog given two contradictory commands.

'And,' I said, pressing my advantage, 'if you felt all this, why didn't you say it at the inquest? Why keep quiet about it then?'

'Bright said there was no evidence, that he could never bring a case. He called it the fifty-one per cent rule.'

'What is that?'

'If there's a fifty-one per cent chance of conviction you bring a case. If it's only fifty-fifty they won't prosecute.'

'And it was fifty-fifty on me, was it? Why not on you?'

'I could prove I wasn't there. You, if you remember, could not.'

'Nor could Mrs Drew, nor could a thousand other people. We don't all account for every minute of our time just in case we might be accused of murder one fine day.' I could hear myself repeating phrases I had trotted out to Knife-blade. 'You haven't answered my question,' I said. 'Why didn't you say all this at the—' I was about to say trial. '—At the inquest? Why not?'

'I don't know. I suppose I felt that as there was no evidence there was no point. It was better to get the damn thing over with.'

'Feeble, Paul. You know that if you had started throwing allegations, the Paul-and-Mrs-Drew conspiracy theory might have started bouncing back at you, and you didn't want to have to handle that.'

'That was an outlandish idea.'

'Outlandish or not, you didn't want it showing its head.'

'Attack is the best form of defence. Same old Millie, shifting the focus onto me. I came here to talk about you.'

That was pretty good for a person as drunk as he was. I was impressed.

'Ah yes, Millie,' I said, 'the amazing actress who can convince anyone of anything. Do you really believe I could do what you accuse me of and then calmly go off to an interview at the BBC? And even get the job? You have a crazy notion of my histrionic powers.'

'I'm sorry, Millie. It's what I believe.'

But his conviction had crumpled a little.

'Then there's nothing to be said. Or done.'

I spoke with a combination of grimness and despair. He lifted his head and looked at me from under his brows. His eyes were bloodshot. He was confused again. How weak he was!

'I've lost everything now,' I said. 'Liza, Mrs Drew. And you. The only real friends I had.'

'But you're becoming a star, Millie. What you wanted. All you wanted.'

'Not all, by any means.'

'But quite a lot. It'll have to do. And you *have* got it, as a direct result of—'

'So have you if it comes to that.'

That hit home.

'Yes, so have I.'

He closed his eyes.

'And it's all *you've* got now, too,' I said.

'Yes.'

'It will have to do for you, too.'

'Yes.'

He recovered a little, by an effort of will. 'But I never wanted it the way you do,' he said.

'Didn't you?'

'No, Millie. Not everyone is driven by ambition as you are. It's hard for you to understand that.'

I was silent. He went on, struck by his new idea. 'I think you're a kind of psychopath, you know, Millie. You have no conscience. You see only what you want. And you'll use any means in your power to get it. You don't care what happens to anyone on the way.'

He was pleased with his little textbook exposition.

'Well, that puts me in a nutshell,' I said. 'Thank you. I suppose you think nothing can hurt me, either.'

'Not much,' he said.

'You're wrong, Paul. *You* can. You have tonight, over and over and worse and worse. You're cruel, crueller than I would be to you, or to anyone. I can't believe the things you have said to me and I can't stand any more of it. I wish you'd just go. And leave me alone.'

'Oh I'll go. I just want you to know that you *are* alone, that's all. That's what you've got out of it. And I hope all the success in the world won't make up for that. I wish you no joy of it. Like I have no joy of it. And I hope you don't sleep at nights, like me. Though I don't believe it, any more than I believe anything could spoil your success.'

Then he left.

# CHAPTER TWENTY-THREE

He was right. I allowed nothing to spoil it. It was all I had. And it would have to be enough. I screwed down the lid on the box containing Paul and I buried it. Deep.

Like they buried Liza.

The funeral was at Blythburgh Church. It was a dismal affair. Apart from five damp reporters, the only people present were Mrs Drew, Paul, myself, and Mrs Drew's cleaning lady who stood at the back of the church in an old black coat that looked as though it dated from the 'fifties and was worn only for funerals.

I had received a cold invitation from Mrs Drew on a sheet of expensive notepaper: 'I had wished it to be a private occasion. However, it might look bad were you not to be there.'

She wielded a lethal subjunctive.

It was private, all right. The three of us separate in the cold church, the journalists preferring to smoke outside. A pale boy helped the priest, standing by his side. The man spoke so quietly he could hardly be heard; the insubstantial sound fluttered up to the angel rafters and dissolved. No bells rang.

The priest led the way to the grave with the boy at his side. Two reporters took off their hats as we passed. Four men carried the coffin, strangers to me. Paul followed it. Mrs Drew walked in front of me, carefully placing her feet on the rough gravel path. She had got so old. At one point she stumbled. I put out an arm to help her. She shook me off. I didn't try again.

The wind was fierce as we stood round the hole in the earth. We were pelted with rain, then slanting sleet. This was a freakish winter. As Mrs Drew had said, it went on and on. She and Paul each threw a handful of earth on the thing when it was lowered in. I did not. I looked away, towards my house. I would not go there today. When I turned back I saw a man standing under the black-green conifers on what passes for a hill in that part of Suffolk. He was small under his black umbrella, and his features indistinguishable at that distance, but I knew who he was.

It was buried, the ritual was over. Mrs Banks helped Mrs Drew over to the church door. We all shook hands with the clergyman. The reporters were huddled outside the lych gate. Showing respect?

At the gate Mrs Drew turned to Paul.

'Goodbye,' she said, 'I hope—' The cameras clicked.

He quickly shook her hand, then walked to his car. Two cameras followed him. She turned in my direction. Her face was disintegrating.

'Millie,' she managed to say.

I put out my hand. She turned swiftly to Mrs Banks and they tottered together towards her car, two old black figures in the sleet, followed by the reporters, bent against the wind.

Knife-blade appeared at my side silently. We stood watching them go.

'That's that, then, Millie.'

'It's that, all right.'

'Cup of tea at your place?'

'I'm not going there.'

'Now? Or ever?'

'Probably both.'

'A-ha.'

'What are you doing here? I thought the case was over now. Unofficially, of course.'

'It was an impulse. That's why I was late. Don't know why I came really. Finish it off perhaps. It's not closed in my head, you see. Thought this might do it.'

'And has it?'

'Maybe.'

It sounded like no.

'Lovely place,' he said, 'even in this weather.'

'Yes.'

'I like it round here. Never came across it before.'

'It has powerful magic, Suffolk. Corn dollies, hag stones.' I was talking for talking's sake.

'Hag stones?' he said.

'Stones with a hole through the middle. You find them round here, all shapes and sizes. They hang them over the doors, the windows, even the fireplaces, all the orifices inside the house.'

'To keep the hags out. I see.'

'Yes.'

'Doesn't always work then, does it?'

'What does?' I said.

'Let's go to your nice house and light a fire.'

'I don't go in for hag stones,' I said.

'I'll take a chance. I'm a brave fellow.'

'All right,' I said.

I don't know why I agreed. I regretted it immediately. Perhaps it was the idea of returning to the flat in London alone; perhaps I wanted to shut out the pictures – Paul staring bleakly across the grave, Mrs Drew refusing my hand; perhaps it was simply the idea of a fire, out of the driving rods of sleet. Maybe I was tired of resisting. Anyway, he was startled by my aquiescence.

'Okay!' he said. 'I'll follow you.'

'What do you think you've been doing for the last three months?'

And I found I didn't mind. He lit a fire, fast, those capable little hands rolling the newspapers, placing the kindling, balancing the logs. He squatted to do it, shoulders level with his knees, balanced, relaxed; he enjoyed it. It was pleasurable to watch him, like watching an animal move about in its environment, no superfluous movement, spare. He didn't speak till the fire was lit. And not immediately then. We sat watching the flames, listening to the house shift.

He said, 'Better than the telly, isn't it?'

'Yes,' I said, 'But don't tell anyone; the telly is my living.'

'I'll keep it quiet,' he said.

We watched it some more, in silence. There was no strain, apart from my uneasy wondering what might be coming next.

'It's over then,' he said.

'You keep saying that. Trying to convince yourself?'

'That's about it. They call me the terrier.'

'Why?'

'Once I get my teeth into a thing I shake it till it gives up the—'

'Ghost?'

'Fight. I don't let go, you see.'

'I do see, yes.'

'This time I had to. People were getting impatient. Now, *I'm* not impatient.'

'I've noticed.'

'No, I'm a very patient man. I kept feeling it was a matter of time, if only I had more time I'd get what I needed. I knew rationally that time could make no difference; in the end I had to face that. Only I still have this niggling feeling that I just need a little more time and it'll fall like a nut from a tree.' He opened his hand and closed it again. 'Like that. Right into my hand.'

It was strange, sitting there watching his hand, knowing, both of us, that I had been – was still? – one of the major nuts about to fall; yet feeling companionable, safe. The conflict between these two sets of knowledge was momentarily acute; my head seemed to be rising into the air, leaving my body behind. It was only a moment; I controlled it. I speculated not for the first time on whether he might have hypnotic powers. He didn't look like my idea of a hypnotist, sitting there slightly hunched, feet up on the rung of the chair, hands round a cup between his knees, his face perplexed in the flames. I laughed.

'What's funny?' he said.

'Nothing.'

He regarded me a while. 'Yes,' he said, 'it's weird.'

He smiled like a fox.

I didn't ask him what he meant; I didn't want to know.

'You want some food?' I said.

'Food? You haven't been here for months.'

'Freezer,' I said.

'Sure!'

He fried potatoes while I did something with some frozen prawns. I laughed again. He got absorbed in whatever he did, with a fierce concentration, relaxed at the same time. He gave another foxy smile.

'Got any lemon?' he said.

I found one in the bottom of the fridge, shrivelled with age.

'Excellent,' he said.

He tasted the prawns and gave them a squeeze of the lemon and a shake of salt and pepper.

'That's better,' he said. So he cooked as well.

'Are you married?' I asked. It had never occurred to me.

'Was,' he said. 'It didn't take.'

'When?'

'Fifteen years ago.'

'Very young.'

'Yep.'

'You didn't like it.'

'I liked it. She didn't.'

'How long?'

'Three months.'

'Three months! You weren't a terrier with her, then.'

'I told you, I always know when I'm beat. Took longer to get split than it took to get spliced. This is a meal fit for the gods. Nothing like some unexpected lunch to cheer a bloke up. All it needs is a bottle of Montrachet. Don't suppose you keep a wine cellar, do you?'

'Sorry,' I said.

'No, I thought not; you're a philistine.'

'Thanks.'

'True. Your work, that's all you ever think about. Never relax.'

'You have to be relaxed to do my work.'

'That's deliberate relaxation. You work at it; you relax when it's necessary. I'm talking about letting go; you never do that. Enjoying the good things. You're like a spring. Wound up for one purpose. You're an athlete,' he said.

I was stung. I was flattered at the same time. So I was wary.

'So are you if it comes to that,' I said.

'Only when I'm working. The rest of it I enjoy.'

'I told you, you're always working.'

'Maybe. But not like you; you're a phenomenon.'

I was starting to hear echoes of my last conversation with Paul.

'There *is* some wine,' I said, 'as a matter of fact.'

'I'm amazed,' he said.

I took it out of the fridge. It was a half bottle of white something-or-other, an unopened first-night gift from a year ago.

'Not bad,' he said.

He opened it with the same expertise he did everything. Without a proper corkscrew, just a thing on the end of an old can-opener.

'This is the life,' he said. 'Cheers.'

He clinked his glass against mine. I felt silly.

It was snowing now, outside, falling on the sea.

'Yes, it's beautiful,' he said.

For a split second I felt swollen with rage. He had to stop hearing my thoughts! I could have pushed my glass into his face. When he turned back from the window I was under control. But my ease had gone. I wanted to weep; I wanted to be alone, without this man watching me. But I was afraid of being alone. Just today.

'Great funeral, wasn't it?' I said. 'For a star.'

'Star, killer, success, failure: doesn't make any difference when you're in the wooden box. Makes it all look pretty stupid, doesn't it?'

I shrugged.

'People make too much effort in this life,' he said. 'Don't you think?'

I shrugged again.

'Never mind, Millie,' he said.

I put my head on the table next to the detritus of the meal, and wept. It was awful. I felt his hand on the back of my neck. I got up and gripped the edge of the sink. I wept there instead. It subsided at last. He handed me a towel.

'I loved her,' I said.

'Yes, I believe you really did.'

'I – don't want her to be dead.'

'No. I don't suppose anyone wanted that.'

'Somebody did.'

'I'm not so sure.'

'What do you mean?'

'Wanting to kill someone and wanting them to be dead are two different things.'

'It's a bit late afterwards.'

'Ah yes. It's too late then.'

I put a corner of the tea towel under the cold tap and bathed my face. I felt better.

'Now you look really terrible,' he said.

'Thanks.'

'Here, have a sip of this.' He offered his glass.

'No, I hate drink.' It was the glass of wine that had done this to me.

'A-ha. You would.'

'Why?'

'You have to be in control. People who like control don't like drink.'

'Maybe.'

'Never really lose it, do you?'

'I just did.'

'Not really.'

'You'd know, of course.'

'I would, yes, I think.'

I felt tired.

'You should lie down,' he said.

'No thanks.'

'But yes. Go on. Go and lie on the sofa. Go on.'

I found myself doing as he said. I heard him padding upstairs. He came down with my quilt and covered me with it.

'That's better,' he said.

I watched the fire, listened to him washing up in the kitchen, whistling through his teeth, no tune, an irritating noise.

He woke me putting logs on the fire.

'Ah, I was trying to do it quietly,' he said. 'I've got to go.'

'So have I,' I said.

'Why weren't you working today?'

'Everyone gets a day off for a funeral, even actors, from time to time.'

'A-ha.'

'What about you?'

'Nothing urgent on. But you never know.'

He disappeared, came back putting on the leather jacket and a scarf.

'Bye then, Millie. Take care of yourself.'

He bent over and put his mouth on mine. I was too surprised to avert it. He was too quick.

'See you,' he said.

I heard the door close, footsteps outside. His car started up. The noise of the engine faded up the lane. I was lying in the same position. I was confounded. I went on lying there, watching the flames.


Bill Warren liked the high life, restaurants, clubs, first nights. I started to chase around with him. He was a lonely man with a lot of friends. We were seen everywhere, photographed, a public couple. 'Just good friends,' we said. It was true: not Bill's fault, but he wanted a wife and I wasn't wife material. We cleared it up amicably after an initial skirmish or two; it was a good arrangement, convenient.

The reporters gather with their cameras outside the theatres every opening night, hoping for a flash of a face the public might know. A few months ago I could have walked in and out without a glance from them; now they pounced, flashed, questioned; and I was sweet.

'Hi, Millie, how's it going?'

'It's going great.'

'When's the series going to appear?'

'September.'

'Looking forward to it?'

'You bet!'

We had finished the studio stuff. We were filming the location bits now, mainly South London streets. Apart from the filming it was in the can; we were on the last lap. The air of excitement had increased if anything.

And summer had come. Paul's play was still running; it had moved from the Almeida into the West End. Bill and I ran into him from time to time, in clubs, always with a girl on his arm, never the same one. We didn't speak. He was a cloud that passed; I was soon in the sunshine again. I *was* the sunshine. 'Millie! Great to see you!' everyone said. They laughed at my jokes, even the bad ones; I felt like Prince Charles. And I had a movie coming up; a small one, the pay wasn't millions, but it would do fine till the series came out. And I was the star of it, again. It was a small pond, as yet, but I was a big fish, and as the pond got bigger, so would I.

We had a huge party for the end of the series. They lent us a hostility room, as they're always called, at Television Centre. Everyone was there, and happy. Joe, the writer, cornered me.

'They've asked me to write another eight,' he said. 'Have you heard?'

'A whisper,' I said.

'How do you feel about it?'

'Great. You can't go wrong.'

'Don't want it to go on forever,' he said.

'No, but one more series can't hurt.'

'You wouldn't mind playing Jackie for another few months?'

'I wouldn't mind playing Jackie forever,' I exaggerated.

'You're so marvellous in it, Millie.'

Writers are so sincere. At the time. Actors are too.

'They're such marvellous scripts, Joe.'

This was real last-night party stuff. It was going on all over the room, late, drunk, earnest groups patting each other on the back so hard the skin was worn off. Next day was going to be bad for everyone; but not for me. I wasn't drunk, and I started the movie in a week. There was work to do. I was a dolphin, leaping to the crest of the next wave; I was flying high.

# CHAPTER TWENTY-FOUR

High? Next day was terrible. Like a morning-after ashtray, it stank. Groping in fog, no details, nothing to touch, glacial. I had forgotten what such days were like – the day after the job ends: peeling off grey sheets at noon, an inch of sour milk in the fridge, wandering down to the shops, desultory reading, going back to bed. The phone doesn't ring; you suspect it's been cut off, like everything else. It is a hangover of the worst kind; it is not caused by drink.

Then the phone rang. I had washed my hair for something to do; it can make you feel better. It didn't.

'John Bright here,' he said.

Who? I thought. 'Oh!' I said.

'I'm – er – in the area, as they say. Thought I might drop in. If you're – free?'

'Okay,' I said, 'give me ten minutes.'

Any other day I'd have put him off.

I got dressed fast, straightened up the flat, opened the window. There was a pleasant evening out there; bird-song; it was a surprise. The only thing I could do with my wet head was wrap it in a towel; that annoyed me. I regretted already letting him come, decided to get rid of him.

I'd go down when the bell rang and tell him I'd changed my mind. The bell rang. I had my hands in water, washing up. When I got onto the landing the woman downstairs was letting him in. I'd have to move house.

He came up light and fast as usual. We met at the top of the first flight. I nodded, stiff. He gave the towel a glance but didn't mention it.

'Millie.'

'Hi.'

'Brought you these.'

He handed me a bunch of pale pink-ivory roses wrapped in newspaper, droop-headed roses, not the shop kind.

'From the garden,' he said.

'Whose?'

'My own.'

'You have a *garden*?' I was flabbergasted.

'A-ha.'

'Well. Thanks.'

Unwrapping the roses I drew blood; they had a lot of thorns.

'I've rung you a few times before,' he said. 'You're not in much these days.'

'That's right. I'm out a lot.'

'A-ha.'

He was jingling his change. We were both awkward. His squint seemed worse. I'd forgotten how unprepossessing he was. He'd got smaller than I remembered, too. But he'd lost none of his spring; he was still like a runner at the starting tape.

'What did you want to see me about?' I said.

'About? Nothing. Just to – say hello.'

'Oh . . . Hello.'

Stupid clever stuff. I embarrassed myself. His mouth tightened at the corners; not a smile, but trying.

'Well, sit down then,' I said.

'That an order?'

'If you like.'

He did, leaning forward, hands clasped between the knees; he was tense. I was dealing with the roses. Their scent was heady stuff. A garden where he grew roses. Astonishing.

'What are they called, these roses?' I asked.

'Albertine.'

I turned, pleased.

'Like Proust!' I said.

'Christ, Millie.'

'Sorry.'

'I'm a policeman . . . Proust!'

'Okay.'

'Proust . . .'

'Actors get a lot of time to read.'

'No need to make excuses.'

'Nice roses anyway.'

'I tried three times as a matter of fact.'

'What?'

'The sentences were too long.'

'I'd have thought, as a policeman, you'd be keen on long sentences.'

He groaned. I apologised.

'It was a heavy night last night, end of term party.' I said.

'You don't drink.'

'No, but I talk. And get talked to.'

'A-ha.'

There was an uneasy pause.

'What do you do next?' he said.

'Small-budget movie.'

'Any good?'

'Very.'

'Good part?'

'The lead. And good.'

'Things still going well then?'

'Oh yes.'

'A-ha.'

There was another pause. I broke it.

'If I hadn't been in, what were you intending to do with the roses?'

'I had contingency plans.'

'I see.'

'Some old lady in the street.'

I smiled.

'Fancy going out somewhere?' he said.

'I've just washed my hair.'

'Oh really? Thought the towel was for my benefit.'

'Ha.'

He wasn't getting any less nervous. Nor was I. I found it suddenly hard to get my breath.

'Have you been avoiding me, Millie?' he said.

'Yes.'

'Why?'

I shrugged.

'Because I kissed you?' he said.

I rubbed my face. I did not want this conversation.

'Me?' he said. 'Or any man?'

'I don't know what you mean.'

'I mean is it me you object to, or would you run away from any man who got – close?'

'I mean I don't much care to talk about it.'

'I'd like to know.'

'Why? What difference does it make?'

'A lot, to me.'

'Oh.'

I was floundering. I sucked my finger.

'Your roses have thorns,' I said.

'All roses have thorns.'

'Yours more than most.'

'No jokes, Millie. Come on.'

I let out my breath. 'I don't know,' I said. 'I don't know.'

'You can do better than that. If you try.'

'I don't want to try.'

'A-ha.' He was at a loss.

'It's not you, in yourself—' I was hesitant. '—At least I don't think it is. It's—' I got up. 'For Christ sake,' I said, 'one minute you're interrogating me down at Gestapo Headquarters in the firm belief that I'm a murderous psychopath, the next minute you're—I don't get it. And what I don't get I don't like.'

'That was my job. The job's over; I told you.'

'You also said it was not over for you.'

'That's my problem.'

'Excuse me: you suspected – believed – believe – that I killed Liza Drew. Now you're coming to my flat bringing me roses. That's *my* problem.'

'Suspicion, belief, nothing. I was doing my job. It's my job to find out. I was trying to find out.'

'And maybe you're still trying to find out. How do I know?'

'The case is closed.'

'Not officially, you said. And it's not closed for you. The "person or persons" are still unknown. You're not a man to give up, you've said that yourself.'

'I also told you I know when I'm beat. I was beat on that. It's over.'

'I don't believe you.'

'Anyway, what does it matter?'

'What does it *matter*?'

We were standing shouting at each other with stiff arms and fists clenched; veins stood out in his forehead.

'Yes.' He was breathless. 'Even if you had killed Liza Drew, what does it matter?'

'You're mad. You have a criminal mentality. How can I . . . You think it's perfectly okay that you bring me roses and . . . in the belief that I'm a murderer! I'm supposed to get cosy with you knowing that's what you think about me – it's a nightmare.'

He rubbed his eyes.

'It's a nightmare,' I said again, quieter.

'Yes,' he said. 'It's weird all right. Nothing weirder. I know that.' Quieter still.

The air in the room settled a bit; shifted anyway. He lifted the bottle of Scotch. There wasn't much in it.

'May I?' he said.

'Yes.'

His hand shook when he poured, but it all went in the glass. Deft as ever. Shaken but not stirred. Noticing his hands had a peculiar effect on me. As always. A slow turning-over of my insides. I didn't like it. I didn't want to know what it meant. It robbed me of my strength, my power to fight. I'd depended on that power all my life. I couldn't let go of it now.

He offered me the glass. 'You?' he said.

I shook my head, then reached out my hand. I took a sip. It burned. I shuddered and handed it back to him.

'Nice medicine,' he said.

He swallowed the rest, put the glass back on the table by the roses and folded his arms. He'd calmed down, but not all the way. He spoke seriously.

'I'm a good man, Millie. I'm not a bad man. There'd be no point lying to you. I could say I was convinced you didn't kill her, that there was no doubt in my mind. It wouldn't be true and you wouldn't believe it. What I'm saying is, it doesn't matter to me one way or the other. It doesn't matter because even if you did it, you're still you, and it's you I like. It makes no difference. I'm not being a policeman when I'm with you.'

'That's like saying I'm not an actor when I'm with you. It's not true. It's what we both *are*. It defines us, it's the air we breathe. And it matters to *me* – that you could think—'

'It shouldn't. And anyway. There are the – compartments.'

'What do you mean?'

I was shocked. He had used my word.

'You know all about the compartments,' he said. 'You put things in them, you shut the door, you turn the key. You throw the key away.'

'I don't—'

'Yes, you do. I recognise it. I do it too. You've tried to put me in one, but you can't; I won't stay in. I keep getting out and coming back.'

'With roses.'

'A-ha.'

I looked at the roses. I wished they'd die.

'I don't want . . .' I stopped.

'To get involved?' he said.

'What an original way of putting it.'

'I'm not trying to be clever.'

'That makes a change.'

'But you are involved, Millie. You don't want to be but you are. Christ, you must be! It can't just be me, I'm not an adolescent, I don't just imagine these things. Do I? Maybe I am crazy. I don't think so though.'

'I don't like—'

'What? Being touched? Kissed? That stuff. Is that it?'

I laughed. 'You must have been talking to Paul Mannon, the famous psychiatrist with his doctorate from the Actors' Centre.'

'Oh,' he said. His eyebrows went up; I'd made a mistake, a bad one.

'No,' he said, thinking fast, 'I never asked him about that. I should have done. Why didn't I? I don't know.' He was puzzled. 'So Paul thinks you're frigid, does he?'

'Oh go away,' I said. 'I can't stand this sort of conversation. I've got to dry my hair.'

He laughed.

'It's not funny.'

'Yes it is,' he said.

I started to rub my head furiously with the towel.

'What about Bill Warren?' he said. 'What does he think?'

'Bill Warren?' I looked at him. 'Bill Warren is—'

'Yes, "just good friends", I know.'

'It's true,' I said.

'Is it?'

'Yes.'

'Oh.' He was thinking again.

'Oh,' he repeated. He'd suddenly got cheerful. 'I thought you were being a loose woman, Millie.'

'Not me,' I said, wishing he didn't so often surprise me into the truth. No one else did. It was dangerous. And it wasn't fair. I wrapped my hair up again. I had to get this over with. I spoke slowly.

'I really do want you to go,' I said. 'I have enough in my life. I have what I want. I don't want you – messing it up. You've got to get out of it and . . . leave me alone. I've asked you before and you have taken no notice. But I'm serious: I really am asking you to go. And not come back. Not with roses. Not with anything. I don't want you around.'

He was still cheerful.

'So you think I can mess it up, do you?' he said. 'Well, you're right. I can. I do. I want to. I don't want to be put in my compartment. I won't stay there. I'm out and I'm staying out.'

'I want you out of my life.'

'Oh no, I'm staying in that. I like it there.'

'But I don't.'

'Yes, you do.'

'Oh God.'

I wanted to scream, break things. I looked at him helplessly. He grinned. That did it.

'You remind me of my father,' I said. 'I hated him.'

The grin stopped. 'That's serious,' he said.

'Yes. It is.'

He revived a little. 'You didn't always hate him,' he said.

'I did. Always. He was a nasty, rattish little man.'

'Like me. I see.'

'With a squint,' I said. He winced.

'You know how to hit where it hurts, Millie.'

'No more than you.'

'No. But still.'

I walked towards him, a moving weapon. 'No but still. I want you out, I told you that, and I'll use anything I've got to get you out. If it means hitting below the belt, too bad. I'll hit and I'll go on hitting till you're down.'

We were almost nose to nose.

'You might count me out to nine a few times, but I'll be up on ten.'

'You don't know how hard I can hit.'

'I'm getting an idea.'

'Well, go on getting it.'

'Your father eh? That's interesting.'

'Get out.'

He put his arms out and closed his hands behind my back. He held me against him. I started to shake. He pressed his hands flat against my back. I wanted to push him off but my arms were pinned to my sides; anyway, I was shaking too much. He moved his right hand up to the back of my neck and held it; his hand was warm, dry. The shaking got worse. We were both making noises, I like an animal, trapped, moaning, 'No, no', he soothing, 'There, there. Sh, sh.' He pulled my head towards him, the side of his face pressed against the side of mine. 'Don't,' I said. 'Don't, don't.' 'Sh,' he said. 'Sh, sh.' It was stupid, terrible.

He was rubbing my back now, roughly, like drying a wet dog. I felt like a wet dog, shivering. 'There's no danger, Millie, there's no danger, you're safe.' We were near the roses, his warmth, their scent. I opened my eyes.

The summer evening was still outside, a smooth sky, yellow and blue.

The shivering started to subside.

'There,' he said. 'There. Not so bad, is it?'

I was exhausted. He rocked gently, his face still against mine, We breathed slowly. I did feel safe. It was an illusion but for the moment I let myself sink into the illusion. It felt good, peaceful, rocking in the gentle evening light.

'Oh Millie,' he said.

Safe? I depended on myself; to depend on someone else was no part of my plan. I was in great danger. It was a trap.

'No,' I said.

We moved our heads to look at each other.

'No?' he said.

'No.'

He held my head, one hand on either side of my face. He touched first my eyelids, then my mouth, lightly with his mouth. I didn't shake. I didn't stiffen.

'There,' he said. 'Never mind.'

I didn't know what he meant. I don't think he did either. I didn't pull back or flinch. I didn't even control the desire to. I didn't feel the desire to. I couldn't understand.

'Never mind,' he said again. 'Don't worry about it. It's all right.'

Worry about what? What was all right?

'It's all right,' he said again.

'Don't say that.'

'It's all right.'

'Don't say it. Whatever else you say, don't say that.'

'Now? Or ever?'

'Ever. Don't say it.'

'Okay . . . What's bad about it?'

'Everything. Nothing. Don't say it, that's all. I can't tell you, but don't.'

'Okay . . . Anything else I can't say?'

'Nothing that springs to mind. I'll let you know.'

The bad moment was over.

'Okay.'

Diffused, like the pale sky.

'Nice, isn't it?' he said, turning to look at it.

'Yes,' I said.

'Fancy a walk?'

'Yes!' I said, surprised. 'I do.'

'You'll have to take the towel off. Shame.'

It took only a minute to dry my hair. I didn't mind him being there, watching me.

We drove to the Heath and walked till after sunset. Trees, people, dogs racing. I was as calm as the water in the ponds. The ducks could have floated on me. It was a new sensation and I knew it wouldn't last, but I let that go, for now. We didn't talk much.

He asked, 'So who's this Albertine?'

'His girlfriend. A boy in real life, you gather. Rides a bike. Capricious, beautiful, cruel.'

'Good name for my roses then.'

'Yes, beautiful and thorns.'

He laughed.

It was dark when he dropped me at my door, a soft warm night, not like England in any season. Before I got out of the car we sat staring ahead. He turned and took my face in both hands again, touched my mouth with his.

'Sleep well, Millie,' he said.

He took his hands away. We sat.

'Shall I call you?' he asked.

I thought. Or appeared to think.

'Okay,' I said.

He laughed. 'I will then. Get some rest. You need it. So do I. You're an exhausting woman, Millie.'

'You can talk.'

'But worth it.'

'That I doubt.'

'Oh yes. No question.'

'Goodnight, then.'

'Night.'

The smell of roses filled the room, even with the window open. I had that yellow sky inside of me in place of my lungs. I went to sleep like a child. Not the kind of child I had ever been; the kind you read about in fairy tales.

# CHAPTER TWENTY-FIVE

It didn't last. Next day I dreaded seeing him again. I studied the film script; it took my mind off him. Bill Warren rang at seven. We met in town and ate together. He drank a lot. I left him early, carousing in a club, and went home. I was bored.

The rest of the week passed like that, working by day, out with someone in the evening, generally Bill. By Friday I was bored rigid but I had stopped dreading the phone; I had decided he wouldn't ring.

He did.

'Like Indian food, Millie?'

'It's okay.'

'I'll pick you up around eight. If that's okay?'

'It's okay.'

'Sounds as if everything's okay.'

'More or less.'

'That's okay then. See you at eight.'

I shut the front door behind me as he drew up. He was amused.

'Well timed,' he said.

'Mmm.'

We ate at a place in Willesden.

'Location's not so hot,' he said, 'but the food's good.'

It was. Time went fast. I wasn't bored.

The night was warm when we came out into Willesden Lane.

'Walk on the Heath?' he said.

'In the dark?'

'Why not?'

There were people drinking wine in the grass and swimming in the ponds. I had never seen that before. The air was thundery, close. An owl was making a noise. We stood under a tree listening to it. He took my hand and held it tight. Then he put his arms around me and held me. I didn't mind. I seemed to let out my breath for the first time for days.

'I go to Cornwall on Sunday,' I said, 'for the movie. I'll be there three weeks.'

'A-ha,' he said into my hair. 'I'll be here when you get back, you can't escape.'

'Three weeks' parole.'

'That's about it.'

'I'd like to escape.'

'But you can't.'

'We'll see,' I quoted him.

'We will, yes.'

I laughed. I didn't know why. I didn't know what I was doing standing under an oak tree on Hampstead Heath in his arms in the dark.

He dropped me at my door, didn't attempt to come in.

'See you,' he said.

'I suppose.'

'Gracious to the last,' he said.

I smiled.

The movie was tough but fun. I was in bed by nine-thirty each night with tomorrow's scenes, up and on location by six-thirty each day. Sunday was the only day off, spent walking on the Lizard in the sun, or the rain. I came back to London dazed, as though I had been away for months, off the planet somewhere.

The next two weeks were spent shooting the London scenes, mainly in and around a boat moored at Chiswick Mall. It was then I decided to leave my flat and live on a boat; it would suit me, I knew. I told Knife-blade on the phone.

'About time,' he said.

'Why?'

'That soulless flat. Landlady's furniture. Things are looking up.'

'Perhaps I'll change my mind,' I said.

'When do we meet?'

'Not till the movie's over. Two weeks.'

'Don't you get a day off?'

'Sunday.'

'What do you do then?'

'Sleep.'

'Then what?'

'Study Monday's scenes.'

'Enjoying it?'

'It's the only life.'

He laughed.

Saturday was a naked-in-bed scene with an actor called Greg. The dread had started a week before and the closer it comes, always, the worse it gets. I thought it was just me till I sat next to Greg in the make-up chair at six a.m. He was nearly as white as I was.

'Millie,' he said.

'Yes?'

'I've got a bottle of brandy.'

'Have you?'

'Like some?'

'I don't know.'

'It's the only way to get through it, believe me.'

'Brandy makes me ill.'

'It won't.'

'I might forget my lines.'

'You won't.'

'Okay, I'll try it.' I'd have tried anything.

We'd got through half the bottle by the seventh take and there were four more takes. For once I didn't throw up, for once I didn't hate drink. I took a taxi home, though I felt fine. I brushed my teeth hard and had a bath before pulling the cool sheet on top of me and passing out.

When the door of my room opened I had no idea whether I was awake or asleep, like one of those slow-motion dreams in which you want to run but your limbs are too heavy to move. Knife-blade was silhouetted against the dim landing light. My mind slowly worked out that the woman downstairs had let him in; I hadn't heard the bell. He closed the door softly. It was dark in the room, only the light from the red square of window. I heard a motor horn and a dog barked. His shadow stood looking at me? He started to take off his clothes, unselfconsciously, as if he were at home. It was so like the scene in the movie that until his body was stretched next to mine I still wasn't sure I was awake. He made a sound something between a groan and a whimper, a sound my imagination couldn't have supplied, like a woodland animal coming home to its nest.

This had to happen. I had known I couldn't escape it indefinitely. It might as well be now. I prepared myself to endure, to lie like stone. Faking was all right with other people; it wouldn't do for him. His warm dry hands moved lightly, my hair, my face, my arms, my legs, my feet; his mouth, also warm and dry, brushing my skin. He continued to utter small whimpering groans. It was a forest creature in my bed, not a man; something in its natural element. It was curious: he even smelt of clear water, cut grass. My teeth were clenched, my body stiff, with this light kiss like a zephyr running over it. His face stroked mine over and over, his mouth brushing my lips from side to side, like feathers, like air, like leaves. I began to have visions, clear as hallucinations: woodland clearings, a white horse in sunlight. I was entering a nightmare of ecstasy. I had to get out. I started to fight, gripping his hard hands, pushing against him with my hip bones, my arms, my knees. He fought back; and that's how it was to the end, gripped, strained in combat, pushing him off, out, anywhere away from me, groaning, fighting. I was screaming silently, 'No, no, no.' He was saying 'Millie, Millie, Millie!' over and over again; and then I was drowning in a black sea, down, down; a silken wave lifted me, dropped me, lifted me again. I was on its back, it threw me, anywhere, on the black water, in the black water. I clung to him to save me from the terrifying sea. I was a ship, fragmenting, he was holding me together, we were one small body thrown, shuddering, in the dark, flashes of light on water, sickening descents into depths. I was drowning with him. I was shuddering. I was dead.

He was sitting on the edge of the bed, with water in a glass; he was stroking the hair back from my forehead.

'You passed out, Millie. You passed out.'

I took the water and drank it, all of it. He took the glass from my hands. I was crouched in the corner where the bed met the walls. I wanted to get out of the bed but I was trembling.

'You're shivering,' he said.

He fetched my dressing gown. 'Come on. Put it on,' he said.

I got myself to the edge of the bed. He pushed my arms into the sleeves. I tried to stand but my legs were weak; convalescent limbs. He helped me up and to the window where I supported myself by holding on to the back of a chair. I couldn't speak, and he didn't.

He came and touched my back. I flinched. He took his hand away but continued to stand behind me. I could feel his warmth; and his smell, like grass, like biscuits.

After some time he moved away and I heard him rustling in the dark; he was starting to put his clothes back on. I turned. I didn't want him to go; I was afraid to be alone. He came to me half-dressed and held me.

'I'm not going,' he said.

He sat me down with him, holding me. I was helpless.

'We need some coffee,' he said.

I heard myself laugh, shakily, from a distance.

'Simple things, Millie, simple things.'

I didn't take my eyes off him as he prepared the coffee. Watching the precise movements of his hands touching the jar, the kettle, the cups, gave me that swooning sensation that threatened to drown me again. I no longer doubted what it meant. I shut my eyes.

'Here you are.'

The heat of the cup revealed the coldness of my hands. I was still shivering. The hot liquid burned my insides, like the cauterisation of a wound. The manufacturers of instant coffee granules would have been gratified by its effect. The spasms of shivering started to subside; then stopped. The room began to appear again, in pieces: the table, a chair, the corner with the wardrobe, the carpet, my feet on the carpet, his feet next to mine, his bare knees. I looked at his face. I felt like Lazarus.

'I said you needed coffee,' he said.

'And you're always right.' My voice was paper-thin.

'Oh yes.'

We looked at each other.

'It never happened to you before, Millie?'

I shook my head.

'A-ha.' He nodded, thought for a moment. 'Well, don't worry,' he said, 'it might never happen again.'

'What do you mean?'

'Joke,' he said.

'Oh. I see.'

He lay back on the bed and laughed. 'Oh Millie,' he said.

So I didn't sleep that day. It rained continuously, warm summer rain; we were marooned on the island of Sunday. There was a flower struggling to open inside me. Joy, I suppose it would be called. I fought against it. In the evening I said:

'You have to go now.'

'Why?'

'I have to work. I can't work with anyone here, it's private. I'd be embarrassed.'

'Okay.'

I was taken aback by his acquiescence.

'What will you do?' I said.

'Go and see my old mum. I owe her a visit.'

'Where?'

'Guess. South Norwood.'

'Joke?'

'No.'

I wasn't laughing. Flowers are easy to kill.

'Millie, you look amazing, wonderful. What happened to you?' The director on Monday morning.

'Nothing,' I said.

'Spend yesterday in the beauty parlour, darling?' said the costume boy.

'It's the make-up,' I said.

'Like hell it is, dear.'

It was odd to have become transparent. It was odder still not to mind. Memories of his hands, on my back, my knees, my face, kept thickening my blood if I closed my eyes, even to blink. I felt connected with everything, everyone. I was bewildered, invaded by a weakness I couldn't afford. I was too weakened even to desire my former strength. I was letting it happen. I had no choice.

He turned up Monday evening with a toothbrush. He prepared a salad with his customary skill. At nine he said:

'I'd better go now. Let you work.'

'Yes.'

I clung to him. Me. Millie Hale.

'Yes, go,' I said.

He handed me the toothbrush ceremoniously.

'May I keep this here?'

'No,' I said.

'This is an entirely new extremely expensive toothbrush. What am I to do with it?'

'Keep it about your person,' I said.

'I see. Don't push your luck, John.'

'John . . .' I said.

'Ah, at last.'

'What?'

'You used my name. Things are looking up.'

I was walking through a landscape I didn't know. I *was* a landscape I didn't know. At four years old I had a recurring dream which fell short of nightmare only by the strength of my will. I was running across a flat marshy country with tufts of high grass, like Suffolk, like the moon. I had to keep running because every few steps revealed a hole of bottomless depth and you never knew when the holes would come. I never fell into one of those holes, I leapt them all, night after night, by keeping on the move and never looking back. I would wake breathless, sweating, having escaped this time, just. The dream came back to me vivid, complete, as he stood in the doorway and left.

'Millie, you look marvellous!' became the cry.

'It must be my movie,' the director said.

'That's right,' I replied.

'It's success,' Bill Warren said.

'Not yet,' said I.

'She's in love,' said the costume boy; they always know everything.

'Like hell,' I said.

'Who is it, Millie?'

'Bill Warren,' said Greg.

I laughed.

They could think what they liked. Love? It wasn't anything like my idea of love. Knife-blade wasn't anything like my idea of what I wanted: small, wiry, strong, dangerous, with his sharp face, his snapping eyes, his nosey London voice. He had broken the fence, trampled it down. It was the last thing I wanted on earth. If this was love I wouldn't give it the name; it was terror, slavery, joy, rage, hunger, power, need. It was too much for me.

I would see him only on Sundays. He turned up on Saturday night. My excuse for not seeing him oftener was work, and work I did, but that wasn't the reason; the reason was fear. Someone opens you to that much joy, they can make you tell them anything; there wasn't anything I wanted to tell. I hoped I could kill my need by little usage. It didn't work. In spite of the movie, Monday to Friday crawled, the weekends galloped by. I didn't tell him that, but he knew.

The movie overran by a fortnight.

'When it's finished we'll go to Suffolk,' he said. 'I'll take some leave.'

'No,' I said.

He grinned.

The movie finished on Friday; we went to Suffolk on Saturday. I'd never seen the grey North Sea blue and gold before. He cooked startlingly good meals, we walked in the woods and along the empty shore. On Tuesday we ran out of milk and went into Saxmundham for supplies. We came out of the shop laughing, and walked into Mrs Drew.

# CHAPTER TWENTY-SIX

She stood paralysed. So did I. Knife-blade looked amused. Nobody spoke. Then he said:

'Good morning, Mrs Drew.'

She looked from him to me and back again to him. She saw everything. And we saw that she saw.

'How are you, Inspector Bright?'

'I'm fine, Mrs Drew. How are you?'

'Much the same as the last time we met, thank you.'

She let the words hang. 'And you, Millie? You are looking . . . well.'

She was having difficulty believing what she believed. I didn't reply and the silence stretched.

'Where are you staying?'

She included us both in the question.

'I'm staying with a friend,' said Knife-blade, smooth as silk.

'I'm staying in a cottage,' I said, like a cart over stones.

'It's a small world,' said Knife-blade.

'Exceedingly.' Like cracking ice.

Again, silence fell. We were jostled by people going in and out. None of us noticed.

'An odd place to choose for a holiday, I should have thought.' She was not pretending to be polite.

'I like it down here.' Knife-blade was implacably cheerful.

'Millie always did, of course,' she said. The jade green eyes were slimy with dislike.

'Yes,' I said. 'I always did.'

'That hasn't changed, it seems.'

'No. That hasn't changed.'

'I congratulate you, my dear.'

'On what?' said Knife-blade, calling her bluff.

'Her ability to survive.'

'A quality we all need, Mrs Drew.'

She turned the eyes on him. 'And which some of us possess to a greater extent than others, Inspector.'

'That can't be denied.'

His cheeriness was getting on her nerves. I knew he would go too far.

'Are your superiors aware that you are associating with a former suspect in a murder case?'

'Associating!' said Knife-blade.

'They might be interested to know.'

'There was more than one suspect, Mrs Drew.'

'But not more than one killer, Inspector.'

'Are you threatening me, Mrs Drew?'

She was irresolute for a second. He was alarming when he got quiet.

'Are you threatening Miss Hale?'

She looked at me and let the eyes rest.

'I believe my attitude to Millie has not changed,' she said, 'unlike yours, it would seem.'

'Well—' He was brisk. '—I'm sorry you feel as you do, but it is understandable. However, I wish you well. Come on, Millie, I'll help you with these.'

He took a bag of groceries from me, the one with the protruding bottle of wine. She looked at it.

'Goodbye, Mrs Drew,' he said.

She watched us leave.

The car was round the corner. He had to drive. My foot would not have been able to control the clutch.

'Don't let her get to you, Millie; she's an old bitch.'

'She could always get to me. And she could cause real trouble for you.'

'How?'

'What she said. Report you. For "associating with a suspect".'

'No law against it. You were "eliminated from inquiries".'

'She could get the case re-activated.'

'Unlikely.'

'She has nothing else in her life – now.'

'She has too much at stake. She was a suspect as much as you.'

'She wouldn't be if she tried to revive the case.'

'She won't.'

It was that night the nightmares started, however.

We made love and lay under the cool quilt watching the moon. I must have fallen asleep before him. I started to feel hot. My body burned, not damp and sweating, but scorching and dry. The heat was coming from the bed itself, from the mattress, and the bed was the narrow one I slept in as a child. It burned hotter and hotter; I thought, it is going to burst into flames. I heard a throbbing noise like a distant engine. The bed throbbed. I was on a ship, pulsing and rocking. Still in the dream, I woke. I sat up. There was smoke coming from a spot in the bed down by my feet. I beat the smoke down. It died away but the heat persisted. I lay down again, felt an acute searing sensation near my thigh, sat up again. Smoke was issuing from that point in the bed; I beat it down; it came from the other side, at my knee; I flailed at it; then from near my waist, my shoulder; each time I beat down one source of smoke another started somewhere else. Then flames started to appear, first in one part of the bed, then in another. I was terrified, couldn't scream, knew it wasn't a dream because I was awake, and woke to find my arms lashing about and Knife-blade trying to hold onto me.

'Millie, Millie, you're okay, you're okay, it was a dream, you're okay.'

My body was still burning. I said, 'The bed's on fire.'

I was searching all over it for signs of charring. It was intact. I got up and splashed water on my face. I couldn't get back into that bed. I still wasn't sure I was awake. Perhaps there was no end to the wakings within the dream. If I went back to the bed the burning might start again. I couldn't. He couldn't persuade me no matter how he tried. At last he went back to sleep. When he woke me in the morning I was in the chair. I told him I couldn't remember the dream. He knew I was lying.

'You said the bed was on fire.'

'I don't remember.'

'A-ha. Okay.'

It happened again the next night. He got up with me and tried to

comfort me but I couldn't bear his hands on me, my body was too hot.
Also the dream had again contained two awakenings and my sense of
reality had gone.

The next night in the dream when the flames appeared all round
me and I was trying to beat them out, suddenly my father's hands were
there, charred black, trying to fight the flames and pull me out. They
were more terrifying than the fire. I tried to fight them off; I woke
and they were Knife-blade's hands. I floundered against them till they
gripped me and I woke; I mean really woke.

'What is this, Millie? You've got to tell me.'

'I can't.'

'You've got to talk about it.'

'I can't.'

'You must. You'll go crazy if you don't.'

'I can't.'

'Stop saying that. You can.'

'I need water. I need cold water.'

He put me under the shower. It shocked me into consciousness.

'Are you here? Am I dreaming now?'

'You're not dreaming, Millie. I'm here.'

He wrapped me in a towel. We sat in the chair, I in his arms. I was
half asleep when he said:

'What is it that frightens you?'

And I, without thinking, said, 'My father.'

'Your father?'

'My father frightens me.'

I started to cry in that helpless breathless way a baby does.

'How? What does he do to frighten you?'

'He . . . touches me.'

'Oh Christ!'

'He says it's all right. It's not all right. *It's not all right.*' I was screaming,
high. '*It's not all right!*' I was rocking backwards and forwards on his
lap. Devils were coming out of me. He held onto me, stopping me from
flying off. In the midst of it I had a vision: men in white coats, putting
me into a white van. The spasms died down. He wiped my face with a

corner of the towel, then he picked me up, put me on the bed and lay beside me holding my hand.

'When did this happen, Millie?'

'I was nine the first time.'

'Did you know what was happening?'

'Not the first time, no. I'd had a nightmare. He got into my bed. He was comforting me.' I laughed.

Knife-blade said, 'Sh, sh.'

'Then it started to happen once a week. He used to go to the pub on Saturday night. He came to my room when he got back.'

'Did you try to stop him?'

'I didn't know how. I used to say no, go away, in whispers in case my mother heard, but that's what he always said: 'It's all right, Millie, it's all right; it's all right, honest, Millie, it's all right.'

He wiped my face again.

'You're safe now,' he said. 'It's over now.'

'I asked my mother to stop him coming to my room. "Why?" she said. I didn't know how to say it. "I don't like it," I said. "Nonsense, he's your own father," she said. "Don't be so silly." And I knew she knew. That's when I knew I was on my own. I hated her worse than I hated him. She didn't try to stop him; or maybe she did. I don't know. I saw no signs of it, there were no rows as far as I could tell and he was there in my room on the dot next Saturday night. So I made a plan. I stole a hammer from his tool kit in the shed. I took it to bed with me. When he came in I pretended to be asleep and when he came close to the bed I hit him with the hammer over and over again. I couldn't reach his head but I nearly broke his arm. He got the hammer away from me. I thought he'd kill me – I wouldn't have cared if he had, I'd have killed him if I could – but he didn't, he scurried out of the room like a scared rabbit. He never came near me again. It was never mentioned. I never got punished. But he changed after that. He'd been a cheerful little man. He became shifty and sullen. He hardly spoke. It was the same with her. It was a silent house. Hate and shame. That's all there was. It's all I ever had.'

'You never told anyone this before?'

'No.'

'Why?'

'They'd realise how – leprous – I am.'

'Unclean, unclean. I see.'

'I ring bells.'

'You do that all right.'

'You took no notice.'

'I knew I had to break a dam.'

'You shouldn't have bothered.'

'It was nae bother, as my mum would say.'

We were silent.

'What about Paul Mannon?' he said.

'What about him?'

'He didn't break the dam?'

'No.'

'But you made love?'

'I pretended.'

'And he didn't know?'

'No.' I recalled my last conversation with Paul. 'Yes,' I said. 'I don't want to talk about this any more.'

'Okay.'

We lay like two empty pea pods till the sun came up and after. He was dropping with sleep but he stayed awake with me.

'How do you do it?' I asked him.

'It's the job,' he said. 'You get used to it. You get a technique.'

The job. A technique. He had a technique for everything. So did I, but I was losing mine; what else might I be impelled to tell?

He treated me like a convalescent all day, tucking rugs round me, bringing me things on trays. I felt empty, clean, purified. But weak as a baby, learning to walk all over again. That night I slept with his arms around me and I didn't dream. The next day I was convinced that devils had really gone out of me, that I could start again. I was wild with excitement, hope. He said at night, 'Calm down, Millie, take it quietly, or you'll be ill.'

'Anything you say – "John".'

I put his name in quotes, like he used to say 'Miss' Hale.

'Twice,' he said. 'Careful. I'd like to know what you call me in your head.'

'I'll never tell you that.'

'We'll see.'


A few days later he went up to the village for a walk. He came back looking blank.

'What's the matter?' I asked.

'Nothing. I think.'

'Something. I think.'

'Mrs Drew's on the warpath.'

'You met her again?'

'Worse.'

'What *could* be?'

'I phoned headquarters. Just to see if there was anything I should know about.'

'And?'

'Inspector of Operations has had a letter.'

'From her?'

'A-ha.'

'Oh no.'

'A-ha.'

'What will happen?'

'Nothing, I think.'

I felt sick.

'Don't look like that, Millie. There are often weird letters after a case like this. Usually anonymous.'

'But not this one.'

'Not this one. But it's nothing to get upset about. He'll ignore it, write a polite reply.'

'This one maybe. What about the next? And the next? She's not a woman to be put off with polite replies. She won't give up. She's a boa constrictor; she'll squeeze you to death.'

'She can't win. I've done nothing wrong. My – er – "involvement" with you didn't start until I was off the case.'

'You can't prove that. They'll say you didn't investigate me sufficiently.'

'There were witnesses to my investigation of you.'

'That questioning at the station could have been a put-up job. We could have arranged it between us, easy. I'm an actress; I could have been pretending scared; we could have arranged that you would stop the questioning where you did. Or I needn't have been in on it at all. You stopped the questioning where you did because you wanted me not to be the one, you were prejudiced in my favour. Why did you stop it there, why—'

'Shut up, Millie.' Like a slap. I was shocked. 'That's enough,' he said, quieter. 'This is what she wants: not to reopen the case, just to get under your skin. She didn't like you looking happy.'

'She never liked me at all.'

'Don't let her win. You're a survivor like she said. And we're two against one.'

'That's where she's got us.'

'No one's got us. We're okay; we're more than okay, Millie, we're better than anything.'

'You think?'

'I think. Don't you think?'

'I think.'

'Well then.'

'Okay.'

We forgot about it. Most of the time. Anyway, we didn't mention it much. On Sunday his leave was up. We closed the house on two weeks of turmoil and happiness mixed, and went back to sticky summer London.

I started some dubbing on the movie. Even on the scratchy little print in a tiny Wardour Street dubbing theatre I could see it looked good. It was a thrill. Dubbing was hard, gave me a headache from the top of my head to the soles of my feet, but I got better at it, like riding a bike.

Knife-blade came round to tell me he'd had a chat with the Chief Inspector.

'He's not taking it seriously. He wrote to her defending my integrity. She hasn't replied.'

'Yet,' I said.

'If she gets a lawyer on to it it might be different. He doesn't think she will.'

'He doesn't know her.'

'But I do. A bit. I don't think she will either. How do you look in the movie?'

Great!' I said.

He laughed.

'It's true. The scenes after I'm supposed to have fallen in love with Greg I'm like – it's amazing. I – fly.'

'I wonder why?'

'I wonder,' I said.

When our hours off coincided we looked at boats. Boats were cheap; and they floated. You could take off in a boat; where could you go in a house, except upstairs? No one could catch you in a boat. Why would anyone live in a house?

They were doing a big hype on the series; well, big for the BBC. The days I wasn't dubbing were taken up with interviews and photo sessions. We were making the cover of the *Radio Times* and a two-page spread inside. We were getting the kind of coverage usually reserved for wild animals or sport; they were pinning a lot on us. It should have been scary. I wasn't scared.

At the press showing of the first episode down at Television Centre there was unheard-of applause. A lot of white Chateau BBC was drunk; but not by me. I was still playing Liza with the press; it was a good act, they liked it. And they liked the show.

Two days later the previews appeared: 'The first episode is searing and shocking.' 'The casting is impeccable throughout.' 'Millie Hale, newcomer to TV, unbeatable.' 'Riveting performance, not to be missed.' 'If the rest of the series lives up to this, the nation will be glued to its collective seat on Wednesday nights.'

I watched it alone. Knife-blade was working. He watched his video the next day.

'I knew you were good, Millie, but I didn't know you were that good. I feel a bit – awed,' he said.

'That'll be the day.'

'You're going to be a star.'

'About time too.'

'What about me?'

'What about you?'

'Where do I come in?'

'Do you want to get out?'

'Still, it's weird, me tied up to a star.'

'Not as weird as me tied up to a policeman,' I said.

The Sundays were more excited than the dailies and on Monday my agent was ecstatic.

'Lots of enquiries, darling. People are thrilled. We must take our time and not rush into anything.'

'Anything you say, Dorothy.'

After the second episode the letters started to come in: weirdos, cranks, bedwetters, the sort of stuff Liza used to get; and some normal stuff from ordinary people too. Among the second batch was a letter from Paul:

Dear Millie,

Mrs Drew has been in touch with me. She saw you with the rat-like  policeman and believes you to be having some kind of 'thing' with him. I find this hard to believe, though with you I now think anything is possible. Is that how you prevented yourself being charged? Seducing the law? I shouldn't be surprised. Mrs Drew wishes me to join forces with her in trying to get the case re-activated. I am considering my position and taking advice.

Paul Mannon

# CHAPTER TWENTY-SEVEN

'He's trying to frighten you,' Knife-blade said.

'He's succeeding,' I replied.

'Are you going to answer it?'

'What do you think?'

'I think you should ignore it.'

'And hope that it will go away?'

I showed him my reply. It had taken me two days to write.

Dear Paul,

Your letter came as a bad shock. I suppose you intended that. I knew Mrs Drew would try to make trouble but I didn't think you would join forces with her. My friendship [It had taken a long time to find the word.] with John Bright began after he was off the case. I dare say you will find that hard to believe but it is true and therefore futile to try to prove otherwise. You must recall how friendless I had become at that time, how friendless we had all become. I regret the loss of your friendship more than I can say.

'As I wrote that I was amazed to discover that it wasn't true,' I said.

'Oh yeah?' Knife-blade looked sceptical, but went on reading.

If you and Mrs Drew did try to reopen the case and destroy John Bright's life and mine, it could not be worse than that.

Millie.

'Don't appeal to them, Millie,' he said.

'What else can I do?'

I tore the letter up; in the end sent one saying:

Dear Paul, don't do this, it can only reopen the wounds, cause heartache and pain, to no avail. Don't let Mrs Drew influence you in this. Yours, Millie.

'You can't change anything,' Knife-blade said.

It's creepy being recognised by strangers. It started to happen in earnest after the showing of episode three: the corner shop, the tube, everywhere you go, you lose your normal right to anonymity walking down the street. I didn't like it at all. Which is odd, considering how famous I wanted to be. It frightened me: 'Hey, you're Thingy in that new series!' I stood accused. 'Yes.' Where did we go from there? They were people I didn't know.

I pumped up great injections of my Liza persona to deal with it. I became sweetness itself, impervious. Three days and I was handling it like a pro.

Knife-blade didn't like it either, but was amused.

'It's the price, Millie.'

'Quite high.'

'You pay for everything.'

'It can't be pleasant for you,' I said.

'No skin off my nose. I'm good at keeping out of sight.'

He was, too. After a gaggle of fans had got their autographs and gone, he would reappear at my side. He had the knack of dematerialising at will. I envied him. I felt increasingly hounded, needed to hide.

I bought the boat at the end of September. It was moored at Richmond and was called *The Egg*. I didn't change its name. There was hardly a thing to move out of my flat, only clothes and a few books. I had been there for years and gathered no moss. I looked around it for the last time. It looked just the same without me as it had looked with me.

'We've been happy here though, Millie.'

'Yes,' I said.

The boat was our burrow. It was dim downstairs with silver flicker-ings of watery light. Knife-blade fixed shelves and made a garden on the roof, high trellis and climbing plants. There were other boats moored as adjacent as a housing estate but it seemed everyone was there for the same reason as me: to get off the edge of the world. They were not sociable; they left us alone. I spent my time painting the boat, cleaning it, and reading scripts, none of them offers I couldn't refuse. It felt like a holiday, my first. Knife-blade was busy on a case. He wouldn't talk about it except, 'I've got to nail this one, Millie. Can't afford two failures in a row.' He didn't say why. He didn't need to. His chief had received a letter from Paul. It said he and Mrs Drew were 'consulting' about the action they should take. The threat hung over us; we ignored it; what else could we do? We were aware of the need for cover, however. We didn't go out together in public; if I went to a first night, I went with Bill Warren; to lunch with friends, I went alone; to a party, alone or with Bill. Knife-blade was my secret. I'd never minded secrets, I liked them in fact but previous secrets had been my choice and this one was not.

Knife-blade said, 'It's only for a while. This'll die down, it always does.'

'She won't drop it, she has too much at stake.'

'Revenge? Clearing her own name by smearing yours?'

'No. Paul. It's got him in touch with her again. She'll keep him there as long as she can.'

'Ah, I hadn't thought of that.'

So we clung to the boat. It was our raft.

The Royal Court offered me a play, a new one. It was good. It started in a month. And Knife-blade got his man. He staggered down the stairs one night round two a.m., red-eyed and thick of utterance.

'I've done it, where's the Scotch?'

'How?'

'He confessed. I knew he would in the end. I questioned him for four hours.'

He had only questioned me for two.

He wrapped himself around me that night like a child, nuzzling into my neck.

'Oh Millie, what would I do without you now?'

I lay awake till morning; not even the boat could rock me to sleep.

And in the morning the letter came: 'Mrs Drew and I have taken legal advice. There appears to be a good chance of proving police negligence.' There followed some remarks on my ill-gotten gains and, 'You will be hearing from our solicitors in due course.' The letter had been forwarded from my agent's address. She was under orders to tell no one where I was. Knife-blade was still in a heavy sleep. I decided not to show him the letter but he knew the moment he opened his eyes.

'What's the matter, Millie?'

'We have to split up.'

'For Christ sake! Just 'cause I got drunk last night!'

I laughed miserably. 'Yes, you know I can't stand drink.'

'Well, why then?'

'Because you are going to be in big trouble. If we split now they won't have anything to base their case on. We've only been seen together once – we think. That can't last; it's dangerous.'

'Millie, we've got nothing to hide. I did my job properly, I always do. They can't get me on that.'

'They can get you on me.'

'Are you happy with me?'

'No. Miserable.'

'A-ha.'

'I never knew what happiness was before.'

'Well then.'

'Well then nothing. You're not a child, you're a clever man. You're putting yourself on the line for nothing. For me. It's stupid. It's criminal.'

'You're what I want.'

'Destroying your life.'

'You're the other half of my equation, Millie. I'm not throwing it away now I've found it. It took me a long time.'

'What about the other half of *this* equation?'

I threw the letter at him. He read it quickly and rubbed his eyes.

'Does your chief know about us?' I said.

'Yes. Better to tell the truth from the start.'

'So it makes no difference then?'

'What?'

'Whether we part or not.'

'No! It makes no difference!'

He threw himself on the bed, legs in the air, pulling me on top of him.

'You come with me when I go, Tiger; they can't do anything to us.'

'Tiger?' I said.

He squinted up at me. 'A-ha, it's what I call you. It's what I called you from the start; snarling away at me from behind all that hair. Tiger,' he said.

I laughed and went on laughing. He still didn't know my name for him.

'What's so funny?' he said.

But he couldn't make me tell.

'Come on, Millie,' he said.

He gathered me up and I stopped laughing and started to weep.

He went back to work in the afternoon. I rang Dorothy to say yes to the Royal Court.

'I'm sure that's the right decision, Millie,' she said. 'It will consolidate the success.'

'Sounds very grand, Dorothy.'

'And the movie has got distribution, darling! It's opening at the Gate in six weeks.'

'That was fast!'

'Your success in the series has helped, Millie.'

'Oh.'

'By the way, darling, there's a journalist, Harry Loach, who wants to interview you. He's called me four times this morning. Here's his number. It's a nuisance you being so elusive, Millie.'

'Sorry, Dorothy.'

'Never mind. Take care, darling.'

'I will.'

It's not wise to alienate the gentlemen of the press. They don't fight by the Queensberry rules. I rang him.

'Oh, Millie, thanks for ringing back. Can I come and see you?'

'Well, Harry, I'd rather not. I've just moved house and you know what it's like. Things are in an awful mess. Won't the phone do?'

'How about me taking you out to lunch?'

I ground my teeth. 'Okay,' I said. 'That would be nice.'

'Tomorrow?' he said.

'Lovely,' said I.

We fixed a place in Soho, one o'clock.

'Thank you, Millie, that's ever so nice of you.'

He didn't know how nice.


He was a depressed-looking little man with a limp moustache and the watery eyes of a drinker who chain-smoked. He pulled out my chair with drooping gallantry. The restaurant was packed. Italian waiters flashed smiles and outsize pepper grinders; there was a lot of noise. He had gin for lunch, with three mouthfuls of spaghetti vongole and five cigarettes. His fingers were the colour of a walnut chest of drawers.

'Congratulations on the series, Millie, it's making a lot of noise.'

'Thank you. Yes, it's very gratifying.'

'Your big chance, would you say?'

'Yes, it was. I'm just glad I didn't make a hash of it.'

'And now you've got the movie coming out.'

On it went, the same questions, the same silly answers. I knew the script. It was easy to be modest and charming; I was lulled. Then he grew more intimate.

'And what about your – private life – Millie? How's that going?'

I stiffened, but not so's he'd know.

'Oh fine,' I said.

'Anyone – special?'

'No, no one special. I've been working too hard.'

'Don't see you about with Bill Warren so much these days. That still on?'

'It never was "on" as you put it'—Careful, don't get tetchy.—'We really were just good friends. We still are, that hasn't changed, it's just that we're not working together any more. I'm very fond of Bill.'

'You've got so private lately, I thought there might be a new man.'

'Oh no, I've just been moving house.'

Damn. Why had I let him panic me into reminding him of that?

'Ah yes. Where are you living now?'

'Richmond.'

'Oh, lovely spot. Maybe we could do some pictures there? "Millie Moves House" stuff, eh?'

'Oh no, honestly'—I was so sweet it hurt my teeth—'now that I'm recognised all over the place I really would like to keep that sort of private, you know. And anyway, I told you, it's an awful mess.'

'Okay, okay. Later on maybe, when you're more settled.'

He sank himself into another gin, by way of dessert.

'Now, Millie—' The watery eyes swam closer as he leaned in and coughed, dropping ash on the tablecloth. '—I know it's a while ago now but erm . . . the case of Liza Drew . . .' He took a long drag. 'How would you say you felt about that these days?'

Oh no. I recognised him now. He was one of the crowd who had interviewed me at the time; made my name, you might say. He had privileges.

'It's still painful. I don't like talking about it much.'

'No, no, no. But . . .'

I waited while he gave his lungs another fix.

'You see,' he wheezed, 'no, erm, culprit was ever found, isn't that right?'

'Yes, that's right.'

'Yes. Now, how did you feel about that?'

'Well, you can imagine, it made it even worse. Never to know. Anything.'

'Yes . . .' The fish eyes focussed somewhere beyond my left shoulder. 'I hear they might be going for a second inquest.'

The stained fingers ground out a stub in the full ashtray. My head felt strange.

'A second inquest?' I said.

'Ye-es. Had you heard about that?'

'No. I hadn't. Why? Have they found some new evidence?'

'I don't know, Millie.' He smiled. 'I thought you might be able to tell me.'

There were large yellow teeth under the moustache.

'Well no, I can't,' I said. 'How did you hear about this?'

'Never reveal my sources, Millie.'

I thought for an instant he had said 'sauces' and was referring to the gin.

'Please tell me,' I said, oh so gently. 'I'd like to know. It would really be something if they found out who did it after all this time.'

'Well then,' he said, 'as it's you. I was having a little chat with Paul Mannon the other night. He mentioned it, said it looks as though there was negligence at the time on the part of the police.'

'Good heavens! Did he say how?'

'No. Any idea yourself?'

'None at all. They questioned us all very thoroughly, over and over again, everyone who knew Liza, all her fans even, everyone. They said they couldn't find evidence against anyone.'

'The inquest verdict was a bit dodgy though, eh? Person or persons unknown.'

'Dodgy?' I said.

'Yes. Leaves a cloud over everyone. Not an open verdict, see.'

'Oh yes, I see what you mean. But the coroner was careful to point out that everyone who was present at the inquest had been eliminated from inquiries,' I said.

'So how do you feel about it, Millie?'

'About what?' I was playing for time.

'About another inquest.'

He dragged deep.

'Well, I have mixed feelings,' I said slowly. 'On the one hand it's wonderful if they have found new evidence and we find out who did it and why; on the other hand there is a part of me that would like poor Liza to be left in peace.'

'Ah yes.' He sighed and coughed. 'I see what you mean.'

He lit another cigarette from the stub of the one before.

'Do you still see much of Paul Mannon, by the way?'

'Not a lot,' I said. 'We're both so busy, you know.'

'You used to see a lot of each other before the – er – tragedy, isn't that so?'

'Yes, but it was always Liza I was closest to. She was my greatest friend.'

'Ah yes.' The moist eyes oozed sympathy. 'It must have caused a bit of a – gap – in your life.'

'More than a gap,' I said. 'A chasm. But I've been lucky, it's been filled with work. As much as it ever can be filled, that is.'

I was hoping to steer him back towards the subject of work. It was a mistake.

'Oh yes,' he said, 'the series. I heard a little whisper the other day that Liza was offered that part before you. Any truth in that?'

The eyes wavered around me like jellyfish poising to sting. I was at the bottom of the sea.

'Coffee, signorina?'

I was never so glad to see a waiter in my life. I wanted to decline coffee, say I had to go; but it would look bad.

'Yes. Thanks,' I said.

'You, sir? Coffee?'

Harry Loach nodded, without ungluing his sticky eyes from me.

'Yes,' I said when the waiter had gone. 'It's true. But Liza had turned it down before . . . before she died.'

'Oh?'

Not what he'd heard, he implied.

'Because she was pregnant,' I said.

'Oh . . . Ye-es.'

He was thinking, behind the raised tumbler of gin. He saw that made sense.

'Yes, I see,' he said.

The coffee arrived. It burned my mouth. 'And how did you feel, Millie? Stepping into her shoes, as it were?'

'Oh,' I said, dabbing my hot mouth with a napkin. 'I felt terrible at first, of course, when I was offered it. I was going to turn it down. It was Paul Mannon actually who persuaded me I should do it; for Liza's sake, he said. When I thought of it like that I felt better about it. In fact that's what sustained me all the way through, that I was doing it for her.'

My eyes filled up. 'Sorry,' I said, dabbing at my eyes this time. 'I haven't talked about this before. They promised not to make it public, you know.'

'Oh, I heard it strictly off the record.'

I looked at him appealingly through my tears.

'It's a good story though,' he said.

He dropped an inch of ash into his coffee and drank it without noticing. It was a small satisfaction to me.

'I can see it upsets you, Millie.'

'Yes. It brings it all back.'

'It would do, yes.'

'One doesn't really get over such a thing. I probably never shall.'

'No. I can see that.'

I blew my nose thoroughly, then drained the coffee cup.

'I'm sorry, Harry, I'm afraid I have to go now. Hairdresser,' I said. 'I'm already late.'

'Well, thank you ever so much for giving me such a lot of your time, Millie. I know you're a busy girl these days.'

'You're welcome, Harry. Sorry I got a bit – emotional. Thanks for lunch.'

'On the paper,' he said, showing the yellow teeth. I left him paying the bill.

I told Knife-blade. He looked worried.

'He was round the station today,' he said. 'He wanted to talk to the Chief. The Chief was busy. Then he wanted to talk to me. I was busy. The Chief called me in. He says if it gets into the press we might not be able to avoid an inquiry into police conduct.'

'It's my fault,' I said.

'No, Millie.'

'Oh yes.'

'No.'

He could always comfort me. Trapped and hunted though I felt, we spent evenings and nights in a joy so wild it frightened me. Happiness had rendered me ill-equipped to deal with the hunters. Before, that lunch would have been a walkover for me; now not only was it a struggle but I hadn't handled it well. The performance had lacked conviction; my heart wasn't in it; my heart was engaged elsewhere. '*Each man kills the thing he loves.*' Old Oscar Wilde certainly knew what he was talking about. I was leading Knife-blade into an iron trap that was going to take off more than a leg.

The story did not appear the next day, nor the day after that; I wondered what he was keeping it for.

On the third day I went to see Paul. I had nothing to lose.

# CHAPTER TWENTY-EIGHT

His mouth dropped open when he saw me on the step.

'Hello, Paul.'

He wanted to shut the door in my face but he was a polite fellow. I had the advantage there.

'You might as well let me in,' I said. 'I'm not going to go away.'

He was about to say something but lost his nerve. He hesitated between fight and flight, but finally stood back to allow me through.

'Thank you,' I said.

The flat was a mess. All trace of Liza had gone. There was a layer of dust on everything; even the lace curtains were grey. He still did not speak. I saw no point in beating about the bush.

'I was interviewed by Harry Loach the other day,' I said.

Paul folded his arms but said nothing.

'You told him about trying to reopen the case.'

His face was pale under the olive skin. He did not look at me.

'You knew he would use that information. You were using him to threaten me.'

Still not a word. I sat down and rubbed my face, laughing unsteadily. I had to try another tack. I spoke more gently.

'Paul, why are you doing this, really? Have you asked yourself?'

I saw he was shaking. Was it anger, hatred, loathing? Fear?

'Paul,' I said.

He walked to the window. 'I do not wish to discuss this,' he managed to say.

Oh yes, he had been spending time with Mrs Drew.

'Please, Paul.'

I stared at his back in the silence and waited. At last he said:

'I have no need to tell you anything. I did not invite you here.'

'You're going to destroy two people's lives, you owe me an explanation.'

He turned on me breathing hard, the white of his eyes was red.

'Owe!' he said. 'Owe? You have already destroyed four lives, you bitch.'

'How?'

'How? You killed Liza, Millie. Liza was carrying a child. I loved Liza. Her mother loved her. Now there is no Liza, there is no child, there is nothing for us now. Four lives.'

'You don't *know* that. You *believe* it. You can't *know* it because it isn't true.'

He clenched both his fists and banged them against his forehead twice.

'God,' he said.

'Your belief and Mrs Drew's is not enough to base a case on. There was no evidence.'

'There is evidence of police negligence,' he said.

'You have said that and said that but I can't see it. John Bright hounded us. It was he who first made you think it was me, it was he who turned you against me, for heaven's sake.'

'He just confirmed what I knew already and didn't want to admit to myself.'

I let that go. I had to stay calm.

'Why should he turn you against me if—'

'I don't know. He's a very unorthodox fellow, isn't he? Just how unorthodox we are going to find out.'

'You suggested in your letter,' I said, 'that I could have convinced him I was innocent by "seducing" him, as you put it. But you saw how I was with him from the start – from the very first questioning at Mrs Drew's house – I've never been so unpleasant to anyone. And that local bobby was there at Mrs Drew's place; he would confirm that.'

'He would also confirm that Bright insisted on driving you back to London. Why did he do that? There are no witnesses to what went on on that journey, are there, Millie?'

My stomach turned. I had forgotten that.

'On that journey,' I said, 'he questioned me about Mrs Drew. And about you. I refused to say a word against either of you. Then or ever.'

'We have only your word on that. And you know what I think of your word.'

Silence fell. For the first time he looked at me. His eyes wavered but didn't move away.

'Paul, you don't really believe this accusation, do you?'

He had calmed down. 'I don't know what I believe, Millie. I want to find out. No answer was discovered; I have to know why. All I know is that Mrs Drew saw you with John Bright. She watched you together before you saw her. She saw what was going on. And I can see it myself, Millie. You've changed. You're glowing – and that's not just success and all those things you wanted so much. It's something else. I recognise it, you see, because I had it myself. I had it for a long time. And you took it away from me. I can't imagine such an un-prepossessing little runt giving anyone such happiness as he appears to be giving you, nor can I understand what he could possibly see in you, but "*chacun à son chacune*," as someone said. There's no accounting for taste.'

I saw him through a red film. I wanted to wring his handsome neck.

'It's envy then,' I said. 'You have lost your happiness so you want me to lose mine.'

'Call it what you like, Millie, I don't care. I believe that man could have arrested you and he didn't. I want that looked into. I have the right.'

'The day we met in the police station he questioned me for two hours.'

'Then he should have questioned you for two more.'

'Can't you just accuse me without implying negligence on his part? Can't you find a way of doing that?'

'We have taken advice. This is the way to do it.'

'Paul, we were friends for a long time—' I was floundering.

'Don't give me that stuff, Millie, it makes me feel sick.'

It made me feel sicker. 'You're going ahead with it then?' I said.

'We're going ahead with it.'

'Even though Mrs Drew may have been in London at the time Liza was killed and lied about it to the police?'

'No suspicion attaches to Margaret.'

'She might get hit by some of the flak she is aiming at me.'

'She is innocent; it won't hurt her, as long as you are properly investigated at last.'

I sat and looked at him. A weak childlike man, wafted by whatever breeze blew. Once I could have convinced him of anything; now the breeze was from the east.

'Hasn't it occurred to you,' I said, 'that Mrs Drew has got what she wanted through this? The woman is crazy about you; she'd do anything to get you back into her clutches. That's what this is all about. She's got you where she wants you again. Well, perhaps not quite.'

'That beastly little policeman of yours convinced me of that for a while; it's rubbish.'

'It's true. She didn't start drinking again because of losing Liza, it was because she was losing you. I expect she's stopped the drinking again now?'

'You are being spiteful, Millie.'

I laughed. '*I* am being spiteful!' I said.

'She is a good, upright woman who wants justice.'

'She's an evil selfish witch who wants revenge. And you.'

'You'd better leave, Millie, before you say anything else you might regret.'

'I regret nothing.'

'You will.'

At the door, as a last throw, I said, 'Paul, please think about all this. Whether it will do any good. And whether you haven't been led into it by Mrs Drew.'

It was not a clever thing to say. He went white.

'I am not in the habit of being led into anything. I am my own master. And I have given it all the thought it needs.'

Never point out their weakness to the weak. Liza had made him feel strong. That was perhaps her greatest gift to him. Liza was cleverer than I. I had discovered that.

'That's it then,' I said cheerfully. 'Goodbye, Paul. And good luck.'

'You sound as though you meant that.'

'I do.'

'I can't wish you the same.'

'No. But you could say goodbye. It's the end of a beautiful friendship after all.'

He was puzzled. 'Goodbye then,' he said.

'Shake hands?'

He slowly put out his hand. I gripped it. I'd like to have thrown him down the steps but I never learned judo. Shame.

'Convey my respects to Mrs Drew. Wish her all the best from me,' I said.

His face was puckered with mystification. I let his hand go. I smiled.

He was still standing at the top of the steps as I drove off. I waved as I passed. He almost raised his right hand but stopped the reflex; put it in his pocket out of harm's way. I laughed.

I laughed a lot that day whenever I thought of his face. And more the day after when Harry's article appeared: 'Mixed Feelings Says Millie' was the headline. It was all there, including, 'The police were not available for comment.'

I did a lot of shopping while I laughed. I bought asparagus. I bought two dozen oysters. I bought a bottle of Sancerre (Knife-blade had trained me well) and strawberries. I cut my hand opening the oysters and was bleeding when he came down the stairs.

'What have you done?' he said.

'Lost a fight with an oyster.'

'What's all this?'

'It's a feast.'

'What are we celebrating?'

'Everything. Happiness, success, life, you, me. How about it?' I said.

'Count me in. After I've bandaged your hand.'

He put down a carrier bag, and the newspaper with the article.

'What's in the bag?' I asked.

'Champagne.'

I put it in the fridge. He came back with the bandage.

'One mind—' I said.

'—With but—' he said. 'No point in going into mourning. We're not dead yet.'

He put his arms round me. We stood there some time, my bandaged hand touching the back of his neck.

'Opening oysters is a skilled job,' he said.

'You'd know all about that.'

'Oh yes.'

He set to work while I washed strawberries then made a salad: watercress, spring onions, avocado pear. I set the table: white tablecloth, dark blue plates, candles, roses in a bowl.

'Champagne,' he said.

We took the bottle and glasses up to our garden on the roof. It was a warm evening. The water was smooth and black, gold flecks on it. We sat hand in hand, scoffing the champagne. He'd fixed a bucket for lowering the bottles into the water, not as smart as a silver ice bucket but more ingenious.

'Millie has mixed feelings,' he said.

We laughed.

'Going down with the ship,' I said.

We laughed.

'Pity I'm not a bishop,' he said. 'They'd make good headlines out of that.'

'Actress seduces bishop in confessional.'

We laughed.

'You should have seen Paul's face.'

I laughed and laughed.

'You didn't go and see him?'

'I did.'

'Millie, you're mad.'

'Explore every avenue,' I said.

'Leave out the dead ends.'

'You're right; he is one.'

'His face what?'

'When I wished him luck.'

'You didn't.'

'I did.'

We laughed right through the bottle of champagne. Then we made love, very slow and silent on our roof behind the trellis. We were visible only from a low-flying helicopter and there wasn't one. Then we ate dinner. Candlelight and roses. And oysters go down easy. We finished the Sancerre in bed. Afterwards I held him. I said:

'John.'

'My name again.'

'John.'

'A-ha?'

'What will you do?'

'If they sack me?'

'Whatever.'

'Become a bishop.'

'Seriously.'

'I don't know. Lots of things I've always wanted to try if I had the time: work with wood, travel. Read Proust.'

'Be serious.'

'Tell you the truth, I don't know. I've been at it twenty years. Didn't figure on an early retirement. If they give me the sack they'll probably put plenty of money in it. I'll have time to sort out what to do next.'

'Are you sure of that?'

'Oh yes. I've put in some good work for them in my time. They won't want to give me the push. It'll only be if they're forced.'

'The art of forcing the force.'

'A-ha.'

'Can you imagine doing anything else? Happily?'

'No but I haven't been trying long. Give me time. I only started this morning.' He showed his beautiful teeth in the dark above my face. 'The main thing I imagine these days is being with you; that's all that matters to me, Miss Hale.'

I closed my eyes.

'Me. That's the reason you're in this mess.'

'Sure is.'

'Well?'

'Worth every minute.'

'Not forever. I've said it before – you're a policeman like I'm an actress. It's the air you breathe.'

'Don't know yet.'

'I know.'

'I'm a cheerful fellow, Millie, I can turn my hand to anything. I don't cry over spilt careers.'

'What about the humiliation? You've been so clever all your life. They'll make you look foolish.'

'Yes. But they won't make me *be* foolish.'

'You think you won't mind. But you will.'

'I know I will. But not for long.'

'You'll blame me.'

'Maybe.'

'And you'll be right.'

'No.'

'Yes! John—'

He put the hands he was so good with gently over my mouth.

'I'm responsible for my own actions, Millie. I chose you. I don't regret the choice. I won't ever regret the choice. At the same time, if I'd been able to find evidence against you, or if I'd been able to bully you into a confession, I'd have arrested you, make no mistake about that, Miss Hale. Make no mistake about that.'

He moved his hands and kissed me.

'And nobody can prove otherwise,' he said, 'because that's the truth.'

'Truth,' I said. 'John—'

'That was a great celebration you organised tonight, Millie. If there was any thought in your mind of a farewell party, forget it. I'm in the soup now whether you're around or not and I'd rather be in it with you around. I've been there before; I'm an unorthodox fellow; it doesn't keep you out of the soup. I can handle it.'

'Not a soup like this.'

'We'll see.'

'What you always say.'

'So no brave goodbyes, Millie. Understand?'

'I understand.'

We didn't sleep much. He left fairly red-eyed in the morning.

'For someone who used not to drink, Millie, you look pretty good on it.'

'You look terrible.'

'I'll look better tonight.'

'I can't wait.'

I held him tight. Then watched him cross the plank, as we called our little wooden bridge to the towpath. I watched him go up the lane. He waved at the corner. Then he disappeared.

I went straight back in. I had a shower and got dressed. I cleaned up the debris of the night before, made everything shipshape, as you might say. I had a busy day ahead of me. I had letters to write.

# CHAPTER TWENTY-NINE

The first was to his chief:

> You know his methods are unorthodox; just how unorthodox you are about to find out. While he was pursuing the investigation into the death of Liza Drew, you started pushing him for time. He tried to get a confession out of me. He was brilliant, I have to admit. But I am an actress and I was good too; he didn't manage it. There was no evidence, as you know, so a case was not brought against me.
>
> What you do not know is that he did not give up at that point. After the inquest he wormed his way into my confidence, made me trust him, and in the end he got his confession. I told him everything in a letter this morning.
>
> I am telling you this in case he tries to protect me in some way. He's a great policeman, he's good at his job, no one better. I was clever, but he was cleverer.
>
> I am confessing to you, as I have to him, that I killed Liza Drew in January of this year. Yours, Amelia Hale.

The next was to my mother:

> There's not a lot of money in the bank but what there is is yours. It may come in useful. You won't see me again, but you haven't seen much of me since I left home anyway. No hard feelings, Millie.

Then to my agent:

> See you, Dorothy. (In a manner of speaking.) Sorry about this.

There'll be some fuss but it'll die down. At least you got some commission out of me at last. If the movie makes money I'd like you to have the royalties; you deserve them. Say sorry to the Royal Court for me. Affectionately, Millie.

I scribbled a note to my bank, giving instructions as to the sale of the boat and the house in Suffolk, proceeds to go to my mother. Then I sat. I walked up the lane and posted the letters. Then I came back and sat again. I looked at the flickering light of the water on the walls. I put on a jacket and went up to the roof. There was no one about. I settled myself into a chair.

Dear John Bright,

Alfieri says there are two kinds of envy: 'That which takes root in base minds, displays itself in hatred against everyone possessed of the smallest superiority, and in a desire to injure and deprive them even of what cannot benefit themselves; the other, which emanates from generous souls, is evinced under the name of emulation, by an ardent longing to obtain the same superiority . . . Thus we see how imperceptible is the line which separates the germ of our virtues and vices.'

I agree with him about the imperceptible line but I don't believe in the 'generous souls' and the 'base minds'. Envy takes the form of emulation when you have hope; when the hope goes, it turns to hatred and revenge.

You got it right in almost every detail, of course. It was when you described that deadly Tuesday of mine that I almost told you the truth. She did tell me about the job on the Monday night. She threw me the script:

'Shall I do it or not, I wonder? It would be a marvellous part for you, Millie.'

'I'm not likely to be offered it.'

'No.'

It was her cool 'No'. I had to go and splash water on my face.

And I didn't sleep that night. But on the Tuesday she phoned me again. It was dark when I went round, late.

'I've got to tell you, Millie, I can't keep it to myself any more.'

While she couldn't have Paul's child I had hope. As you pointed out. She was radiant with her secret. She was wrapped in a duvet, lying on the sofa. She had taken a sleeping pill, too excited to sleep.

That was lucky, wasn't it?

'What about the job?' I said.

'The job? Oh that! I can't possibly do it now, isn't it wonderful?'

The job I'd have given my eyes for. And Paul's child.

I was behind the sofa looking down at her. She had never looked so beautiful. I waited till her eyes closed drowsily. Then I picked up a cushion and lowered it onto her face and held it there. There was an astonished pause from both of us. Then she started to struggle. She lunged like a harpooned whale, like a bucking horse. I had to lie full-length on top of her, use more strength than I knew I had, but I won. There were fifteen years in that fight. I was fighting for my life, not against hers. The bucking and heaving and gasping stopped. I lifted the cushion and looked at her.

Her hair had come off in the fight. She was completely bald.

It was a wig, of course, over a stocking-cap, that she wore sometimes when her hair had not been done. I picked up the wig and put it on, laughing uncontrollably. She was like a broken doll lying there but there wasn't a mark on her. Or on me. Her arms had been pinned behind her head by the cushion and my weight and the duvet had protected both of us from outward signs of harm. I was so lucky it drove me wild. I put my old coat on her; I dressed myself in her fox fur jacket. You've seen what I look like got up like her – phenomenal, isn't it? I felt wonderful. I put some old slippers on her feet. And an old beret on her head. I heaved her off the sofa, got one of her arms round my neck and lugged her upright out of the flat, round to her car, onto the back seat. You wouldn't believe the weight. But my strength seemed boundless. It was the early hours; there was no one about. I went back for the duvet and covered her with it. I didn't know what I was doing. I drove my car round to my flat, leaving her where she was. I wanted more. I wanted to hurt her more. I'd had the spirits of salts ever since she stole Paul from me. I wanted to destroy her face then, too. I got the bottle from under the sink, and some rubber gloves. I was starting to think, if you can call it that. I remembered the house she'd asked me to visit with her. 'Okay, Liza, we'll go and see the house!' The night raced by. I don't know what I did; part of it must have been spent in a sort of trance. In the morning I did a full make-up job as Liza; it took hours, my hands were shaking. My agent rang about the interview. I had a quick bath and finished my preparations. I took a huge laundrette bag, the spirits of salts and the gloves. I drove to Swiss Cottage but did not park in King Henry's Road. I put on the wig just before getting out of the car. I went into the flat to collect the cushion I'd used, wash up my coffee cup, that sort of thing. Then I drove her car just like you said, with her dead on the back seat, and her shoes on the seat beside me.

It was hell getting her into the house. She wasn't as stiff as you might expect, perhaps because of the duvet? James Hadfield would know! I used it to drag her in, so's not to mark her delicate dead flesh. Getting her clothes back onto her was a terrible job but I did it in the end. Then I took the bottle and unscrewed the cap. The fumes nearly knocked me out. I poured it into her open mouth. A dusty smoke arose as though something were being burned. I was disappointed because there was no immediate effect. Quite a lot of it spilled round her mouth down to her ears. I took the stocking off her head and her hair sprang out. It was alive. I'd like to have cut if off. I turned her head away – it was hard to move now – and arranged the hair over the face. I drove out of there in my interview clothes and the wig, took off the wig, left her car in the lane, walked to my own car with the laundry bag containing the wig, the duvet, the cushion, the gloves, my old clothes and the bottle; sat in my car to wipe Liza's face off my own; and drove to the interview. I threw the laundry bag into the back of a garbage truck in St John's Wood and watched the evidence get chewed up. I was lucky every inch of the way, not clever like the coroner said.

You see, Liza Drew was a bitch. Lovely, warm, vulnerable, generous, she was all those things all through like Brighton rock; but for one reason only – in order to get her way. She became my friend at drama school because I was the best – she thought the talent might rub off; and I was taken in. She took Paul away from me because he was mine. When she got success for herself and didn't need to bathe in mine, when I lost everything, she treated me like a shabby old coat. She didn't throw it away in case it came in useful, but she sure as hell didn't wear it for best. Eight years is a long time to suffer such knowledge in silence when you have nothing of your own. I didn't hate Liza Drew. I wish it had been as simple as that. When I told you I loved her it was the truth. I loved her. I wanted to be her. I wanted everything she had. And *I* hated her, wanted to destroy her as I believed she had destroyed my life. I know well now that my life was crushed before Liza came into it and that the saving of my life was you and that if I hadn't killed Liza I should never have met you. And on and on the ironies go. Like my returning to the house to 'discover' her because I was impatient to come into my inheritance. Ah well. It's over now. I saw a movie once where a man kept a revolver under his pillow for just such an emergency as this. With me it's pills; they're my insurance, my power, like the spirits of salts. They're here on the table in front of me. I'll take them and at the right moment roll into the river.

Goodbye and thanks for everything.

Millie Hale

Then I wrote to him:

That's the public version, my darling John, but it's all true, every word.

I played my scenes well, John, didn't I? My best performance ever, and only you will ever know how good. If you had gone on questioning me that day you'd have broken me. Did you realise that? Is that why you stopped? It tortures me that I shall never know.

John, you cured me. You brought the world up close for me so I could touch it, enter it. You killed all the nightmares, my father, everything; you closed all the wounds.

Such joy, John.

But it couldn't go on. 'It doesn't matter,' you said. But it did. It was always there. When we were close like one dolphin on a wave, my secret was there between us like a great cold rock weighing me down. I could only let it drown me, not both of us.

I love you. And I wish. And good luck.

Millie.

PS. I told your chief you tricked me into this because you just couldn't bear to fail. Stick to that story or you fail me. Make this worth my while.

I read through the public confession and added:

John Bright, you did it, you succeeded, you made me confess. I did it just the way you worked out. Very clever. But then you've been the cleverest thing all along. Congratulations on a fine win. You're a champion.

Millie Hale